SAVAGE PEACE

*To Jo,
with thanks and
all my best wishes.

Freddie P. Peters*

Also by Freddie P Peters

RIVER SWIFT VIGILANTE THRILLERS

KILL SWITCH

NANCY WU SMART WOMAN CRIME THRILLERS

BLOOD DRAGON
SON AND CRUSADER
SAVAGED INNOCENCE

HENRY CROWNE PAYING THE PRICE THRILLERS

INSURGENT
COLLAPSE
BREAKING POINT
NO TURNING BACK
SPY SHADOWS
IMPOSTOR IN CHIEF
RED RENEGADE

SAVAGE PEACE

A River Swift Vigilante Thriller

FREDDIE P PETERS

Shadow Network Press

London

Copyright © Freddie P Peters, 2025

The right of Freddie P Peters to be identified as the author of this work has been asserted by her in accordance with the Copyright, Designs and Patents Act 1988.

All rights reserved. No part of this publication may be reproduced, stored in or introduced into a retrieval system, or transmitted, in any form or by any means (electronic, mechanical, photocopying, recording, or otherwise), without the prior written permission of the publisher. Any person who commits any unauthorized act in relation to this publication may be liable to criminal prosecution and civil claims for damages.

Without in any way limiting Freddie P Peters's exclusive rights under copyright, any use of this publication to "train" generative artificial intelligence (AI) technologies to generate text is expressly prohibited. The author reserves all rights to license uses of this work for generative AI training and development of machine learning language models.

Cover design by Lizzie Gardiner
Typesetting by Susan Hood

This is entirely a work of fiction. Names, characters, businesses, places, events, and incidents are either the products of the author's imagination or used in a fictitious manner. Any resemblance to actual persons, living or dead, or actual events or localities is purely coincidental.

This book is sold subject to the condition that it shall not, by way of trade or otherwise, be lent, resold, hired out, or otherwise circulated without the publisher's prior consent in any form of binding or cover other than that in which it is published and without a similar condition, including this condition, being imposed on the subsequent purchaser.

E-book ISBN: 978-1068672279
Paperback ISBN: 978-1068672286

www.freddieppeters.com

Chapter 1

The birds had been circling in the cloudless March sky for a while, riding the thermals. River had noticed a couple of them as she stopped her bike along the mountain ridge. She had decided to take a break from her long ride along Interstate 15 to Saint Ab, Utah, her destination. The travel mug of coffee she filled at the small B&B where she had stayed overnight was still warm, and now that she was getting near to her father's hometown, she was in no hurry to reach it.

She laid the mug on the ground and stretched the muscles of her back. She was tall and fit, but the drive on the Yamaha from Denver had started to take its toll. She picked up her coffee again and resumed her observation, raising her eyes to the sky once more. A glint of sun pierced the foliage of the tree next to which she'd stopped, and she shielded her blue eyes from it.

River had stashed her binoculars in her duffel bag, which was strapped to the back of the bike. She thought about taking them out, but in the end, she didn't need them to recognize the pattern vultures make in the sky once they've spotted a dying prey. By the time she finished her coffee, leaning against her rented Yamaha Super Ténéré, at least thirty of them had gathered in the sky, forming a kettle—a large circle in which the birds wait for an animal to die. She had seen this in Africa, where she and her parents had lived for a while. Her parents explained that this was part of the cycle of life, but as a child, she found those birds gross.

What her parents hadn't told her, and what she discovered in school, was that vultures aren't only interested in scavenging animals: A dead human will do just fine. The young boy who'd furthered her education had taken delight in giving her the gory details. River had let him speak, then just turned her back and ignored him for the rest of the week. It was going to take more than that for her to show she was scared. The thought made her smile . . . already defiant at such a tender age.

River checked her watch. It was time to pack up her travel mug and go if she was to arrive on time at her brother's house for lunch. But a change in the pattern of the vultures' kettle stopped her from putting her mug away. She surveyed the ridge on which she'd stopped to take advantage of the morning sun and the rugged yet stunning scenery. If she moved to the left and climbed to higher ground, she might see what was attracting the attention of the birds.

She picked up her backpack, stuffed the travel mug in it, and shouldered the pack. The terrain was steep and the ground rough. River slid a few times and stopped to check that she was taking the best path to the top of the hill, then reached it a few moments later. She now had a clear view of the valley below and what was catching the attention of the scavengers.

Someone was lying down there. River shivered. Her experience as an air force medic, identifying the wounded and the dead, made her certain that the person had little time to live.

She turned around and scrambled down the slippery slope as fast as she could. She gunned the engine of her bike and rode to the edge of the rim. She could see a path that led straight down to the canyon. The trail looked steep, but she could tell that other bikes had been down there from the looks of the tire tracks they'd left behind.

River had no time to lose. She rode as fast as she could, slipping dangerously close to a couple of boulders yet forcing the bike back on track each time. Sending up a cloud of dust, she hit the bottom of the canyon, then revved the engine and sped to where the person lay.

The young woman was slumped on her side, her clothes dirty

from having been worn for far too long. The smell that rose from the ground next to her told River she'd been sick. River stopped the bike and stood it on its kickstand. She dashed to the girl, knelt, and gently turned her on her back, pushing away the matted dark hair from her face. Her breathing was so shallow that River took a few seconds to detect it. She found a very faint pulse when she checked her small wrist, noticing rough marks on it. She opened one of the girl's eyelids. Her pupil was constricted to the size of a pinprick.

"Shit. It's an overdose," River mumbled.

She dropped her backpack to the ground and yanked out her cell phone, checking for signal. But deep in the gorge there was nothing, not even a single bar. River put the girl into the recovery position, took her biker jacket off, and covered the girl's thin body with it. River was torn: She didn't want to leave the girl in such a vulnerable position, but without a vehicle to transport her to hospital, she was going to die—if she could make it that far.

River started the bike again and followed her tracks back to the ridge. The incline felt steeper than she'd expected. She revved the bike to give it more speed. Standing on the foot pegs, she selected the least rocky part of the path and managed to avoid the boulders she'd almost crashed into on the way down. She trimmed her pace a little to avoid sliding backward over gravel and got over the rim. River then let the gas out, riding the bike down the dirt trail fast and finally reaching Interstate 15.

She stopped abruptly, got her cell phone out of her backpack, and checked again. Reception was weak, but at least she had some. She dialed 911 and waited for a response.

"State the . . ." The voice was garbled, but River replied anyway.

"I'm reporting the overdose of a young woman. Near the intersection of Interstate 15 and the Silver Rim path."

"Repeat . . ." more jumbled words.

River repeated herself, but the operator still couldn't understand. She cut off the conversation and looked around for help. She was twenty miles away from Saint Ab. She wouldn't get better reception until she cleared the Black Mountains. Fortunately, the bulk of a truck materialized in the distance, and as it grew closer, River started her bike again and sped in its direction. She was riding in the opposite lane, flashing the bike's headlamp so she could attract the trucker's attention. He flashed his headlights back and sounded his horn but didn't slow down. River turned the bike into his lane and rode toward him, right in his path. This time the friendly horn toots were replaced by a staccato of angry and rapid warnings. River kept going. A battle of wills had begun, and River wasn't one for backing down.

The brakes of the truck started to scritch. She saw a plume of smoke coming out from underneath the tires. It was going to be close. The semi only had fifty yards to go. River swung her bike out of the way at the very last moment. The truck stopped. Its driver shoved open the door of the cab, got out, and started to hurl insults at River.

She rode the bike back, stopped, dismounted, and walked to the man, putting her hands up in a show of apology.

"I'm sorry, but I need to use your CB radio to call for help," she said. "A young girl is dying in the canyon near the Silver Rim."

The man's anger vanished instantly. He climbed back into the cab, lifted the radio's mike, and keyed the microphone button. River was expecting 911, but instead a man's voice came on, sounding more friendly than official.

"Mad Dog, I'm on patrol now."

"I know, Dale, but we have a situation. There's a young girl who needs help near Silver Rim."

"What sort of help?" The voice now sounded focused.

Mad Dog handed the mike to River.

"Hello, Officer. I stopped your friend because I couldn't get a signal and make the call myself. A young girl is dying in the canyon just below the ridge. I'm on a bike. I can't take her to the hospital, and it's desperate. She hasn't got long to live."

"Get to the rim. I'll meet you there in five minutes."

River handed the mike back to Mad Dog. "Sorry about the scare earlier on."

The big man shrugged his shoulders. "What scare? Ain't a small bike with a girly on it that's gonna panic Mad Dog." He then smiled and gave her a thumbs-up. "Good luck. Hope the girl makes it."

River turned the bike around once more and sped toward the rim. In the distance, the flashing lights of Officer Dale's car showed he was on his way. River reached the dirt trail a moment before he did. He stopped his car in a flurry of grit and rolled his window down.

"Where is she?"

"Just over the ridge. In the canyon below," River said. She didn't wait for an answer and took the dirt trail that led them back to the spot where she had stopped for coffee. Overhead, the number of vultures had increased, and some were making some low passes already.

Dale looked up at the birds and said, "I don't have time to get around to the canyon with the car. I'll have to carry her back."

"If you have a blanket, we can do that together," River suggested.

Dale got out, heaved an old blanket from the trunk of his car, and followed River down the pathway to the canyon. It was as treacherous on foot as it had been with the bike, and they slipped and slid as they reached the bottom. River ran to the place where she'd left the girl. She knelt, took her jacket away, and turned the girl gently on her back. She checked for a pulse, and this time it had almost disappeared.

"We need to hurry," River said as she turned toward Dale.

He had already stretched the blanket on the ground and moved to the other side of the girl.

"Has she OD'd?" he asked.

"I think so. Why?"

"Drug cartels are using these young Latina girls as mules. And by the looks of it, one of the bags she was carrying inside her has burst open. They collected the rest. And I don't even have some Naloxone with me."

Dale pointed to a place not far from where the girl lay. River had assumed that the soiled ground was the result of the girl being sick, but she now realized that the girl had been forced to move her bowels to release the bags her intestines contained. River briefly closed her eyes.

Monsters.

Dale had already put the girl on the blanket when River stood up.

"I'll tie that end so she doesn't slip as we go up the slope. You take the front part," Dale said as he tied a solid knot with the two ends of the blanket.

The girl's face was ashen white, and River's heart sank. She pushed the thought of death away. She had to believe the girl would survive, at least long enough to identify the men who'd done this to her.

Dale picked up the back end of the blanket, and they both started to move uphill. Again, the uphill climb was hard, yet it took less time than River had anticipated. As soon as they cleared the ridge, they put the girl down. Dale wrapped the blanket around her, took her in his arms, and ran to the car. River couldn't help but admire the man and the way he'd handled the girl's soiled body—no hesitation. His only interest was making sure he gave her a chance to live.

"I'll follow you," River shouted as she reached her bike.

Dale answered with a wave of his hand through the window of the police car. They retraced their steps, reached Interstate 15, and darted toward Saint Ab, lights and siren blazing. Traffic was light when they hit the outskirts of town, and they went through several red lights before the hospital appeared in the distance. Dale gave it a final push and rushed into the emergency offloading bay. River arrived only a few seconds later. She stopped and stormed into the ER, simply lifting the visor of her helmet.

She stopped one of the nurses and said, "We have a young girl suffering an overdose. She's critical."

"Show me," the nurse said, already moving toward the entrance.

They rushed through the sliding doors, but then both women stopped. Dale had taken the girl out of the car and laid her on the ground. A medic was kneeling next to her body, stethoscope in hand but head bowed. Dale lifted his head to face River and shook it. She was gone.

"No," River cried. "No," she repeated as she, too, knelt next to the girl.

River felt a sob rise in her chest. She'd seen her fair share of death on deployment, each equally tragic. But the death of this young girl shattered her more than she expected. Perhaps the hard shell she'd created to deal with being part of a medic extraction team that deployed in combat was softening. Or perhaps it was the girl's youth that touched River so. She slowly moved a few strands of hair from the girl's face. She hadn't realized until now, but the young Latina had been beautiful. Her face was still lovely after all she'd gone through and even now in death.

Dale laid a friendly hand on River's shoulder.

"I'll speak to my colleagues. They'll take care of the body."

"And you'll find the fuckers who did this," River said, standing up slowly.

Dale's silence was deafening.

River was going to be late, but she just couldn't let it go. Dale called the morgue while the doctor and nurse who'd tried to help dealt with the body. They put the girl on a gurney, covered her with a sheet, and wheeled her inside the hospital.

"This is gang-related, I presume," River said after Dale hung up.

He nodded and gestured toward the main road.

"There is a nice diner within walking distance of here. I guess you and I could do with some coffee."

River checked her watch quickly. She hesitated. Her brother liked punctuality, but instead of making her excuses, she gave Dale a brief smile, and they both walked to the diner. She toyed with the idea of texting Luke, her brother, but he would start questioning her. Better make up some excuses when she got there. She removed her helmet, released the scrunchie that held her shoulder-length blond hair, slipped it over her wrist, and hung the helmet over her arm.

Memories of the place where she was due to meet her brother and his family flooded her mind. She hadn't been back to her grandparents' home for more than ten years, shortly after her parents' death. At that point, Luke had decided to move into the old house, and he needed to discuss their inheritance. River signed the papers he presented her with. She didn't care about the money, although she was certain that Luke, for all his faults, wouldn't treat her unfairly. She opened an account with a local bank, and he transferred the money he owed her into it. She hadn't touched it since.

At the Red Benn Diner, Dale pushed the door open and let River go in first. A couple of waitresses who were serving customers stopped and acknowledged Dale with a smile. He returned the greetings with a friendly nod and walked toward the far end of the long window. He slid into the last booth, as did River.

"Black coffee with cream on the side?" he asked.

"Black coffee, no cream, no sugar," River said as she shrugged her biker jacket off.

"Hullo, Dale. What's it gonna be today?" one of the waitresses—Frankie, according to her name tag—asked.

"Two black coffees, one with, one without."

"How about some of them pancakes you like?"

Dale hesitated, moving a hand to his waistline, and then shook his head. "Trying to stay in shape, you know."

Frankie gave him a naughty grin. "It all looks in very good shape to me."

Dale's cheeks seem to color a little. His fair skin and freckles must have been a disaster when he was a boy. His light brown hair was cut short, almost in a buzz cut, although River wasn't sure he would have been military material.

Frankie turned around and went to get two cups, the coffeepot, and cream. She came back, poured the coffee, and left them to it.

"Tell me about the gangs," River said before taking her first sip.

"I gather you're not from around here," Dale said as he poured a large helping of cream into his coffee.

"Just visiting my brother, Luke Swift."

Dale blew a few times over his steaming cup and said, "The doc who lives in his grandparents' home?"

River nodded but didn't volunteer more.

Dale got the hint and carried on. "Saint Ab looks like a nice, friendly, clean community, yet we sit squarely in one of the trafficking corridors used by Mexican cartels to move drugs and people around the country. They use illegal immigrants as mules to carry the drugs, and then, once they've recovered the drugs, they ship the girls across state lines for prostitution."

River waited a moment before asking her question. She recalled her tours in Afghanistan, where poppy growing was the most lucrative business for farmers. Poppy culture had been used by the Taliban to fund its terrorist activities, and it'd been impossible to rout out the drug trade from the country, no matter how hard the army tried. The poppy fields of Afghanistan kept fueling the production of most of the cocaine that landed in Europe and even the States.

"What is it that these cartels are importing? Cocaine?"

Dale shook his head. "The cartels I know of smuggle fentanyl. The raw materials originate in China, but the drug is actually produced in Mexico and sent across the border in its final form. That's what an FBI agent told us at the police station a little while ago, anyway."

River understood the power of fentanyl. It was used to control pain, and River had seen plenty of cases in which it helped soldiers suffering from extreme combat injuries or needing amputation. With that came the risk of dependency, so the drug had been tightly controlled.

"Where in Mexico do the cartels cook the drug? And how do they do it?" River asked.

Dale frowned. "I don't fully understand how the cooking works. But the labs move around a lot to avoid detection."

River gave him a kind smile. "Don't worry about not understanding about the preparation. I do because I'm a medic. Although I would have to research how *exactly* fentanyl is produced. A drug requires precursors, but I don't know which with fentanyl. In any case, I know that's what they cook in a lab to create the final product."

River and Dale had been sipping their coffee as they spoke. But something didn't sit right with his story. Then again, she reasoned, Dale wasn't part of a narcotics squad. A fentanyl overdose would kill its victim in one to three hours, whereas it had taken River and Dale more than an hour to get the girl to the hospital. And if what Dale had said was true—that the smugglers had forced her to release the drug parcels she'd ingested—she would have been at the bottom of the gorge for more than two hours at least.

Dale stood up slowly. "Thank you for your help. If you leave me your number, I'll keep you in the loop."

"Are you going to ask for an autopsy?" River said as she rose to her feet.

Dale shrugged. "That depends on Sheriff Andersen."

"Do you mean that because she was an illegal immigrant we don't need to know what killed her?"

Dale lowered his voice. "Sheriff Andersen isn't inclined to spend public money on . . . Jane Does from other countries. Also a reason why we're not carrying much Naloxone."

River cocked her head. "But you're going to want me to come to the station and make a statement, right?"

Dale grew a little uneasy, but he seemed to acquiesce.

"You lead the way," River said, picking up her helmet and jacket, "and I'll follow with the bike."

River covered the cost of the coffees with a ten-dollar bill, then made her way to the door and waved at the waitress who'd served them before leaving the Red Benn Diner. She and Dale walked back to the hospital, where they'd left their car and bike. Dale was silent, and River felt that he was almost certainly considering whether he should lead her to the police station or not.

"If it's not convenient to go to the station now, I can come back later. But you might not be there by then," River said as they reached their respective modes of transportation.

"Let's do this now," Dale said.

Just as River expected, Dale was keen to be there when she gave her statement. Perhaps he thought that letting her meet with Sheriff Andersen on her own wasn't a good idea after all.

Dale got into his car and led the way. They stayed on the outskirts of Saint Ab and reached a red-brick structure that looked well kept. A sign bearing the word POLICE was affixed next to the main entrance but was obscured by a tree. Shrubs had been planted around the perimeter, making its squat architecture look less severe.

Dale drove his car to the back of the building while River parked her bike near the front. She took her helmet off and waited for Dale. He parked and made his way to her.

"If you want some results for this girl, let me handle Sheriff Andersen," he said.

"Sure—you're the officer on this case."

And I'm a medic who's not resting until she knows who's responsible for that girl's death.

Dale entered the premises first. The door slid open, and a puff of warm air blasted over them. The woman who was manning the reception desk lifted her head and nodded as she recognized Dale, but didn't smile. She hardly looked at River and returned to whatever she was doing. Dale and River crossed the reception area and made their way to the rear of the building, where there was a large room filled with rows of desks. It was almost lunchtime, and Dale's colleagues seemed to have left to get their sandwiches. On the right-hand side, the sheriff's office door was open, and River could see a large bald man there tucking into some food. River could tell what it was by the aroma: Sheriff Andersen was enjoying some tacos. At least he wasn't opposed to Mexican food.

"Jackson." Andersen's voice boomed across the room. "What's this 'bout the illegal you found?"

Dale's face dropped. "We found her at the bottom of the canyon near Silver Rim, Chief," he responded, walking toward Sheriff Andersen's office with River in tow. He stood on the threshold as if waiting for instructions. Perhaps Sheriff Andersen didn't like his taco consumption to be interrupted.

River watched as the big man licked his fingers and proceeded with the next taco in the box. He took a large mouthful, started chewing, and said, "Ove'dose?" He swallowed his food, took a swig of Pepsi from an extra-large cup, and raised an eyebrow.

"That's right, Chief, and Ms. . . ." Dale fumbled, not remembering River's name.

"Swift," River said softly.

"Ms. Swift found the girl and called for help."

"What with?" Andersen said before stuffing the rest of the taco in his mouth. He chewed a couple of times and swallowed. "Ain't no reception in those parts."

"She stopped a trucker and used his CB to make the call."

Sheriff Andersen must have thought that River's resourcefulness deserved his attention. He strained to take a better look at her. River seized the opportunity and stepped forward.

"I'm here to make a statement. And I'm happy to help your CSI team if they need more details about the death. I'm a medic, so I can describe what I observed when I first encountered the victim." River wasn't sure whether her choice of words was right, but she tried to sound as confident as she could.

Andersen was about to tackle the last taco, but his hovering hand withdrew from the cardboard box. "You have forensic experience, then?"

"Some. I helped MPs with their investigations when I was deployed in Afghanistan." River and Sheriff Andersen exchanged a quick yet venomous glance.

"Which regiment?" Andersen shot back.

Sheriff Andersen seemed to have little understanding about how the US Air Force worked.

"Special Operations Surgical Team, assigned to the 24th Special Operations Wing at Hurlburt Field." River almost stood at attention, but she'd be damned if she would do so in front of an individual as revolting as Andersen. She wasn't going to tell him she'd left the military, either. Andersen might be more reluctant to tackle someone who still had the backing of the air force.

The sheriff grimaced. He wasn't expecting this level of detail or that River's credentials would be that impressive.

She took advantage of the moment and said, "Let me know when the ME proceeds with the autopsy. I might be able to give him some helpful information."

Andersen just nodded, and Dale seemed to think this was the right moment to step in.

"Time to take your statement."

"Sure." River turned around to follow Dale, hoping she'd spoiled Sheriff Andersen's appetite.

Dale directed River to one of the interview rooms. He closed the door before he said, "I know you mean well, but you don't want to make an enemy of Sheriff Andersen."

River chuckled. "I'm afraid that train has already left the station. But thanks for the advice."

Dale smiled. He turned to the notepad that lay on the table and said as he sat down, "So, Ms. Swift, would you care to tell me what happened?"

Chapter 2

The dilapidated ranch looked abandoned from afar. It wasn't many miles away from Saint Ab, yet it was remote enough that no one ever checked the place. Alfonso pushed the pickup truck harder so that he could get to his meeting earlier than expected—a trick his father taught him. That way, the men working for him never dared slack off. He drove right to the entrance of the main house and stopped. The wood of the steps had collapsed. Part of the roof had been blown away by a storm, and the walls were crumbling in places.

Alfonso ran a hand through his thick mane of dark hair, adjusted the sunglasses that shielded his brown eyes, got out of his truck, and took one step to get to the bottom of stairs and one giant stride that propelled him directly onto the porch. The porch had lost its roof, too, but the part of the house where he was having his meeting was still intact.

The door opened, and one of the Cruz Cartel's men greeted him.

"Hola, Alfonso. Todo esta bien ahora."

"En Inglés," Alfonso said with a frown.

He'd told his men he wanted them to speak English so that they could blend more easily into their surroundings, and Luis was no exception. It always took a second attempt for Luis to follow instructions. In fact, all Alfonso's men seemed to take their time when following instructions. They never did that with his father, whose men almost anticipated his instructions and followed them to the letter.

Disobeying Señor Gonzalo Carlos "El Diablo" Cruz-Coronel had devastating consequences for whoever dared to—and their families.

"All is well now," the man repeated with a harrumph.

"You mean you found the girls?"

"One of them is dead, but we managed to get most of the chemicals out of her before she died. All the others are on their way to Vegas."

Alfonso should have clapped Luis's shoulder, but instead he simply nodded. He moved further inside the derelict house. The rest of his couriers had already moved the last batch of drugs out. It was on its way along Interstate 15 toward central Utah and Salt Lake City. It would then follow its course to Saint Louis and Chicago for partial distribution and then ultimately arrive in New Jersey, where the last batch would be sold. His father's cartel, the Cruz Cartel, had done well in California, but Señor Gonzalo had ambitions for himself and his three sons. Alfonso was the youngest, following in the footsteps of his brothers—reluctantly.

When Alfonso arrived in the back room of the ranch, he found an old man tied to a chair, his head dropped over his chest. Luis had already interrogated him and found out how three of the girls he was smuggling into the United States had almost escaped.

"He's just an incompetent fuck," Luis said over Alfonso's shoulder.

Luis's English didn't need improvement when it came to insulting someone.

Alfonso walked closer to the chair. The man must have sensed that someone was approaching. He jerked his head up. The eye that wasn't swollen shut was wide open, and he tried to speak. Only a garbled sound came out as he coughed up some blood. Luis moved to the chair and slapped the old man across the face.

"Enough," Alfonso said with steel in his voice. "I want to hear it for myself. Give him some water and let him speak."

Luis grudgingly walked to a table that stood in the middle of the room. A couple of implements he must have used to persuade the man to talk were scattered over the tabletop next to a jug of water.

He picked up one of the plastic tumblers next to it and poured a small amount of water. He returned to the old man and brought the tumbler to his lips. Water dripped down his chin and naked torso as he tried to drink, but he managed enough. He licked his cracked lips.

"Tell me what happened," Alfonso said.

The old man paused to gather his thoughts. Luis was about to hit him, but Alfonso stopped him with a curt show of his hand. Then the old man started his story.

"One of the girls started to fall sick. I could see on her face she wasn't faking it, and—"

"How did you know?" Alfonso interrupted. He grabbed a chair, turned it around, and straddled it, sitting across from the old coyote.

"Her face was pale. She seemed out of it." The old man swallowed and turned toward Luis. Alfonso nodded, and Luis helped the man to some more water.

"I checked her pupils—they'd started to get smaller. You've got to know these things when you run mules across the border. When it's time to get them to release what they hold."

"So you decided to stop the truck and give the girl a laxative?"

The old man grimaced in disgust. "I didn't, but the two girls who seemed to be her friends did. I told them to."

Alfonso considered his reply for a moment. Coyotes could be so finicky about what they would and would not do when taking illegals across the border. It was okay to beat them up or let them die if they couldn't follow orders, but giving mules a way to release the drugs they'd ingested seemed to be too much for their fastidious selves.

"And the girls took advantage. They ran away instead of going back to the truck," Alfonso said with a disapproving sigh.

The old man shifted in his seat. It wasn't looking good for him.

"Señor Alfonso, it's the first time it happens to me. The problem was that the bags that came out had started to burst open, so I was trying to salvage what I could."

Alfonso turned toward Luis. "We lost ten out of the fifty bags she was carrying," he said.

Alfonso sighed again. "Do you know how much money you cost us?" This wasn't a question that required an answer, but rather a justification for what was coming next. Alfonso stood up and shook his head.

The old man hesitated. "I'll repay you, Señor Alfonso. It's the first time it happens." The old man's chin wobbled as he spoke.

Alfonso might have accepted the offer. After all, it was true: This coyote had a good reputation, and he would have almost certainly found the money to compensate the Cruzes for their loss. But Alfonso had been tasked by his father with furthering the cartel's business and securing new routes that went deep into the United States. In doing so, the Cruzes were challenging one of the biggest drug organizations in the world—the Sinaloa Cartel—and this required one thing: a show of brute strength that told the world that the Cruzes meant business.

Luis stepped forward. He was eyeing the old man with greed, wondering how he would finish him off. But Alfonso drew his gun, aimed, and fired. The old man's head jerked back. Luis looked at Alfonso, surprised and then angry.

"Clean up the mess," Alfonso just said. He wasn't going to indulge the psycho his father had assigned him any extra pleasure. He'd had his fun already. It was good enough that the old man had to die, and the news that he had found a sorry end at the hand of the youngest Cruz brother would carry weight.

Alfonso turned around, ignoring Luis's furious glance, and wondered how long it would take for him to stop feeling comfortable turning his back on Luis. His father had been indulging the young man. They were perhaps much closer to each other than Alfonso would ever be with his father. They shared the same savagery and pleasure in inflicting pain. Still, for the time being, Alfonso felt safe enough.

He'd successfully completed a degree in chemistry in Mexico and had been helping the cartel create fentanyl from its precursors—the components used to create the drug. These were imported from China, and previously these substances hadn't been controlled by the

Chinese, Mexican, or American authorities. Recently, though, they had attracted the attention of the Americans, and China had agreed to better control or restrict their exportation. It was now more difficult to produce fentanyl and smuggle it to the United States.

This is where Alfonso proved his worth to his father. He'd managed to create not only fentanyl but also its precursors in one of his father's clandestine labs. The final product was even more potent than the original Sinaloa fentanyl. Now the Cruz Cartel had an advantage over the other drug lords, and it was time to capitalize on it.

Alfonso left the farm and headed in the direction of Saint Ab. Another lot of girls was due to arrive in a few days' time, and he needed to make sure this delivery went smoothly.

River read her statement one more time. Satisfied, she picked up the pen that Dale had left on the table and signed the piece of paper. She glanced at the clock on the wall of the interview room. She had around quarter of an hour to get to her grandparents' place, which now was Luke's family home. They agreed on a 1:00 p.m. lunch, because he would finish at his medical practice around 12:00 p.m. and wouldn't be going back to work that afternoon. They would have time to chat.

Luke had been surprised, not necessarily pleasantly, to hear from River, but he hadn't pushed back when she said she'd like to pay him a visit. She'd made up a reason—something about leaving the air force and taking some time to reconnect with friends and family. She felt bad about not being more truthful, but she couldn't explain that the object of her visit was to ask Luke about a piece of paper she had stolen from a Washington, DC, lobbyist named Chuck Clery.

Clery had died at the hands of a notorious arms dealer, but more important, the paper River had stolen included a mention of River and Luke's parents, who were both physicians employed by Doctors Without Borders. She now wondered whether they actually were, as they were said to have been, the unfortunate collateral victims of a turf war between two warlords in the Democratic Republic of the

Congo. River had never asked Luke what personal effects of theirs he'd eventually received from the DRC, but now she wanted to know. Perhaps she might find an answer to the question that was now haunting her.

River picked up her jacket, helmet, and backpack. She'd scribbled her cell number on a piece of paper and had left it on top of her statement and was about to leave the room when Dale opened the door. He didn't look happy, and that confused River.

"It's all good. I've signed the paper," she said.

"Someone's here for you," he replied, taking the papers from her.

River frowned and came to the door of the interview room. A few steps away, her brother was talking with Sheriff Andersen, and the conversation didn't look friendly.

"Shit," River blurted out. "How did he know?"

"Told you. He's one of those SOBs you need to be careful about. Plus, your brother is well known in Saint Ab."

Luke hadn't changed that much since the last time they'd seen each other. He was perhaps a little heavier around the waistline, but his wavy fair hair still resembled their father's, and so did the way he held his tall body—slightly stooped. For a moment River thought she could see her dad only a few feet away from her. Her throat tightened, and she bit her lip.

Luke must have felt that someone was observing him, because he turned his head in her direction. She tried to smile but wasn't sure she succeeded. Luke frowned and waved her closer. A gesture he used to make whenever he was assuming the role of big brother. Whatever Sheriff Andersen had said to Luke, it had annoyed him. River wouldn't forget this: If Andersen was a mean SOB, she, too, could be the greatest pain in the ass he'd ever meet.

Be careful what you wish for.

River walked across the open space and reached the two men. Sheriff Andersen locked eyes with her. She read triumph in them. A misplaced feeling, she thought, but Andersen wouldn't know that just yet.

"Sheriff Andersen tells me you're seeking to interfere with an autopsy process," Luke said.

River turned to her brother and smiled. "How nice to see you again, Luke. I missed arguing with you, too, so it's nice to pick up where we left off. And no, I did not offer to interfere with an autopsy, but to help. I was the first responder in an emergency situation—I found a young girl who had OD'd. I thought my experience as a medic might be of assistance."

Luke's face dropped, and his anger subsided. He hadn't kept in touch with River since she'd entered the air force, a move her parents disapproved of. And it seemed he hadn't anticipated that the sister he'd last seen eleven years ago had morphed into a confident woman whose experience might well have overtaken his own.

River donned her jacket, slung her backpack over her shoulder, and started toward the door, turning around to see whether Luke was following. He was still standing where they'd just had their spat.

"Are you coming?" River said. "We're going to be late for lunch."

Luke took leave of Sheriff Andersen with a curt nod that was perhaps less subservient than the sheriff might have liked. River didn't say goodbye to Dale, not wanting to drag him more than she already had into the showdown between her and his boss. She walked out of the Saint Ab North Police Station and got on her bike. Luke walked toward her, but she anticipated his question.

"Yes, I recall how to get to Grandpa and Grandma's house. I'll see you there."

She revved the engine, put her helmet on, and eased the bike onto the main road. It took a moment for her anger to subside and make way for deep sadness. She hadn't seen Luke for more than a decade and had spoken with him only a handful of times since then, solely for administrative matters concerning the death of their parents. Why did he always have to assume the worst when it came to her?

She stopped at a traffic light and was so lost in thought that she didn't notice when it turned green. No one beeped at her, and she was grateful that drivers calmly waited for her to go.

River blinked back tears and thought about what lay ahead. She was going to a place loaded with memories, some of which she didn't wish to revisit. Her determination wavered as she was waiting for the next light to turn green, but when it did, she maintained her resolve and kept going in the direction of what was now Luke's home. She would have to concentrate on the good memories.

She smiled when she recalled one of her grandmother's stories. Her grandmother, like her daughter—River's mom—enjoyed recounting folktales and legends.

There was an old Cherokee elder who one day sat down with his grandson and said, "Let me tell you the story of the two wolves who live and battle within you. One is noble, courageous, and kind. The other is deceitful, greedy, and angry."

The grandson thought for a moment and then asked, "Grandpa, which of the two wolves wins?"

"The one you feed the most."

River never knew whether the story really originated with the Cherokee people, but she did know which of the two wolves she wanted to win.

It took another fifteen minutes for her to reach the house. Luke had already arrived, and he'd parked his car alongside the sidewalk right in front of the property. River parked the Yamaha in front of his car and killed the engine. She sat there for a moment, taking in the house she knew as a young girl, and realized that Luke had changed nothing about its appearance apart from giving it what looked like a very fresh coat of paint.

The house her grandparents built was on two levels, surrounded by shrubs and a lawn. A rock garden led the way to the porch and the main entrance. River's stomach somersaulted. When she was a child, she'd enjoyed her time there because she'd been allowed to ride her bicycle and explore the wilderness around the city. Luke was often less interested, complaining that there was usually plenty of wilderness wherever they lived with their parents. Their nomadic life, a consequence of her parents' position in Doctors Without Borders, suited River just fine—one year here, two years there.

The door of the house opened, and a woman stood there for a moment. River removed her helmet and waved. Rosa, Luke's wife, had just stepped out of the house. River had met her only once, when Rosa and Luke were dating. She remembered her as vivacious and attractive, with soft brown eyes and large brown curls dropping over her shoulders. She'd liked the woman and had been surprised that Luke had chosen such an outgoing and friendly person. River had learned of their wedding and the birth of their two children through the grapevine. She'd seen the photos on his Facebook page, a page that, strangely, Luke had let her join. River also recalled that Rosa was a doctor with the local hospital, so perhaps they both would have the opportunity to talk some more after lunch.

Rosa came to greet River with open arms.

"It's so nice to see you again after all this time." No hint of reproach in her voice. Just the sheer joy of being with River again.

"It's been too long. I should have found the time long ago."

They hugged.

"Come inside," Rosa said with a smile, her dark eyes sparking with joy.

River opened the luggage box of her bike and took out her duffel bag, and she and Rosa made their way inside. River closed the door behind her and stood there for a moment, bombarded by a mix of emotions—sadness, joy, anger, and . . . puzzlement. She couldn't believe she'd let her differences with her brother get in the way of visiting the only family home she'd ever known and might still ever know.

"Would you like to freshen up before lunch?" Rosa asked.

"If it isn't too much of an inconvenience."

Rosa nodded. "Follow me," she said. "I've prepared the spare room in the addition. I hope you'll be comfortable there. We've just had it refurbished."

River smiled, but her heart sank. It was silly to be expecting she'd be sleeping in the original house. Luke and Rosa had used the bedrooms there for their own kids. But perhaps it was for the best. River wasn't sure she would have liked spending time in her old bedroom—too many memories might distract her from her goal, which was to find out any information Luke might have about the death of their parents.

Rosa and River crossed the inner courtyard. It was perhaps a little greener than she remembered, with more shrubs and another rock garden where cacti of various shapes and sizes seemed to do well. The windows of the addition were open, and Rosa entered the main room first. The scent of something fresh and citrusy welcomed River. The room was very different from what she remembered. Her parents had used it as their own little den as well as a play area for River and Luke. Toys were stored there. Some had belonged to her dad, too.

"That's very kind," River said, dropping her duffel bag to the floor. "I won't take very long."

"No stress. I'm not working at the hospital until late."

Rosa disappeared, and River stood still for a moment. She was grateful that the room had changed so much: It was almost a different place from the one she remembered.

She shook herself from her reverie and made her way to the bathroom, where she quickly undressed and stepped into the shower. She was glad of the opportunity to clean away the morning's grime and wash away some of the images that lingered. She was determined to have the last word when it came to the young girl who was now lying on an autopsy table. Whether Luke liked it or not, she'd find out what happened. For the time being, though, River concentrated on making herself presentable.

She stepped out of the bathroom, dried herself quickly, and took out a pair of black jeans and a white T-shirt from her duffel bag. She rolled them as she packed to rid them of their creases, so they didn't look wrinkled when she put them on. She changed her biker boots for a pair of black Converse sneakers, put on a green pullover, combed her hair, and made her way to the kitchen.

A slender young girl of about seven, holding a tabby cat in her arms, was standing in the porch to the main house. She looked puzzled to start with, then gave River a toothy grin.

"Are you Aunt River?" she asked as she skipped forward.

She made sure the animal was secure in her arms, then she turned so River could better see the cat. "This is Franklin. We don't know how old he is for sure, but he's my cat."

River bent down and scratched Franklin's head. He seemed to like it and immediately started to purr. "You're right. I'm your Aunt River, and that makes you Carmen."

Carmen giggled. She rubbed her plump little cheek against Franklin's head and then started petting her cat. The purr sounded like a small engine, and River chuckled in turn. The door of the kitchen had opened without River noticing, and Luke was standing just outside it. But instead of looking grumpy, he was smiling. River couldn't miss the look on his face as he was watching the scene—total adoration for his little girl.

"Come on, sweetie pie. Lunch is ready. Bring Franklin in and go and wash your hands."

"Franklin isn't dirty. He's a very clean cat," Carmen protested.

"I know, sweetheart, but it's a good habit to wash your hands before food nevertheless."

Carmen sighed and walked inside the house. As her father moved away from the door to let her through, he ran a hand over the mass of her dark hair and turned around to see her disappear toward the bathroom.

"She spends her entire day with her cat. I've never seen such a loving little animal."

"Did you get him when she was a baby? He looks almost as old as she is."

Luke shook his head. "Franklin is a rescue cat. She saw a program on TV, and it mentioned an animal shelter here in Saint Ab. She wouldn't stop talking about it until we went."

"Franklin must be the luckiest cat in the world," River said.

"That's got to be true. He was the oldest cat in the shelter. She'd set her mind on saving one of them, and she did."

Rosa called them in, and both Luke and River walked into the dining room. Carmen was already sitting at the table in the dining area across from the kitchen. Franklin had curled up in a chair next to her and was fast asleep. River noticed that there were five plates around the table and wondered where Jack, Rosa and Luke's son, was. Luke picked up on River's puzzlement.

"Jack is on his way. His best pal lives just around the corner, and they've been skateboarding all morning," Luke said, a little terse. River couldn't tell whether he was annoyed at the lack of punctuality, or whether Jack was spending too much time skateboarding for his father's liking.

The food Rosa had placed on the table looked and smelled delicious, and it made River a little embarrassed.

"You shouldn't have gone to so much trouble," she said to Rosa with a smile.

Rosa grinned and gave a small nod in the direction of Luke. "I just put the food on the table. You need to thank Chef Luke for today's meal. Now that both Carmen and Jack are on spring break, he wants to make our lunches a little extra special."

River felt her cheeks grow warm as she turned toward Luke. He just shrugged.

"After all these years convincing myself I couldn't cook, I bought a cookbook—"

"And the rest is history," Rosa finished as she started to put food on Carmen's plate.

River wasn't sure whether she should bring up the past. Their dad had been happy to help their mom with the food, too, but his culinary skills only extended to pasta with tomato sauce (because the latter came in jars) and omelets (accommodating the leftovers in the fridge).

"I'm afraid I follow the family tradition. I can boil an egg and toss a salad together, but that's about it," she said as she was handed a dish of chicken enchiladas. "We've got a lot of catching up to do," River continued, hoping her remark wouldn't spoil the relaxed atmosphere.

Luke gave her a sidelong glance but then smiled. "This is true, sis. We do."

The bang of the front door slamming shut interrupted the conversation. A moment later, Jack walked into the dining room.

River's throat ran dry. Her father was standing a few paces away from her, only he was now a ten-year-old boy. She recognized the searing blue eyes and the tall—very tall—frame. But what moved River most of all was his smile, open and genuine. Her heart melted.

His jeans were torn at the knees; he was wearing a couple of T-shirts on top of each other. His baseball cap, worn back to front, just managed to contain his unruly dark curls. He dropped his skateboard to the ground and froze for a moment, his confidence suddenly vanishing.

"Jack," Luke said, pointing at the skateboard.

Jack ignored his father and instead asked, "Are you Aunt River?"

River stood up and smiled. "That's me."

He smiled back and stepped forward to give River a hug, as though he'd known her all his life. River hugged him back, although it felt odd to be called Aunt River. She'd never considered herself to be an aunt, but she somehow liked it. Just as she enjoyed it when Carmen had said it.

Jack stepped back, perhaps wary of having been too forward, then he picked up the skateboard and said, "I know—put my skateboard away and go and wash my hands."

Chapter 3

River, Luke, and Rosa had moved to the kitchen while Carmen and Jack had gone back to their rooms. The three adults had cleared the table and loaded the dishwasher while chatting about Saint Ab. What had changed. What was the same. Luke and River sat on the stools that lined the long kitchen counter, and Rosa got busy making coffee.

"Now, that is Rosa's field of expertise," Luke said as he took Rosa's hand and kissed it.

Rosa gave him an amused look and turned toward the cabinets, removing a coffee grinder, filters, and a jar full of coffee beans. River followed her every move. She hadn't seen someone grinding coffee for such a long time. The last time was in Africa. Her mother loved coffee, too, and she traveled around the world with an old electric grinder she'd bought somewhere in Europe.

The sounds of the small motor and the beans hitting the inside of the hopper took River back to a house her parents, Luke, and she shared in the DRC. They had moved there for a Doctors Without Borders program to combat starvation in countries where people had fled conflicts—Rwanda, Somalia, and the DRC. The amazing thing about her parents was that they fitted in immediately with their environment and made their home a welcoming one, even though it needed to be functional, too. On one occasion, their mom had returned from the local market loaded with provisions and a bag of coffee beans. River had observed her for a long time, and that day her mom had let her grind the beans. She'd been so very proud.

Luke must have read River's mind. He extended a hand and touched her shoulder lightly. "I remember the coffee grinder, too."

"Was it shipped back to you?" River's voice wobbled a little.

Luke shook his head. "Very few things came back from Africa."

They both fell silent. The death of their parents, attributed to a village raid ordered by warlords fighting in the region, meant that Doctors Without Borders had to pull its staff from the area. The place had become too dangerous for foreigners, and it was the local doctor and some of the villagers who'd helped gather their parents' belongings. They'd never owned much, but still River would have liked to have had a couple of mementos to remember them by—an old bracelet her mother always wore; her father's well-used stethoscope.

River thought for a moment. She still wanted to take a look at what had been sent to Luke, but the clinking of mugs told her that this wasn't the time to ask. Rosa poured the coffee, then sat next to River, pushing a jug of cream and a bowl of sugar toward her.

"So you had the great pleasure of meeting Sheriff Andersen this morning," Rosa said before taking a sip.

Luke threw his hands in the air. "Just because you don't like this guy doesn't mean you should bring the subject up at the table."

"You don't like him?" River asked, glad she'd found an unexpected ally in Rosa.

"He is the worst sheriff we've ever had, and I've lived in Saint Ab almost all my life."

"What's bad about him?" River took a sip and waited for an answer she suspected would confirm what she'd thought in the first place.

"Don't encourage her," Luke moaned.

River and Rosa simultaneously turned toward him. They couldn't help but laugh. It seemed that their new alliance might be hard to break up.

"My take on Andersen is that he is not only a bully and lazy, but also crooked."

River raised an eyebrow. "That's a pretty direct accusation."

"I know," Rosa said. "I simply wish I had the time to investigate and gather enough evidence about that."

Luke seemed agitated. "There are rumors circulating around the hospital that Andersen has something to do with the increase in drugs in town, but it doesn't mean you should give any credibility to them."

Rosa smiled at her husband. "I know, but the increase in drugs, especially among young people, started *after* Andersen became sheriff."

The ring of Rosa's cell phone interrupted the conversation. She frowned the minute she picked up the phone and saw who the caller was.

"Qué pasa?" she said, jumping from her seat and heading into the hallway to fetch her bag.

River could hardly follow Rosa's side of the conversation, which took place entirely in Spanish. Luke seemed to understand quite a bit of it, though, and he went into the hallway, too. Rosa had her bag and raincoat with her when she returned to the kitchen.

"I'm sorry, but I've just received an emergency call from the ER at the hospital. They need me to come in early if I can. There's been a traffic accident involving several vehicles, and the staff is stretched thin. And speaking of drugs, they've got someone who's OD'd, too."

River stood up. "Do you need a hand?"

Rosa thought as she was putting her coat on. "I would have to get you authorized, but you might be able to help."

River ran back to her bedroom and grabbed her backpack and biker jacket. Rosa was already in the car. Luke looked at a loss, seeing the two women go. River planted a kiss on his cheek and said, "Thanks for lunch, bro. That was really delicious. I'll be back as soon as I can."

River ran to her bike, straddled it, and followed Rosa all the way to the hospital. She recognized the parking lot and the ER entrance, but this time she followed Rosa deep inside the building to the doctors' changing room, where Rosa opened her locker, took out a clean medical gown, and handed a spare one to River.

"You can't make any decisions. I haven't gotten you authorized yet, but you can report to me and let me know who needs what. Luke tells me you were a medic with the air force. You're used to seeing nasty wounds."

River nodded. "I can assess and let you know who's to be prioritized."

They both walked out of the changing room and followed a short corridor that led them to the dispatch area of the ER, where people were lying on gurneys, covered with blankets, and hooked up to IVs. River set to work immediately—lifting sheets and blankets gently, asking for names, and making sure that her intervention was efficient yet kind. She sent a man whose legs must have been crushed by the collapsing dashboard of his car to the front of the line. He needed immediate surgery if he was to survive.

She moved swiftly down a row of patients until her eyes fell on someone she thought she recognized. But it couldn't be. The young girl of this morning's incident was dead. As River got closer, though, she knew immediately that this girl was related to the Jane Doe. She called to Rosa, who swiftly came to her side.

"Is this the patient who OD'd?" River asked.

Rosa nodded and checked the paperwork hanging from the side of the gurney. "They've given her naloxone intranasally."

River opened one of the girl's eyelids. "She's not out of danger yet . . ."

"And?" Rosa said, picking up on River's hesitation.

"I'm certain she's related to this morning's victim."

Rosa frowned, and for a moment River thought that perhaps she didn't believe her, but then Rosa grabbed hold of the gurney and started pushing. River came alongside her and helped Rosa push it toward the elevator. She pressed the Call button a few times. As soon as the elevator arrived, they got in and rose to the third floor. There Rosa went to the nurses' desk, spoke to the head nurse, and returned.

"They're going to find a room for her and start treatment again. You might want to stay with this girl. She'll need a friendly face when she wakes up. I've got to go back."

River nodded. "I'll stay with her."

A tall woman named Martha—the head nurse, according to her name tag—came alongside the gurney and said, "I hear from Rosa you were a medic with the armed forces, so you know what's at stake, right?"

"She needs more naloxone. Her pupils are still constricted, and her breath is too shallow."

"Let's get her into one of the rooms on this floor," Martha said.

Both women pushed the gurney, with Martha taking the lead. They turned onto a long corridor and got to a room halfway down, then stopped. Martha opened the door and started pushing again. River helped position the gurney in the middle of the room.

"I'll get one of the nurses to set up the bed, and I'll return with the naloxone," Martha said as she left the room.

River turned to the girl and studied her face. She now was sure of what she'd said to Rosa: This girl and the Jane Doe awaiting autopsy were related. They had the same high cheekbones and exquisite lips—they were beautiful girls. River's anger flared up at the thought that one of them had her life cut short because of the greed and callousness of drug traffickers. River would do whatever she could to make sure the person clinging to life in front of her not only lived but also was freed.

The sound of voices getting closer redirected River's attention. Martha arrived with another nurse. They immediately busied themselves with making the bed and setting up the medical equipment—blood pressure, heart rate, and oxygen monitors as well as a saline drip. As soon as the bed was ready, River helped the other nurse transfer the girl onto it.

Martha was preparing to administer another dose of naloxone.

River covered the girl's body with the sheet and light blanket that were at the foot of the bed. Martha took a cotton swab that was on the table next to the bed, found a place on the girl's thigh, swabbed it clean, then gave her the intramuscular injection.

The girl groaned, but despite the complaint, it made River smile. She was coming around.

"She's going to be fine," Martha confirmed, running a kind hand over the girl's forehead. "I don't know whether Rosa told you, but we have an epidemic of these at the moment."

"Is it fentanyl?" River asked.

Martha nodded. "Imported from China, trafficked by the Mexican cartels, and unfortunately distributed by a mix of cartels and locals. But I doubt this kid is from around here. I'd say she's one of their mules, and something has gone wrong with the packaging."

"I think you're right. I was on my way to Saint Ab this morning and found another young girl in the same condition . . ." River's voice trailed off, and Martha picked up on it.

"I guess she didn't make it, then."

"No. And I had a little disagreement with Sheriff Andersen about performing an autopsy."

Martha rolled her eyes and said, "We all know what Andersen is up to, but no one has the guts to confront him."

"Perhaps he's managing to help the traffickers without leaving much evidence behind," River suggested.

"There may be some of that, too." Martha sounded skeptical. "Still, if you want to know whether there was an autopsy and what the results were, you should ask Rosa's husband, Luke."

"Really? I know he's a GP, but I didn't know he's a coroner, too."

"He isn't, but he shares his GP practice with Harry Wilson, and *he* is a coroner."

"Harry Wilson." River couldn't believe her luck. Harry and River's father had met at college and gone to medical school together, but unlike her father, Harry had returned to Saint Ab to become a GP. It made sense that Luke might want to join his practice. The advantage for River was that she knew Harry well enough to speak with him directly without using Luke as an intermediary.

"You know him?" Martha said.

"I should have mentioned this earlier, but I am Luke's sister, and Harry was friends with our father."

Their conversation was interrupted by a scream. The young girl had started to thrash around in the bed. Both women turned to her, Martha checking the girl's vital signs and River trying to calm her down. The girl's eyes opened, darting from Martha to River in fear.

Martha started to speak in Spanish to her, and River didn't need to understand the words to know they were soothing. The girl's rigid body relaxed gradually, and she started crying. Her heavy sobs shook her delicate frame, and River gently took her hand, squeezing softly.

She added her own reassuring words to Martha's. "You're fine now. I'll make sure the people who did this to you don't come back."

Martha nodded and asked another question, which this time River understood. The girl hesitated and then said, "Dolores Morales."

"Guatemala?" Martha asked with a smile.

The girl hesitated but then nodded.

"It's okay." Martha's beeper sounded, and she checked it. "I've got to go. I'll come back to check on you."

She gave Dolores a reassuring smile and then went out the door, leaving River and Dolores alone.

River dragged a spare chair next to Dolores's bed and sat down. "Do you understand English?"

Dolores nodded again and then said in a heavy accent, "I learned it with my father."

"That's good. Then I think what we should do now is to make sure the police protect you from—"

Dolores grabbed River's arm, terror in her eyes. "No, please. No police."

River was taken aback by the strength of Dolores's plea. Perhaps the girl had witnessed something during her ordeal that warranted that fear. River took her hand in hers and patted it. "That's fine. If you don't want to talk to them now, we'll do it your way."

Dolores's face softened a little. She was still frowning, but her expression became more peaceful. River changed tack and then asked, "How many of you escaped?"

"Two of us, because my cousin had fallen ill, and the coyote was trying to get her to . . ." Dolores stopped, trying to find the words.

"To get her to release the drugs contained in her stomach," River suggested.

"But Teresa could hardly stand. I think the bags inside her had broken open a long time before we discovered she wasn't well."

River nodded. She didn't have the heart to tell Dolores that her cousin didn't survive. She asked how Dolores had managed to escape the coyote.

"We ran down the canyon, and then we spotted a steep path that led to the top of the cliff, so we climbed it. It was like climbing some of the steep volcano slopes at home, except that here the earth is red and not black."

"And then once you were over the ridge, what happened?"

"We kept running. It was dark, but there were no clouds, and the moon was out. My friend Cristina was in front, and we discovered a trail, but then . . ." Dolores's breathing had become labored, and she was getting agitated again.

"That's all right," River said. "Take your time. You're safe here."

Dolores nodded, then carried on. "I started to feel dizzy, and I had terrible cramps in my stomach. I knew the same thing was happening to me. Cristina made me stop and said she was going to find some help."

Dolores hid her face in her hands and started sobbing again. River took the girl in her arms and held her for a moment. "I promise you I'll find the people who've done this to you, and I'll make sure they'll never hurt you again."

River waited until Dolores stopped crying. Her friend Cristina must have found help as she said she would, and that person must have brought Dolores to Saint Ab's ER. She wondered whether that same person had contacted the police. Her guess was that he or she hadn't.

Dolores face softened a little more, and her head relaxed on the pillow. Her eyelids fluttered, and she drifted off to sleep again. River waited a moment and then took her cell from her jeans pocket. She needed to find out more about fentanyl and the way it was trafficked into the United States.

Dale had mentioned that the cartels no longer imported the drug itself but rather its precursors—its chemical components. River used her cell to search for information. She found a Congressional Research Service paper that detailed China's involvement and the various trafficking pathways that were used. The paper confirmed that importing precursors was now the norm. But these precursors were also controlled more rigorously than they had been. Still, having precursors would enable a good lab to create large quantities of fentanyl.

River browsed further through the web and found articles and other papers all pointing to the same supply chain—China, Mexico, and the United States, where the drug was distributed through various routes and where an increasing number of Americans were becoming involved with the trafficking.

River thought it very odd that she couldn't find the answer to a simple question: Why did people do it? Fentanyl was highly addictive and incredibly powerful, but what pushed people to consume it in the first place? Was it too readily prescribed, and then once they were addicted, people couldn't stop? What did the big pharmaceuticals companies do to regulate its use?

Someone knocked at the door softly and then entered. Martha came over to the bed.

"I need to use the restroom," River said to Martha. "Are you free to stay for a moment?"

"Go ahead. I want to check how my patient is doing anyway," Martha said with a smile directed at Dolores.

River slipped out of the room, leaving Dolores in good hands. She found a quiet corner in the ward and made her first call. Dale picked up on the second ring.

"It's River. Do you know who's doing our Jane Doe autopsy?"

Dale's voice dipped to a whisper. "Let me find a better place to speak to you."

He hung up, and River started looking for a secluded place to take his call. Dale's timing was impeccable. He called back just as River spotted a corner she'd selected for its privacy.

"A guy called Harry Wilson. He's a GP but doubles up as a medical examiner."

River hesitated, then said, "I know him from when I was a kid. My father and he were friends, did med school together."

"Luke Swift and he share the same practice—and . . . and of course, Luke is your brother." Dale sounded happy that he put two and two together and managed to make four.

"That'll make it easier for me to get the results of the autopsy, then."

Dale thought for a moment. "You still want to get involved?"

"Do you really think Sheriff Andersen is going to pursue the case?"

"No. He'll do what he did with the other ones," Dale said. "And that's not right."

"This is what I propose we do," River said. "I'll speak to Harry directly. You see what you can find out on your side, and we can meet at the Red Benn Diner again—say, in a couple of hours' time."

"Sounds like a plan." Dale sounded enthusiastic: He'd finally found someone who cared.

River hung up. She hadn't mentioned Dolores or the fact that she now knew the name of the Jane Doe because she wanted to make sure that Dale, unlike Sheriff Andersen, was on the right side of the law. Still, she needed to protect Dolores from the cartel men, who must be looking for her after her escape.

The ring of her cell phone interrupted her thoughts. It was Luke. But instead of berating her for not having returned yet, he was apologizing.

"I've got to get back to the GP practice," he said. "Harry has had to take the afternoon off, and I need to cover for him. I'm very sorry."

Luke sounded genuinely upset, and she chastised herself for thinking that he would be in a bad mood again. She had to let go of the past and accept that he, like her, might have grown to become a different person.

"Not to worry," she said. "I'll find something to do. What about Carmen and Jack?"

"She's going to a birthday party. She'll be picked up by one of the mothers. Jack has left on a school trip already."

"Let me know if you need me to collect her after that."

"On your bike?" Luke said with horror.

River didn't know what to say to that. She wasn't used to dealing with children in a parental capacity, and she skirted the question.

"Of course not. I assumed you would lend me your car."

Luke didn't sound entirely reassured when he said, "Okay."

"You let me know."

River hung up and went back to Dolores's room. When she entered, she saw that Dolores was sound asleep, and Rosa was now at her side. Rosa turned around and stood up.

"I've given her a mild sedative. She'll be out for a couple of hours," Rosa whispered.

"We need to assume that the cartel men are after her, from what she's told me," River said in a low voice.

"I'd say we need to speak to the police, but I'm not sure they will do her any good. At least not the local cops."

"She was scared of the idea, too, but we need to get her some sort of protection." River paused. "Do you know a young officer called Dale Jackson?"

"Not very well. Why?"

"He was the one who helped me with the young woman I found in Silver Rim canyon. He sounded genuine."

Rosa shook her head. "Let me speak to a few people here. Sheriff Andersen is not the only one who's on the take."

"In the meantime, it might be a good idea to delay entering her name in the hospital system," River suggested.

"I'll make sure it's not there, and if it is, I'll remove it."

"I have something to do but should be back within two hours." Rosa squeezed River's shoulder gently. "You go. I'll keep an eye on her."

River made her way back to the changing room, where she picked up her jacket and helmet, and dumped the used gown into a dirty laundry basket. Once outside the hospital, she checked Google and found that Saint Ab had only one coroner's office that performed autopsies. She got on her bike and made her way there. Traffic was flowing, and she arrived fifteen minutes later. She parked the Yamaha away from the main entrance. Why have her bike identified if she could avoid it? She wasn't sure Sheriff Andersen had men following her, but if he didn't now, he would soon.

She entered the reception area of the building, which resembled the police station—squat, modern, efficient—and approached a desk manned by a middle-aged woman dressed in a severe dark suit.

"I'm looking for Dr. Harry Wilson," River said.

"Do you have an appointment?" the receptionist asked in a surprisingly friendly manner.

"I'm afraid I haven't. I just arrived in town this morning. I'm visiting my brother, Luke Swift."

River waited for an instant. Mentioning the name of her brother did the trick. Suddenly she was part of the family, and the woman nodded.

"I'm the person who found the young girl Dr. Wilson is about to autopsy. I thought maybe he'd like to know what happened. I also happen to be a medic with the air force."

The woman smiled broadly and picked up the phone. River followed the receptionist's end of the conversation and deduced that Dr. Wilson had already completed the task. River wasn't a trained pathologist, but it seemed to her that he had been awfully fast.

"Dr. Wilson is getting changed. He'll be with you in a moment."

River thanked the receptionist and sat down on one of a group of uninviting chairs. Then again, this wasn't a place where people held cozy meetings. She turned toward a window that overlooked the small parking lot. A few palm trees extended their shadows over the cars. A silhouette appeared as a reflection in the window, and River turned to face the man who stood behind her.

Harry Wilson had changed since she last saw him. His hair had gone almost completely white, and the line etched into his forehead had become deeper. His thick, black-rimmed glasses gave his face a harshness she didn't recognize. He must have realized the effect his appearance had on River, because he swiped the glasses off his face and shook his head, surprised. "River," Harry said, opening his arms. "It's been such a long time."

River forced a smile and accepted his embrace. They hugged for a moment, then Harry stood back to look at her with the benevolence she remembered.

"You look good, and I hear you're a medic with the air force."

"That's right," she said. She wasn't going to elaborate about not being the sort of medic who stayed at camp and tended to the wounded, but rather the sort who flew into the battlefield to rescue operatives hit during a mission.

They stood there for a moment, remembering that the last time they'd seen each other, River and Luke were burying their parents.

"Let's find somewhere nicer to chat," River said.

Harry nodded. "I was about to suggest the same thing. There is a lovely diner not very far from here."

They crossed the parking lot, turned at the street, and kept going for a couple of blocks. Harry was full of questions for River, the way an old friend might be. River gave him the sort of information she wouldn't mind getting back to Sheriff Andersen. Harry was a coroner, and she was sure that he and Andersen talked. Even without malevolence, Harry might tell Andersen something about her she didn't want him to know.

Harry stopped in front of a small bay window and looked inside. The diner was busy, but he pushed open the door and went in. A woman waved him in, came out from behind the counter, and went to a table at the back of the long room, which she began to wipe clean.

"What would you like?" Harry asked.

"Just water, please."

"Un café e un agua, por favor, Louisa," he said.

"Ciertamente, Dr. Wilson."

Louisa went back behind the counter and busied herself making fresh coffee.

"When did you become a coroner?" River asked as she sat down.

Harry thought about it for a moment. "Must be five years or so ago."

"It's an odd job, isn't it?"

"You mean dealing with the dead rather than trying to save the living?"

"Something like that."

Their drinks arrived. Louisa laid a cup, a small coffeepot, a glass with ice, and a bottle of water on the table. She smiled and left them to it. Harry poured and pushed the glass toward River.

"I see it as a way to help victims find justice," Harry said after drinking some of his coffee.

"That's true. It's part of the discovery process." River wrapped her hand around her glass and carried on. "Speaking of which, what did you find on the Jane Doe?"

Coolness flitted across Harry's eyes, but then he tried to smile. "I can't disclose any of it to you, River. That's the way it works. Otherwise, I might compromise the case."

"Do you think a case will be brought to the courts? She almost certainly is an illegal immigrant, and cartel victims seldom find justice."

Harry shifted on his chair and took another sip of coffee. "Why do you think she's a cartel victim?"

"Because she had OD'd, and someone had made her empty her bowels to get the bags she was transporting. It doesn't take a genius or a medical expert to know she was a mule."

Harry nodded.

"The question is whether what she was carrying was fentanyl or something else," River added.

Harry's face dropped, and the coolness River had seen in his eyes was replaced by fear. He took a couple of sips of coffee. It seemed like her question had hit a nerve.

River continued. "Everyone knows fentanyl is being trafficked into the United States through Mexican drug cartels. But the latest, most perverse way of importing the drug is through precursors—the key ingredients of the drug—and then cooking it here, on US soil. Problem is, even precursors are now tracked and are illegal to sell unless they come with a specific authorization, so it's worth trafficking them across the border, just like the finished product. The difference is that they are less expensive, so losing some isn't as bad as losing the fentanyl itself."

Harry was frowning. "How do you know all this?"

"I have my sources," River said as she finished her water. She wasn't about to admit that her source was called Google.

"You should stay away from all this," Harry said as he finished his coffee. "It's not a good idea to get involved with cartel business."

"So this young woman was killed by precursors, then," River said, taking a gamble.

"River." Harry extended his hand and grabbed her wrist, squeezing tight. "Listen to me. This isn't a game, and you don't have the protection of the armed forces behind you. This girl isn't worth it."

If Harry had slapped her in the face, the effect would have been the same. River agreed with what he said first—it wasn't a game, and she certainly no longer had the might of the military behind her. But no, this girl deserved every ounce of justice she could get. River's parents had spent a lifetime dedicating themselves to helping others, and such a statement went against everything they had believed in and stood for.

"I hear you, Harry." She could hear her voice tremble. "I'll bear what you said in mind."

She rose slowly, took a ten-dollar bill out of her wallet, and left it on the table. Harry didn't have the time to offer to pay instead. River was already out the door, gasping for air. She walked a few paces and stopped, breathing deeply and exhaling slowly. Where was the Harry her father had called his oldest friend? More important, why had Luke agreed to join his practice? Perhaps Luke harbored the same view of illegals. River shook her head. She shouldn't make assumptions until she'd spoken to her brother.

River jogged to the parking lot where she'd left her bike. She turned back once, but Harry hadn't left the diner yet. She straddled the bike, started it, and made her way to the Red Benn Diner, where she hoped her conversation with Dale would be more productive. She was damned if she was going to give up on Dolores and Teresa—the young girl lying in the morgue.

Chapter 4

She felt a text ping in her jacket pocket and stopped to check who was trying to reach her. It was Dale: He was on his way to the Red Benn. The thought brightened River's dark mood. She arrived there only a few moments later, parked the bike, and walked in. Dale wasn't there yet, but the table where they'd sat in the morning was free. She took a seat and waited.

Dale pushed the door open a few minutes later, scanned the room, and spotted River. He crossed the distance quickly. River hadn't noticed how athletic the young man was. He slid opposite her and sat back. His face was red, and River could tell he'd been running.

"What happened?" she asked.

"I had to disappear really fast. Sheriff Andersen was looking for me."

A thought floated in River's mind, but she pushed it away. She'd consider the timing of her meeting with Harry Wilson and Sheriff Andersen's sudden interest in Dale later.

"What have you got for me?" River asked as one of the waitresses approached with two mugs and a coffeepot.

"Anything else for you good people?" she asked with a smile.

"Pancakes and maple syrup, please," Dale said.

River raised an eyebrow.

"I eat food when I'm stressed," Dale explained. He seemed to have something else to say to River, but wasn't yet sure how to broach it.

"Let me start with my news," River began. "I went to see the coroner, Harry Wilson."

"How did you know he was on the case?"

"Because he and Luke, my brother, share the same practice, and he asked Luke to stand for him this afternoon. It was only natural to figure that he'd been asked to work on the Jane Doe case."

"It could have been another victim."

"Why? Do you have that many suspicious deaths in Saint Ab?"

Dale shook his head. "I guess not."

"He wasn't that happy to see me. He was a very good friend of my dad, but today I somehow didn't recognize him."

The pancakes arrived, and they waited for the waitress to turn away before continuing.

"Maybe the coroner job doesn't suit him. But when Sheriff Andersen asks you to do something, most of the time, you do as you're told," Dale said before tucking into his pancakes.

"Andersen got him appointed coroner?" River said, almost to herself. The Utah Department of Health and Human Services appointed the state medical examiner, who then appointed medical examiners for each county. Sheriff Andersen seemed to be well-connected.

"That was five years ago, I think. A year or so after Andersen was made sheriff."

"In any case, Harry wasn't very talkative, but I got the sense that our Jane Doe OD'd on precursors and not fentanyl."

Dale's fork hung in the air at the news. He twirled it around a few times and put it down. "Do you know what that means?"

"That the cartel people who bring the precursors into the United States cook fentanyl here—on US soil—in some clandestine lab."

"You're pretty clued in for someone who isn't law enforcement." Dale looked impressed.

"I'm a medic, and I have a good source of information called Google."

"Wow—you can find all that on Google?"

"You just need to know where to look."

Dale demolished half his plate of food before he took a sip of coffee and leaned forward. "I found something when I was helping bag our Jane Doe's clothes," Dale whispered.

River leaned forward, too. "Is it drugs?"

"No. It's a photo," Dale looked around. There was no one close to their table. He fidgeted in one of his pants pockets, then slid a grimy picture across the table. River smiled at the thought. Dale had just taken evidence out of the police station.

"Should you be doing this?"

He shrugged. "I just kinda borrowed it."

River looked at the image: three smiling girls, two of whom she recognized—Teresa and Dolores Morales—and one who had to be Cristina, the friend who had managed to save Dolores's life. They were wearing brightly colored dresses, and despite the dirt that covered the photo, River could tell that the girls were happy. She pointed at the two girls she knew and said, "These are Teresa and Dolores Morales. I think the name of the other girl is Cristina."

Dale's eyes widened. "How do you—"

"It seems that you and I don't like doing things by the book, so I guess I feel much better about telling you something I'd like to keep under wraps for the time being."

She waited for Dale to acknowledge what she was asking of him. He nodded and whispered, "All right."

"Dolores Morales is in the hospital. She, too, suffered an overdose, but unlike her cousin, she was much luckier. She survived."

"But shouldn't we offer her protection?" Dale asked. "The cartel men must be looking for her everywhere."

"I sort of mentioned that to her, but she looked more scared about the police than the cartel men."

Dale was about to protest but must have thought better of it. "I suppose she's scared to be sent back across the border."

"There's that, too," River said, "but there's also something else." River waited for a reaction from Dale.

He cocked his head.

"We can't discard the possibility that some people at Saint Ab North Police Station are linked to the cartel."

Dale shifted in his chair, and for a moment River thought she had made a terrible mistake. He must have read the thought on her face and shook his head.

"If you're thinking I'm doing all this because I'm one of them, I'm not. I know you have only my word for it, but I want to get justice for those girls. That's why I got the picture out."

River liked Dale, and her instinct told her she should trust him, but she couldn't afford to make a mistake.

"Okay, then. What's the story about Andersen? I want all the dirt." She took a sip of coffee and sat back.

Dale sighed and pushed away the last bite of pancakes. The idea of having to tell River about what he knew or suspected seemed to make him lose his appetite.

"Sheriff Andersen isn't from Saint Ab or even Utah. He's from Nevada, from a town close to Vegas—or that's the official story. As soon as he arrived, he got rid of some of the older guys and replaced them with younger police officers."

"Who weren't from the area, either," River said.

"And then things started changing. People around town were complaining that the police were a little too tough on small mistakes but let the big things slip, like theft and drug abuse. And then these illegals started to appear."

"By 'appear,' you mean they were alive?" River took another sip of coffee.

"No—dead people. Usually women, but not always. Then things got better, but Andersen never caught anyone."

"So either he knows the traffickers and got them to be more careful, or they found a route that avoids the town altogether. Or perhaps both."

"And then there's Sheriff Andersen's lifestyle." Dale let it hang.

"Way over his pay grade."

Dale nodded.

"And how do you fit in?"

Dale's cheeks grew a little pinker. He took a sip of coffee and finally said, "I'm a local guy. I guess Andersen decided he needed to get a local on his team." Dale took another sip and then added, "My grades were also just right when I applied."

River didn't want to belabor the issue, but she took it that Dale's performance at school or perhaps at the police academy wasn't that impressive.

"So what? There's more to being a cop than scoring a bull's-eye at fifty yards left-handed. Just like being able to stitch someone up without it showing doesn't make you a good medic. You've got to understand the people you're serving. And I think you do. You care about your community."

It angered River that Dale, who seemed like a decent human being, was disparaged because he didn't want to bully or even shoot people who disagreed with Sheriff Andersen. Dale glanced at River, and she nodded. "I mean it, Dale."

"Thanks. That helps."

"If we can't trust Andersen or half the cops at the police station, who do we go to?"

Dale gave it some thought. "I need to contact a couple of guys I sorta hung out with when I was doing my training."

"That's good," River said before sipping more coffee. "I'll find a way to keep Dolores Morales safe at the hospital until we come up with a plan. But I guess we also need to find out about the routes the traffickers take."

"I can go back to where we found the first Morales girl and see whether I can spot vehicle tracks of some sort."

"Dolores told me there's a path that enabled her and her friend to reach the top of the ridge, but the path isn't visible. You might want to find that path. It could tell us where the other girl is."

"I'll get on it right now," Dale said, eager to get going.

River stood up and smiled. "Finish your pancakes, Dale. You'll need the energy." She was about to take her wallet out of her backpack, but Dale stopped her. "It's on me."

River nodded her thanks, picked up her helmet, and headed to the parking lot. She straddled her bike and checked her phone. She had a message from Luke, asking her to call back.

She dialed his number, and he picked up just before the call went to voicemail. "Does your offer to pick up Carmen from her friend's house still stand? I've got a lot more work than expected, and Harry hasn't returned yet."

"Sure—text me the address. I'll swing back to the practice to pick up your keys, then I'll go and collect Carmen."

Luke texted her both addresses. She noticed that the practice was within walking distance from his home. River checked the time. She had another hour or so before Dolores came to. She just wanted to make sure the girl was safe for the night, and then she'd find a better solution the following day.

River started the bike and drove off. As she was leaving, she looked in her rearview mirror and saw Dale's car heading in the direction of the Silver Rim canyon. River accelerated and rode a little faster than she should have, but the Saint Ab Police didn't seem to be around, or perhaps they were otherwise engaged. The idea didn't reassure her.

When she arrived at Luke's practice, she found a friendly receptionist waiting for her with Luke's keys. River picked them up, rode the bike to Luke's house, and switched it for her brother's brand-new SUV. It took River a couple of minutes to figure out how all the gadgets worked, but she managed to start the car and drive off to collect her niece.

The memory of a cheerful Carmen and her cat popped into River's mind, and she smiled. Carmen was a special little girl, and she could see why Luke seemed so besotted with her. River thought about Jack and his skateboarding, and something melted in her. She could see herself in him—adventurous, probably strong-willed, and taking no notice of Luke. River regretted that Jack was due to leave that evening on a short school trip, but was glad he would be back in a couple of days' time. She was looking forward to spending more time with him.

River checked the address again before ringing the bell at a large house that looked similar to Luke's. River heard voices, kids and adults speaking over one another, then a dog barked, and the door was finally opened by a woman whose smile dropped slightly when she saw River. She must have been expecting Luke or Rosa.

River flashed a wide grin. "My name is River; I'm Carmen's aunt. Luke has been held back at work."

The woman's smile broadened. She extended a hand and said, "Very nice to meet you, River. I'm Maddie. Yes, your brother called to let me know it would be you collecting Carmen. She's ready to go, although she's making the most of her last minutes with my daughter."

Both women stepped inside the house. Carmen appeared in a doorway and launched at River with open arms. River grabbed her and whirled her around a few times. Carmen jumped off and dragged River further inside Maddie's house. "You must meet my friend Emma."

They went into the living room, and the sight shook River. A young girl Carmen's age was sitting in a wheelchair. Toys were scattered around her, and she was finishing a drawing with colored pens.

"I'm almost done," she said. And then she lifted a piece of paper with an air of triumph.

Carmen hopped toward her and picked up her own drawing. The two girls exchanged their artwork with a smile and a hug.

"Come on," Maddie said. "Time to say goodbye."

The girls hugged each other once more, and then Carmen put her raincoat on. River and Carmen left, holding hands, and then got into the SUV. River strapped Carmen in the car seat in the back, fumbling a little with the straps.

"Did you have a good time?" River asked.

Carmen looked at her strangely and said, "Emma's my best friend."

"Silly me. I shouldn't have asked the question."

"That's okay." Carmen grinned. "Do you have a best friend?"

"I do. She's called Karen, and she lives in Alaska."

"Is it far away?" Carmen asked with a frown.

"It's up north, at the top of the world."

"Where they have polar bears?"

"That's right."

"Can I come and visit?"

"Sure. We'll have to ask your mom and dad, though."

River got into the driver's seat, and they took off. She got Carmen to chat about her day and then about Franklin, her cat. When they got to the house, Luke had just arrived. Carmen hugged her dad for a moment and then escaped into the garden to find her cat. River and Luke were left on their own, and it somehow felt awkward. Luke turned toward the kettle.

"Shall I make us a cup of ginger tea?"

"Why not? Thanks." River glanced at her watch. Dolores would be waking up in less than twenty minutes, and River did not want her to be alone and scared. But she couldn't dump Luke and run to the hospital. He was trying to mend the rift that had deepened since their parents' death, and she sensed he was doing his best, offering to make a cup of what they had both enjoyed wherever they went—ginger tea.

Luke busied himself with chopping some fresh ginger while the kettle started to hum. Carmen came into the kitchen with Franklin in her arms, then walked past them, busy carrying on a conversation with her cat, whose purring was almost too loud to be real.

"She loves that little animal," River said.

"I seem to remember us adopting all sorts of pets when we were traveling with Mom and Dad."

River chuckled. "How about the baby hyena?"

Luke shook his head and turned toward River, grinning. "That went down like a lead balloon."

"Still, when we had to give her up to an animal sanctuary, I thought Dad was going to cry," River said.

Luke poured two mugs of tea and gave one to River. He, too, drank it without honey. "I know. I'm not sure who was the most amazed about that—him or us."

They took a few sips of tea, and River thought that perhaps she could venture a question about her parents' posting in the DRC. She took another sip, ready to ask, when her phone rang. Rosa's name was showing on her screen, and she picked up the call immediately.

"She's gone," was all Rosa said. River didn't need a name; she knew.

"I'm coming," River said, and then hung up.

She squeezed her brother's arm. "Sorry, Luke. Rosa needs me now. I've gotta go."

River scooped up her jacket and helmet and ran out of the house. Luke hadn't seemed upset when she simply said that Rosa needed her urgently. He seemed to think the world of his wife, and this gave River a warm feeling about her brother that she hadn't had for a long time.

River got to the hospital as soon as she could, forgetting again about the speed limit. She parked in the staff lot and saw Rosa waiting for her at the entrance to the ER, face drawn and panic in her eyes.

"I went to check for Dolores fifteen minutes ago, and she was gone," Rosa said as River got to her.

"When was the last time someone checked on her before that?"

"Around 4:00 p.m. She was still sound asleep then. I wanted to come by again at four thirty, but we had more victims of this terrible car crash arriving," Rosa said.

"And I could have come earlier, too," River replied, feeling as upset as Rosa. "We need to start looking. You go around the hospital. She might still be here. I'll canvas the town and find some help."

Rosa stepped closer to River and murmured, "But who can we trust? Besides, the hospital will have to report her missing soon."

River thought for a moment. "I'm going to speak to the young police officer who helped me with the other girl, and then perhaps you can give him an update. That might delay things for a while, and then . . ."

"What?"

"Can I take a look at your surveillance footage? I just want to see whether we can track Dolores's moves."

Rosa ran a hand over the back of her neck. "It'll depend on who's in charge. But come with me."

They walked in silence until they reached a glass door at the back of the building. Rosa scanned her pass, and the door clicked open. They kept going, and Rosa stopped in front of another door. She signaled that River should wait as she knocked. It opened after a moment. Rosa slid in, and the door closed again.

The door opened once more, and a small man waved River in.

"Antonio doesn't mind us looking at the video of the corridor outside Dolores's room," Rosa said.

Antonio went to a bank of TV screens. He chose one and seemed to be rewinding a recording, selecting a starting point. River recognized the corridor on the screen. She and Rosa leaned in closer and watched for a few minutes as Antonio sped up the recording.

At 4:57 p.m., Dolores peeked outside the door of her room. She disappeared back inside, and at 5:06 p.m., she left the room, dressed in a pair of jeans, a dark sweater, and white running shoes. She had tied her long dark hair in a ponytail and walked with her head down. She kept going until she reached the staircase and started going down. Antonio switched the camera to follow Dolores. She stopped on a floor below the one she'd come from and reentered the hospital corridors. Then she disappeared.

Antonio shook his head, looking frustrated. "There is a blind spot there. People can walk along this corridor and reach the bank of elevators without being detected."

River felt a shiver run down her spine. Someone had told Dolores what to do, and it was neither she nor Rosa. "Can we take a look at the hospital's back doors?" she asked.

Antonio looked at his watch and shook his head. "My colleague will be back from his cigarette break in a few minutes. You shouldn't even be here in the first place."

Rosa sighed and thanked Antonio. She followed River out of the room, and they retraced their steps toward the glass door, then made their way to the place where Dolores disappeared from view. Rosa and River stood in front of the elevators, deciding what to do.

"You can't leave the hospital," River said, "and it's still worth searching for her here. But I think she's left."

Rosa nodded. "I think so, too. And someone helped her."

"I agree. Let's hope it's not somebody connected to the cartel."

"I can't bear the thought."

"Let's split up. We can call each other if we have fresh news."

River rang for an elevator, stepped in, got off on the ground floor, and left the hospital. She reached her bike and straddled it, but fought the urge to start searching right away. She hesitated—but no, she had to decide whether she could trust Dale completely. She had told him about Dolores, but the young woman hadn't been dragged out of the hospital by thugs. River took her cell out of her jacket and went with her intuition. Dale was a decent guy.

She dialed his number. It rang a few times and then switched to voicemail. She recalled that Dale had gone to the Silver Rim canyon after they met. He wouldn't have any reception there. She hung up and sent a text instead.

New development. Need urgent call.

River started the bike and turned onto the road that led away from the city center. If Dolores had any sense, she would avoid places where people could spot her. River rode slowly along the road and came to an intersection. She stayed there for a few seconds, her frustration and fear for Dolores rising. Applying the same logic, she kept going, away from the city center. She spotted the belfry of a church a few blocks away and took the next turn toward it.

When she arrived in front of the church, she noticed that a few women were lining up at the door, loaded with bags. River stopped and watched as they each dropped their bags at the entrance. The door was open, and several women walked out, grabbed the bags, and thanked the donors.

River got off her bike and took a few steps back. She considered the building and realized that this wasn't a Mormon temple but a Catholic church. Then a woman walked out to pick up some of the bags left outside. River frowned, and then it clicked: Martha, the head nurse she'd been introduced to at the hospital, was helping.

River took her helmet off and made her way to the church's entrance. She waved, and Martha stopped. She waved back and waited for River to reach her.

"Are you helping the church collect clothes for the needy?" River asked.

"We have a lot of immigrants crossing the Mexican border and moving from Arizona to Nevada. Since Saint Ab is right at the border between the two states, we get a large influx of them."

River picked up the last bag of clothes and followed Martha inside the church. "I guess a lot of these people are Catholic."

"That's right, and our church offers sanctuary for whoever needs it, whether they're Catholic or not," Martha said, walking along one of the aisles on the gospel side of the building. She entered the sacristy, and River hesitated. A couple of women walked out and smiled at River. Martha called her from inside.

"It's okay. Father O'Rourke is pretty relaxed about our using the sacristy to store the clothes we collect."

"O'Rourke? Is that Irish?"

"Yep. And he's not an immigrant from way back when. He arrived in Saint Ab twenty years ago."

River chuckled. She recalled meeting an Irish medic from Northern Ireland who'd become friendly with her parents. The accent had been a real struggle and a source of incessant laughter.

"I bet he must have stunned everyone the first time he opened his mouth," River said as she entered the sacristy.

Martha smiled. "He still does."

River put the bag she was carrying down and opened it to take a quick look. Jeans and T-shirts that had hardly been worn.

"Where do people go when they need help? I mean, do they come to the church? Or do they know there's another place in town?"

Martha dumped the contents of one large bag onto a table. "You didn't notice it, but we put a note on the front door and on the side door telling people where to go. It's only a few minutes' walk from here."

"Can they get food and clothes and shelter there?" River asked.

Martha nodded. "Although the facility can't afford to shelter everyone. Only the most vulnerable."

River came close to the table where the donated clothes were strewn. She picked up a pair of jeans and said, "Girls like Dolores . . . who just left the hospital a couple of hours ago without a trace."

Martha's face dropped, and her cheeks flashed red.

"It's okay if you have her," River said. "I just want to make sure she's safe."

Martha sat down, shaken. "She's safe, but now I'm worried."

"You mean if I can trace her back to you and this church, so can the cartel men?"

Martha nodded.

"It was pure luck that I found the church, really."

"But you're not from here. Some of these people are. They're from Saint Ab or around the area. They know what we do."

"Surely yours isn't the only organization that helps people in need. I'm sure the Mormon community does its bit."

"Of course they do. They, too, are generous, but the Hispanic immigrants, especially the undocumented ones, come to this church."

River considered the odds, and she was with Martha on this. Dolores wouldn't be safe anywhere until the cartel men had been dealt with once and for all.

"Is there anyone in town who's been following what's happening with drug trafficking in Saint Ab?"

Martha hesitated, and River came to sit next to her. "Listen, I realize it's hard to know who to trust, but if I was one of them, I would have told the cartel men where Dolores was, and they would have come to finish her off before you had time to get her out of the hospital."

"That's true," Martha said with a slow nod. "I'm going to give you a name—Miguel Lopez. He's a freelance journalist and investigator."

River took her cell phone out of her jacket pocket and recorded Miguel's name and number in her contacts list.

"He's my big brother. Miguel is fearless, and sometimes I worry about him."

River tried to sound reassuring. "I'm not suggesting we tackle the cartel by ourselves. But we need to fight back against them in a way that lasts. I have a niece and a nephew. I don't want them ever to come across drugs at school or college."

"And that's exactly where the drugs will be going next," Martha said.

"I'm probably going to need to talk to Dolores at some point. Not now—but I need to ask whether she can tell me more about the people who helped her. They may have information on the traffickers, might have seen something relevant."

Martha thought for a moment, and River added, "I'll be extra careful, and we can meet in a way you think is the safest for her."

"And you need to look after yourself, too. These people will kill you for less. You're encroaching on their business."

River hugged Martha and left the church. She stopped to make sure she remembered its name—Santa Maria de Guadalupe—and then took down the address of the place where migrants were sent to receive help.

She reached her bike and checked her phone again. Dale had left a message.

Got some tracks I'm following. Call me. I'm out of the canyon.

Chapter 5

Luis didn't expect the fist that slammed into his face. Alfonso had never touched him before, and today marked a first for both men. Alfonso, Luis, and Pablo, Alfonso's number two, had been standing on the ridge of a cliff that cut deep into the surrounding red rock. Luis was thrown to the ground and skidded only a foot away from the mouth of the ravine. He crawled back from the void with terror on his face.

Alfonso waited, Pablo at his side. He didn't like Luis—never had—but the thought that the man may have fallen to his death disturbed him. His father, Gonzalo Cruz, head of the Cruz Cartel, had pushed him to lead their new venture. Alfonso was to challenge the Sinaloa Cartel along one of the better-known routes for illegally trafficked drugs into the United States. Gonzalo had insisted that Alfonso needed a man like Luis, and Alfonso had no choice but to agree.

Luis took a moment to stand up, his face betraying astonishment rather than fear. He brushed himself off, and arrogance flashed in his eyes.

"It is under control. I know where the other girl is."

"But she is still alive and must have spoken about what she saw by now," Alfonso said.

Luis spat some blood onto the ground. "She doesn't know the terrain, and my contact at the hospital tells me she arrived unconscious."

"And mine tells me she had a visit from a couple of nurses, including one who doesn't belong to the hospital staff. So now I want to understand what happened and why these girls are falling ill."

"The coyote you used was too old. He should never have been allowed to lead the girls all the way through Arizona."

That much was true. Alfonso had wanted to use people he knew well to ensure that he could control the flow of girls being led across the border and along the new route the cartel wanted to test. The fewer number of traffickers he used the better: That way, the push into the Sinaloa territory could be kept secret. Alfonso wanted to consolidate his father's position before he confronted the largest and most established cartel in the whole of Mexico.

Alfonso turned to Pablo, who leaned toward him and murmured, "Tiene un punto."

Alfonso took a deep breath and surveyed the magnificent landscape that surrounded them—the hills steep and rocky, the earth red as blood, and the sun beating down on them, merciless.

"You have twenty-four hours to find her and bring her back. I want her alive, and I want to know what she said and to who."

Luis frowned. "Why bother to—"

Alfonso lifted his hand, interrupting Luis. "Do not test my patience again, Luis. I ask you to deliver her alive. This is what you will do. Otherwise, the next time we speak, I *will* throw you down that ravine."

Luis held Alfonso's gaze for an instant but then looked away and walked toward his SUV. Pablo moved to block his path.

"You haven't told me why the girls fell ill," Alfonso said.

Luis stopped dead. "I guess whoever did the packing put too much in the condoms the girls swallowed. We're handling precursors, not fentanyl, so we tried to load as much as possible to maximize the value of the crossing."

"Did you ask anyone whether the precursors were lethal?"

"I did, but I gathered they aren't as bad as fentanyl itself."

Alfonso wasn't sure Luis had asked, and if he did, he might have done it the way he did everything else—by bullying someone into giving him the answer he wanted to hear. He indicated with a dismissive move of the hand that Luis could go, and Pablo moved to the side.

"Twenty-four hours, Luis. And I want the girl alive."

Luis got into his SUV, reversed, and disappeared down the trail that led to the top of the cliff. Alfonso waited until the dust the vehicle was throwing had settled.

"He's a loose cannon," Pablo said.

"I know, but he's my father's loose cannon."

Both men got into their SUV, Pablo in the driver's seat. He drove off in the opposite direction from Luis.

"After you've dropped me at the lab, I want you to go to Saint Ab and find out who these nurses are," Alfonso said.

"Do you want me to check on Luis, too?"

"No," Alfonso said, looking through the open window at the landscape he found fascinating. "He needs to make a few mistakes before I can speak to my father about him."

"I thought you wanted to speak to the girl."

"I do, but if she dies, well . . . what's more important is to learn who these women at the hospital are. What do they know? Then I'll decide how we deal with them."

Pablo just nodded. Alfonso relaxed a little and absentmindedly massaged his right hand. He glanced quickly at Pablo, then let his head drop against the headrest. Why had life made his choices so complicated? He pushed the thought away to concentrate on what he needed to do next.

"One more thing to check: I want to know how many girls crossed the border and how many got delivered to Vegas. Ask on the q.t."

Pablo just nodded. They drove in a comfortable silence for another twenty minutes until they reached a ranch nestled against one of the slopes that led to Apple Valley. The place had been deserted for a long time and was off the beaten track. Alfonso had taken his time choosing the site, despite the pressure put on him by his father. But it was now the best lab they had on US soil, producing fentanyl that the network he'd built was delivering all the way up to Canada.

The buildings had been left to crumble on the outside, but the lab that Alfonso had installed inside was equipped with quality appliances. It meant less risk for the chemists who did the cooking and increased output for the customers. Like Luis, his father was a bully. He'd told him many times that strength in their world went hand in hand with violence, and sparing his chemists' lives seemed unimportant to Señor Cruz. Alfonso wondered whom his father would choose when the time came to designate a successor—him or Luis.

River watched in the distance as the sun disappeared behind the mountains that surrounded Saint Ab. She shivered and zipped up her jacket. Luke hadn't said anything about dinner, but he would be expecting her back for that. That was one thing the entire Swift family agreed on: The evening meal had to be eaten together. Even when her parents had been working, one of them would ensure that their two children would eat with whoever was around.

Still, she had some time before she needed to make her way back to Luke's. She took her cell out of her jacket pocket and dialed Dale. He answered immediately.

"I found some good tracks that lead to a couple of cabins in the mountains."

"That's a *real good* result, Dale," River said, overenthusiastic, hoping Dale would get the tease. "On my side, I found someone who knows where we can find Dolores."

"That's a *good* result, River," Dale said with a chuckle.

"I only meant it as a compliment." River smiled as though Dale could see her.

"I know, and I couldn't resist the reply," he said with a smile in his voice, too, but then he turned serious. "We can't take her to the police station. There's a guy who I think can help us, but I haven't been able to get in touch with him yet. It's getting dark here, so I'll go home and give him a call."

"Call me back if you hear anything. I must get back to my brother, but I have another lead for intel about the cartel."

"I know you've been in the military and all, but these cartel guys are vicious." Dale had switched to his serious-cop make-sure-you-don't-exceed-the-speed-limit-again voice.

"I'll be super careful." River wondered how long a cartel man would last in front of a Taliban fighter—or any other terrorist she'd encountered in the field, for that matter. On the other hand, she'd also read as she was scouring the web for information about fentanyl that the military was the one tackling the cartels in Mexico, not the cops. The cartels were forces to be reckoned with. So perhaps she should heed Dale's advice. River hung up, promising to keep Dale updated.

River made her next call, hoping it wasn't too late. A gravelly voice answered, and she launched into an introduction, assuming Miguel needed details before he agreed to speak to her.

"You're River, the air force medic," Miguel said.

"Oh."

"Don't be surprised. Martha called me to let me know you'd be in touch."

"Then you know why I want to talk with you."

"I do, and I can't wait. Are you free now? My wife runs a nice restaurant downtown."

"I'm visiting family. I need to head back there, but I'll get in touch after dinner if that works for you."

"We're open until late. Call me anytime, and I'll put some feelers out to see what's circulating on the grapevine."

River sent a text to Luke before she started the bike. He responded immediately. As she thought he would, he was expecting her for dinner.

When River arrived, Carmen was already in her pajamas. She was watching TV with a fast-asleep Franklin on her lap. River hugged Luke and then went to kiss her niece. Carmen stretched her arms up, and River managed to give her a hug without waking up the cat.

"We'll have dinner, just the two of us," Luke said. "Rosa won't be back until 2:00 a.m., and Jack has gone on his school trip."

River nodded. "Rosa told me she was on the early night shift."

She went to the kitchen, where Luke had laid two plates on the counter and was making pasta.

"Something simple," he said.

"I'm not complaining," River said as she went to one of the drawers to find cutlery. She chose a spoon and a fork, and the choice made Luke smile.

"Do you remember the Italian medics who showed us how to eat pasta with these?" he said, pointing toward the cutlery River had just laid next to the plates.

River sat down. "I remember their faces but not their names."

"Francesca and Massimo, I think."

River snapped her fingers. "That's right. Plus, she had this brilliant meatball recipe."

"And here we are," Luke said as he placed a large helping of spaghetti and meatballs onto River's plate.

"How come you know the recipe?"

"Francesca had given it to Mom, and I found it—"

A cold wind seemed to blow through the room. River clenched her fork hard. Luke stood in front of her, still holding the pan full of pasta but unable to put anything on his own plate. River forced herself to pick up the spoon.

"It's good that Mom's recipe book was spared." Her voice wobbled a little, and she hoped Luke hadn't noticed. "Anyway, it's found a good home."

Luke poured the rest of the contents of the pan on his plate and ditched the pan in the sink. "She'd sent it to me before . . . you know." Luke made a vague gesture that was meant to replace the words he didn't want to speak.

Mentioning the murder of their parents wasn't something Luke seemed to want to do just as they were about to have dinner. He came around the counter and sat next to River. They started eating in silence, but River forced herself to give an approving grunt after the second mouthful. She couldn't give the food her full attention, but she couldn't let her brother's hard work go unappreciated. Luke nodded and smiled. It seemed that he, too, was moved by the memory of old and better times.

The alarm on Luke's phone chimed. He took the phone out of his back pocket.

"Time to get Carmen and Franklin to bed."

He stood up and went to the living room. River was expecting protestation from her niece, but nothing came. River turned around to see Luke scoop his fast-asleep daughter into his arms and carry her up to her bedroom. He returned a moment later to pick up Franklin. The cat stretched a little in his arms but let himself flop and be carried away, too. River almost didn't recognize her brother. He'd been so impatient and critical when they were children. But perhaps this was what it meant to be a dad.

Or perhaps Luke had felt overwhelmed by the life their parents made them lead—moving from one country to the next, making new friends, and then losing them a year or so later. River had loved it—the new landscapes, the new people and their cultures. Poverty never worried her as long as there was an adventure to be had. She managed to keep in touch with old friends, sharing her discoveries with them. But now she could see it all around her: Luke needed to belong somewhere and build a home that he could call his own for the rest of his days. Returning to Saint Ab was the best decision he ever made.

"You shouldn't have waited for me, sis," Luke said as he returned from putting Carmen and Franklin to bed.

"They're both asleep?" River asked.

Luke sat back down at the counter. "And snoring away." Luke smiled and added, "I didn't know a cat could snore so loudly."

River chuckled and picked up her fork again. She took her time eating a couple of mouthfuls. It was hard to pretend the memory of her parents didn't weigh on her mind.

"It's okay if you don't want to finish it," Luke said.

River squeezed his arm. "Remember what they used to tell us? Finish your food, remembering the hungry of the world."

Luke shrugged. "We're no longer in Africa or anywhere else where there's famine."

"But does every American live with a full belly every day?"

Luke gave her a quick smile. "It's strange you ended up in the military, Riv. You're much more like our parents than I ever was."

"It's another way of helping people, I guess." River didn't want to revisit the old argument that had caused her to have a terrible fight with her parents just a few months before their death. But she wanted to get Luke to keep talking. "I wish I could have explained that better to them when we last spoke, all those years ago."

"Me, too," Luke said.

River frowned and Luke immediately clarified. "Sorry—I mean I, too, had a couple of unhappy conversations with them."

River didn't say anything. Luke would know that she was surprised. It had always seemed to her that Luke had been the perfect son. Good grades at school, helpful with chores, venturing outside the camps only when permitted. He always seemed to be falling in step with what his parents wanted—effortlessly.

He shook his head. "I know what you think. I never had an argument with them, but we ended up having a couple of skirmishes when they moved to the DRC."

"About what?" River asked before taking another mouthful of spaghetti.

"I still can't figure out why it was an issue, but I wanted to come and visit them there. I was getting worried that they were moving to a dangerous country. Also, they weren't getting any younger."

Luke took a sip of water. He seemed to need a moment to compose himself. "I suggested I spend some time with them to settle them into their new home, but they wouldn't have it."

River straightened up. "They didn't want you to come because it was what? Too risky?"

"I know. I didn't get it. I mean, we lived in Rwanda for almost two years."

"At the end I threatened to go to the DRC anyway, and that's when we had a big disagreement. Dad even said he would tell the people in the village not to pick me up when I arrived at the river port."

River watched her brother as he spoke about what must have been one of the last conversations he had with their father. He was holding his tumbler of water so tightly that his fingers had turned white. River was glad the tumbler was thick plastic and wondered whether a glass might have shattered. New lines she hadn't noticed had formed on his forehead, and his eyes were cast in the distance, reliving the exchange with agony.

Luke would never be ready to hear what River had found out about their parents. She would have to go it alone. What she needed from Luke was information. Anything that might help her understand why her parents' names had ended up on the same piece of paper as a man nicknamed Dr. Death, one of the most dangerous arms traffickers in Africa.

"They were right to be scared. What would have happened if you'd been there when the fighters came?"

"I should have gone there at the beginning, when I knew there was something wrong with their assignment." Luke let go of the tumbler and buried his face in his hands. His shoulders started to shake a little. River stepped down from her stool and hugged her brother close, rocking him gently.

"It would have made no difference. Mom and Dad were pigheaded when it came to protecting people's health. They wouldn't have moved."

Luke rested his head against River's shoulder. "This time was different, Riv. I felt it but didn't get it until it was too late."

He was right, of course, but he didn't need to know that.

"And look at me. I'd hardly spoken to them."

River's throat tightened, and both she and her brother remained silent for a while. The sound of Luke's phone made them jump. He took out his cell from his pocket and answered.

"Hello, honey." He mouthed "Rosa" to River.

River nodded and started clearing the plates. She didn't follow the conversation but gathered that Rosa was calling about Carmen.

River then concentrated on her task and what it was she was going to do next.

Luke and Rosa chatted for a little while. River gathered that Rosa must be on a short break. She walked out of the kitchen to give her brother privacy and checked the time. The conversation about their parents was over for now, but perhaps it was still early enough to pay a visit to Miguel's wife's restaurant.

She heard Luke yawn as he came into the living room. "I'm sorry, Sis, but I'm going to go to bed. I have an early start tomorrow morning."

"I'm not ready for bed yet, and one of Rosa's colleagues recommended a nice place to have a drink. I might check it out."

"Sure thing," Luke said.

"Thanks again for looking after me today."

Luke nodded and said a little awkwardly, "It was good to see you."

River waited until Luke had gone upstairs. She gathered her jacket, helmet, and backpack and made her way to La Chica Bonita. Miguel had explained she would find the restaurant on the west side of Saint Ab, close to the road that encircled the city. River was grateful that she knew the town well enough to know where that was and that the main roads hadn't changed much since the last time she visited. She texted Miguel that she was on her way and received an immediate answer. The ride across town was easy, and she found herself in front of La Chica Bonita twenty minutes later.

The restaurant looked inviting, with its red bricks, the curvaceous letters that spelled its name, and its flower beds. River went in and waited at the entrance to speak to the hostess. She eyed the long bar and noticed a man seated at the far end, reading a newspaper that was stretched over the surface. He was sporting a black T-shirt on which a skull had been drawn. The skull was ornate, with flowers and birds, and the colors of the Mexican flag ran down its center and sides. A cigarillo hung from his lips. It wasn't lit, and he seemed to be chewing on it as he read his paper. His thick dark hair was tied in a ponytail. River didn't need to ask. She'd just met Miguel Lopez.

Chapter 6

Miguel must have sensed that someone was observing him, because he looked up and scanned the room. River made her way to him, and he stood up from his barstool to greet her, offering a hand and a warm smile.

"I'm glad you could make the time today. Martha told me about the girl." He pointed to a table at the back of the bar area, and River followed. As he sat down, Miguel raised a hand. The barman nodded and got busy preparing drinks.

"Martha tells me that you do a lot of investigation," River said after she sat down. Miguel had chosen a seat facing the door. She sat at a right angle to him so that she, too, could see who was coming in.

"I do, although I'm not brave enough to do it under my own name. I have a pen name I write under."

River shook her head. "I'm not sure using a pen name makes you a coward. You need to stay alive if you want to investigate your next story."

The tequila shots arrived, together with cups of coffee that looked dark and intense. They raised their glasses, and both took a small sip of tequila, savoring its flavor. Miguel grinned his approval.

"You drink tequila like a Mexican."

"I know. My grandparents lived in Saint Ab all their lives, and my parents were always eager to know how to best enjoy their food and drink."

"But you're not here for the coffee or the tequila. Right?" Miguel said.

River took a sip of coffee and replied, "That's right. There's a teenager in the morgue because she OD'd on drugs. There's another one who's lucky to be alive and has found sanctuary with your sister, and there's a third girl who is probably somewhere close to Saint Ab but in hiding. I'm not resting until I know who's responsible and have brought the SOBs responsible to justice."

Miguel raised his eyebrows. "That's bold, to say the least. I know you're in the air force, but we *are* talking about a cartel here."

River shifted on her chair. She had to come clean with Miguel if they were going to work together. "I left the armed forces a couple of years ago. I was a battlefield medic supporting special ops missions."

"Still, how many times were you deployed? If I may ask."

"Three times. Iraq and Afghanistan."

Miguel took a sip of coffee and then said, "I'll tell you what I've gathered over the past few years. Drugs have always transited from Mexico to the United States along established corridors. One of those corridors starts in California and extends through the Southwest, the Midwest, the Great Lakes, and then the Northeast."

"Is this corridor controlled by one cartel?"

"That's a good question. Cartels usually don't like sharing their routes, but this one is large enough to accommodate shared arrangements."

River took a small sip of tequila. "Who's the prominent cartel in that corridor?"

"Sinaloa is the most powerful cartel in Mexico. It distributes a very large part of all illegal drugs in the United States."

"I presume they distribute everything, including fentanyl."

"That's right, but the method of distribution has changed."

River leaned forward and said, "I gather that most fentanyl is imported from China via Mexico, but starting in 2019, the Chinese imposed strict regulations on it. Then the Chinese gangs started exporting precursors to Mexico because they weren't regulated in the same way as the drug itself."

"True, although since 2024, some precursors are also regulated, so again they're not easy to import, but it's a question of enforcement."

"You mean China doesn't always enforce the law?" River asked.

"That's right, and it's been a roller coaster of counternarcotics cooperation and suspension of cooperation between the United States and China," Miguel said.

River frowned. "You think it's a political tool wielded by the Chinese?"

"Perhaps, or at least it could be, just as Hezbollah ships drugs from the Golden Triangle, in East Asia, to Europe in order to wage their jihad there."

"But there's direct intention when it comes to Hezbollah. I wouldn't say that the Chinese government is directly involved in the shipping of precursors," River said.

"Point taken," Miguel replied. "I simply say that it's a way to negatively influence a country that may be perceived as an enemy. It's a tool."

"Understood. So what's next with the precursors? They cook the drug in Mexico and then import it?" River recalled the conversation with Dale about a clandestine lab on the US side of the border, but she wanted to find out what Miguel's take was.

"That's the idea. Package the precursors so they are difficult to detect at customs, then cook them into fentanyl. I even heard that the Sinaloa Cartel is recruiting young chemistry graduates to work in their labs."

River ran a hand over her face. "That's a disgraceful use of talent, but I presume these kids don't have a choice."

"And the money is good, so . . ." Miguel finished his coffee and waited for River to process the information he'd given her.

"Have drugs always been an issue in Saint Ab?" River asked. "I don't recall my parents ever discussing it."

"No. It started a few years back."

"But why would the Sinaloa Cartel wait until now?"

Miguel gave River an approving look. "If you want a change of job, perhaps you could join me in my investigations. That's another good question. There is a new Mexican cartel that is starting to muscle in—the Cruz Cartel. I found out that they've established direct contact with some Chinese gangs and are offering a better price for the key chemical components. Word is that they have some top chemists working for them and that they have even managed to replicate precursors from their key components."

"That means no Chinese control and as much production as possible."

"Exactly." Miguel nodded and took a sip of tequila.

"But an overdose of precursors is what killed Dolores, the teenager I found in Silver Rim canyon."

"Are you sure?"

River thought about it. "I'll check again, but I'm almost certain."

Miguel nodded. "You should. And then, whether precursors or not, you know what that means?"

"There's a lab in Saint Ab or close by?"

"Yep, and it's cooking drugs as we speak."

"Well, then," River said, finishing her tequila, "I find this lab and the people who run it, and I get rid of them both."

Miguel's eyes widened. "You mean . . ."

River chuckled. "I can deal with the lab, but I'll leave the traffickers to the FBI—maybe." Then she grew serious. "I'm not taking any other passenger on this trip." Except Dale, she thought, but Dale was law enforcement. He knew what he was getting himself into.

"You can't do that on your own, and I'll be damned if I don't participate somehow," Miguel said, straightening up.

River shook her head. "I need information from you, but I don't want you to get hurt. I mend people—I don't send them out to get gunned down."

"Don't tell me you're intending to do this alone. Because I won't believe you."

River sat back in her chair for a moment. Miguel had crossed his meaty arms over his barrel chest and was waiting for her answer.

"You're right. Someone from the police station is helping me."

Miguel rolled his eyes. "Are you out of your head? All those guys are on the take."

"Not sure that's true," River persisted.

"Give me a name."

"Dale Jackson."

Miguel sat back and scratched his chin. "Little Dale. Just recruited less than a year ago. I'd never."

River crossed her arms over her chest, too, satisfied with her choice. Then she said, "Now, there's something I need, and I'd rather ask you for it than anyone else."

Miguel nodded. "All right. What is it?"

"I need a gun, preferably a Glock 19, but I'll take whatever's available."

Miguel made a knowing face. "Can do. But if I deliver, I'm in."

Miguel understood the logic behind River's not buying a firearm herself. Sheriff Andersen would know the moment she walked into a firearms store that she was after a gun, and he would draw the right conclusions from it. Miguel was certain he could get her what she wanted and would have the piece ready for her the following day.

River left La Chica Bonita but didn't head to Luke's house. Luke would be asleep—at least she hoped he would—and Rosa wouldn't be back until 2:00 a.m. She had plenty of time to take a detour to the Silver Rim canyon. She throttled up the bike and rode the road around the city until she reached the outskirts of town. She joined the I-15 and forgot about the speed limit.

She slowed down when the Silver Rim cliff was in view and turned onto the path she'd gone down in the morning. Instead of making her way toward the canyon, though, she decided to head toward the highest point along the cliff. She followed a narrow trail and then stopped the bike to continue on foot. She didn't want to leave the bike parked out in the open, so she decided to hide it behind a large rock. She removed her helmet and left it on the bike.

River used her phone's flashlight to check the surroundings, then waited a moment for her eyes to get accustomed to the darkness again. The sky was clear and the moon bright enough for her to make out the path and avoid the rocks that lay in her way. It took River a good ten minutes to reach the peak, climbing over boulders and sliding a few times over gravelly ground. She stood tall at the top of the mountain and moved slowly around, completing a 360-degree rotation.

She was grateful once more for the binoculars she purchased a few days before her trip. She remembered encountering spectacular views in the Rockies when going on walks with her parents and had thought she might need them. River perused the landscape below her again and spotted what she was looking for—a couple of faint lights in the middle of nowhere. They had to be small, isolated ranches or farms.

River managed to locate the canyon where she picked up Teresa that morning and then ran the binoculars back to the lights she'd spotted. One of them shone a few miles away from the place where the canyon came to an abrupt stop against the flanks of the mountain. The other one was to the left of the canyon a mile away, no more. There was a chance this might be the place where Dolores's Good Samaritan and savior lived, and perhaps Cristina had taken refuge there, too. River identified a couple of landscape markers that might help her find the two places again. She'd send a text to Miguel as soon as she was back. He might know whom these two ranches belonged to.

The wind had started to blow harder, and it made her shiver. She crouched for a moment, zipping her jacket up. Movement in the distance attracted her attention. She was no longer alone on the trail to the Silver Rim canyon. River directed her binoculars toward the spot. A large SUV was climbing the steep slope and then stopped. River thought about the bike hidden behind a boulder and then realized that the SUV's headlights weren't on.

The vehicle stopped, and two men got out. They started to head toward the peak. River made herself as small she could, but if the men decided to climb to the top, they would see her. She looked around. The terrain was too steep to climb down the other side, and even if it wasn't they would hear small rocks being dislodged as she moved down. The men stopped and spoke to each other in Spanish. They both had binoculars and were doing exactly what River had done.

One of the men started climbing up again. Any minute now he would reach the peak and discover her. In desperation, River looked around and spotted a small crevasse to the left of the rock on which she was crouching. She shimmied to the ground, holding on to part of the boulder, and let her leg slide toward the crevasse. It took a few seconds before her feet acquired purchase. She tested the rock below. It seemed strong enough to carry her weight. She then glided down, half her body hanging in the air. The man reached the top of the boulder where she stood only a few moments later. If he looked to his left, he might still spot her.

The two men started to talk to each other again. River couldn't understand all they said, but she got the drift. One of the houses she'd spotted was a place they used. River smiled despite the pain that had started to creep into her back and her arms. The men kept quiet for a while, and she thought they might have moved on, but a sudden burst of words told her that not only were they still around but also that they had found what they were looking for—the ranch on the other side of the canyon.

River's arms had started to shake violently. She braced herself but knew she wouldn't be able to hold on much longer. The men exchanged a few more words. River gritted her teeth. Then she heard footsteps and the roll of pebbles underfoot. She managed to hold on for a few seconds more and then heaved herself onto the rock, utterly spent. She rolled onto her back and took a couple of deep breaths. She picked up her cell as she sat up. She had just enough reception for a call and dialed Miguel's number.

Miguel answered immediately. "Something's up?"

"Do you know the area well around Saint Ab and the Silver Rim canyon?"

"Lived in Saint Ab all my life."

"There's a ranch west of the canyon, about a mile out. Does anyone live there?"

Miguel was thinking. "West of the Canyon . . . west of . . . it's gotta be Old Bill. Bill Barrick, lives on his own since his wife died, and—"

River cut in. "Do you have his number?"

"Don't even know whether he's got a cell."

"I think some of the cartel guys are going to pay him a visit."

"Shit," Miguel said. "You know what? Call Dale. Bill is an old copper. Dale would know."

"Thanks, Miguel. I'll call Dale and then I'm going there."

"I'll see you there, then."

"No, you won't."

"Yes, I will. There is a Glock with your name on it that needs delivering."

"That quick, huh?" River said, surprised.

"Anything to keep a fellow investigator happy."

"Well, then. You sure know how to make friends," River said. "One last question. I can get down the canyon with my bike. But do you know whether I can find a place to get to the other side of the gorge with it? I don't want to have to make a big detour."

"When you reach the bottom, turn left, due south. Quarter of a mile down, you'll find a trail that cross-country cyclists use."

She hung up and called Dale. His cell phone rang until it went to voicemail. She didn't bother to leave a message and called again, then repeated the process until a sleepy yet angry voice answered.

"Who the hell are you?"

"It's River. Wake up. We have an issue."

"Can't you—"

"Call the police station? No. I think I found the other girl who escaped, and she's in danger."

River told Dale what she'd told Miguel.

"It's Old Bill's ranch, all right. What should we do?" Dale sounded panicked, and she could hear him moving around his room, almost certainly looking for his clothes.

"Does Old Bill have a cell or a landline?"

"Don't know. Why?" Dale asked.

"You could have called him."

"But I don't have his number. We haven't—"

"Never mind. Get in your uniform and get there with all lights blazing. Let's hope it does the trick." She was about to hang up but added quickly, "And Dale, don't forget your guns."

She killed the call and ran down the slope toward her bike as fast as she could, sliding on her backside a few times, and grazing her hands on the rocks. She straddled the bike as soon as she reached it and started her ride down the trail, lights off. When she reached the spot where she'd stopped that morning and spotted the circling vultures, she braced herself once more for the descent into the ravine and started the dangerous ride to the bottom of the canyon.

The bike felt a lot more unwieldy than it did in the morning. River's arms were stiff from exertion, and she concentrated on controlling the steady slide. The bike skated a couple of times over large stones. One of them shifted abruptly, sending her on course to hit the boulder she just managed to avoid in the morning.

"Shit," she cried. "Just stay with me." She lowered the gear, using the engine to brake, and shifted so that she could keep both her body and the bike balanced. The wheels of the bike retained good grip, and she accelerated just enough to turn away from the rock she was about to slam into. River kept it together until she reached the bottom of the incline and then stopped. She stood the bike on its kickstand, dismounted, flipped her visor open, and wiped the sweat from her face with the back of her hand. She breathed deeply a few times and slammed the visor down again. She had no time to lose. She must make it to Old Bill's ranch before the cartel did.

River followed Miguel's instructions. The trail she found a quarter of a mile to the south was in good condition. She rode up it with ease.

When she reached the top, she stopped for a moment to get her bearings. A faint light was shimmering in the distance. She started up the bike and switched on the headlight. Whoever was out there needed to know she was coming.

The light that was gleaming in one of the ranch's rooms grew larger until she could see that it was shining on the right-hand side of the porch and that someone was still awake. That person would have a good view of the trail that led to the part of the fencing that surrounded the house and the gate in front of it. River slowed down to a crawl. There was no one in sight—no SUV or police car. She hoped she and Dale weren't too late.

She parked the bike a distance away from the main entrance, got off, and walked to the gate. A large shield gave clear instructions to trespassers.

PRIVATE PROPERTY

DO NOT ENTER

I SHOOT FIRST AND ASK QUESTIONS LATER

This was straightforward enough, but she wondered whether Old Bill's bark was louder than his bite. To her surprise, the gate wasn't locked. She pushed it open, closed it and was greeted by a gunshot in the air.

"Ain't it clear? It says do not enter," a croaky voice shouted from one of the windows on the second floor.

River raised her hands slowly over her head. She then lowered one hand, lifted the visor of her helmet, and shouted back, "I can read, all right, but I have a message for Bill Barrick from Dale. Can I please remove my helmet and tell you what it is?"

Old Bill must have racked his brain but said after a moment, "Dale—the young cop?"

"He's on his way, and so are a couple of cartel guys who are after the young woman you're protecting." River took the gamble.

"Take yer helmet off and keep your hands where I can see 'em."

River removed the helmet and dropped it slowly to the ground. She put her hands up again.

"Can I step forward, please? I don't really want to make it easy for the cartel boys to gun me down. I haven't got a weapon on me."

She thought she heard a chuckle. "That's not a good idea in these parts."

"I realize that. Miguel Lopez is on his way to solve that problem and bring me a Glock."

"You youngsters. What's wrong with a good ol' shotgun?"

"Nothing. It's just that a Glock is what I used as a sidearm when I was in the military."

Old Bill grunted. "And anyway, I never asked no one to a tea party."

"I appreciate that, too, sir, but I think I can hear a car in the distance, and I'd rather not be standing here with my arms up in the air when it arrives."

There was a short silence and then Bill asked, "What's the name of the other girls?"

"Dolores and Teresa."

"Get yourself to the door, hands still over your head."

River collected her helmet from the ground and moved fast, her hands over her head. The sound of a car engine grew louder, but she still couldn't hear a police car approaching. She hoped it hadn't been a mistake to call Dale.

The door opened, and a tall, thin man stood in the frame, his gun pointed straight at River's chest. He was wearing an old cap, the color of which looked so faded she couldn't tell what it had been. Old Bill jerked his head toward the inside of the house, and River went in.

"Miguel is on his way, too?" he asked.

"Couldn't persuade him otherwise."

Old Bill lowered his shotgun and balanced it on his forearm. "I guess I'm gonna have to trust you, then."

He turned around and walked toward the back of the main room. It looked old and yet cozy inside. River could tell that someone had once taken pride in the decoration. Bill stopped in front of a wooden cabinet. He took a key that hung on a chain he kept attached to his belt and opened the cabinet. He took another shotgun out of it and spun around.

"Ain't gonna do you any good if you keep them hands up."

River nodded and lowered her arms. Bill threw the gun at her and said, "I'm gonna kill the lights and hope it's not the only thing I kill tonight. You take the right window. I take the left."

Bill returned to the cabinet and took out a couple of boxes marked HORNADY 300 GRAIN SABOT SLUG. River was taking up a position near her allocated window. He dropped one of the boxes at her feet.

"That should do until your Glock arrives," Old Bill said with a grin.

"And how about me?" A young voice said from behind them.

"Too risky." Old Bill's voice was urgent. "You need to hide upstairs."

River turned around. She immediately recognized Cristina from the picture. She'd tied her long hair in a braid and was wearing fresh clothes that looked too big for her.

"I'm never going back with those men. I'd rather die defending myself," Cristina said with a mix of fear and determination.

River spotted two beams of light approaching fast. "They're coming," she said as she loaded her shotgun. "We could do with an extra gun."

Old Bill muttered a few words and handed his last shotgun to the girl.

"You come to my side, Cristina," he said and switched off the light inside the room. It took a few seconds for River to regain full sight. She loaded five slugs into the gun and heard the other two doing the same.

The SUV stopped in front of the gates. The driver switched off his headlights, and for a moment all was still inside and outside.

But then the car backed up. River and Bill slid open the bottom part of the window at which they'd taken position. The SUV went forward again, ramming the gates and crushing them open.

River, Old Bill, and Cristina started firing at the same time, and a barrage of firepower stopped the car dead. River aimed at the tires and managed to get one of them. The driver reversed the SUV as it was being pelted. River couldn't believe it. The SUV had been upgraded: The body had been reinforced, and so had the windows. The slugs had failed to penetrate the hood or break the glass. The driver maneuvered the car sideways so that the men inside were shielded by the body of the car when they got out. River, Old Bill, and Cristina reloaded and waited for the men's next move.

One of the thugs shouted, "We only want the girl. You hand her over to us, and we'll just go away."

"Which part of NO TRESPASSING don't you understand, you son of a bitch?" Old Bill shouted back.

"Okay, old man. Suit yourself, but it's gonna hurt."

The two men took up a position behind the car. River couldn't be sure, but they seemed to be holding a couple of M249 SAWs, and these were more than a match for their three shotguns.

"Do you have a back door?" River whispered to Old Bill.

"Sure do. You want to sneak up on them from behind?"

"That's the idea."

"It isn't locked," Old Bill said as he slid to River's side. "We'll keep them occupied."

"I ain't giving you nothing or no one," Old Bill shouted.

The discharge of the two machine guns was the only response he got. River was at the back door by then. She left the house and ran along its side. The reddish glow of the muzzle flashes illuminated the night and told River exactly where the men were. The ranch had another low building nearby, perhaps a repair barn of some sort. She ran to it and slammed her body to the wall as soon as she reached it.

The shooting stopped, and the man who'd spoken before made another offer.

"You can see what we can do. So this is my last offer. Hand over the girl, or we're going to shred you to death."

There was no reply, and River worried that the man might be right, and that Old Bill might be hit.

"You won't kill these people if I come with you," Cristina shouted.

River followed the back wall of the barn. She had to get to the cartel boys before Cristina did something stupid.

"I give you my word."

"Swear on the Bible," Cristina shouted back.

River had just reached the corner of the barn, where she could take a shot at the cartel guy closest to her.

She heard a snigger before the man replied, "If I had one with me, I would."

River took aim, and as she did, the blaring sound of a police siren and the flash of its light bars broke through the night. She shot the man closest to her in the legs, then ran back to the other side of the barn. Machine-gun fire tore up chunks of the wood where she had stood. More gunshots came from the house and could be heard in the distance. The man she shot was screaming. Then she heard the slam of a car door and the spitting of gravel as the SUV departed in a hurry.

River ran back to the house through the back door and into the main room. As she'd feared, Old Bill was on the floor, holding his arm. She grabbed a piece of cloth from the kitchen and went to kneel next to him. He was moaning in pain as blood seeped through his fingers.

"Let me take a look," she said as she gently pushed his hand away.

"Thought you were in the military," Bill murmured.

"I was. Medic with the 24th Special Operations Wing at Hurlburt Field."

Bill nodded feebly. He moaned again as River started to apply more pressure on the wound.

"I see a police car and another car getting near," Cristina said as she pumped her shotgun.

"Hang on," River replied. "These are friends coming to help."

"The police?" Cristina sounded unconvinced.

"Yes. Dale is with me, trying to help, and so is Miguel."

Old Bill made a low sign with his other hand, indicating that

Cristina should drop the gun. She came to his side and knelt next to him.

"Is he going to be okay?"

Dale's siren covered River's reply. She heard brakes screeching and two voices shouting. "Are you hurt?"

"Old Bill has been hit," River shouted back.

Dale was the first one to enter, gun still in his holster. Miguel came in behind him, and he'd drawn his gun, although it was pointing down.

"Shit," Dale said as he flicked the light on.

Everybody winced.

"Just as well the shooters have gone," River mumbled.

Miguel ran deeper inside the house and came back with some bath towels. River kept trying to stop the bleeding.

"I'll call an ambulance," Dale said, racing for his radio.

Miguel shook his head. "I'll take him to the hospital in my car. You clear the way."

Dale shook his head. "Twice in less than twenty-four hours."

"I'll follow you," River said as she let Miguel slowly lift Old Bill in his arms and transport him to his vehicle.

Dale was already in his police car, ready to go. River helped make Old Bill comfortable in the back of Miguel's battered old Ford. Cristina sat next to him to make sure he wouldn't collapse. Dale led the way, lights flashing, and siren screaming, with Miguel in tow. River put her helmet on and found that her bike had escaped the shootout. She gunned the engine and followed the others back to the place where her day in Saint Ab had started—the ER.

Chapter 7

River overtook Dale's car, its sirens blaring, and arrived at the ER entrance of Saint Ab's hospital first. She parked the bike to the side and ran through the doors to the reception desk.

"Is Dr. Rosa Swift still around?"

The nurse at the desk looked displeased. "Are you here for an emergency?"

"An old man is about to arrive. He's being brought in by the police and suffers from a gunshot wound to the arm. I'm a medic. I did what I could, but he needs immediate attention."

The nurse stood up, looking toward the entrance, and made a call.

"I'm also Dr. Swift's sister-in-law," River added.

The nurse nodded. "We have an emergency gunshot wound arriving now," she said into her phone as the flashing lights of Dale's car shone through the ER doors. She put the phone down, went around the desk, and said, "Dr. Swift is on her way. I'll help you with the wounded in the meantime."

She and River ran to the doors. A few seconds later the sound of a gurney rolling toward them made them stop. Rosa and a male nurse were pushing the gurney, and they overtook them as they went through the doors. Dale had parked his car farther up the drive, and Miguel had stopped right in front of the ER entrance. He opened the back door, giving them access to Old Bill, and Rosa and her colleague took over.

Cristina slid out of Miguel's car to follow Old Bill as he was rolled into the hospital. River stopped her and shook her head.

"The cartel has eyes and ears everywhere in this town, and this hospital is no exception," she said.

"River is right," Miguel added as he came alongside them, watching anxiously as Old Bill disappeared from view. "We need to keep you safe. It's too late to call on my sister, but I can take you to my home. My wife won't mind, and then I'll speak to Martha tomorrow."

Cristina looked at River for guidance.

"Martha has been looking after your friend Dolores. She's a nurse here but also helps migrants at the Santa Maria de Guadalupe center."

Cristina muffled a cry with both hands. "Dolores is safe?"

River wrapped her arm around Cristina's shoulders. "Yes, she is, and so are you now. But you need to go. The more you stick around, the more likely that someone will spot you."

Cristina squeezed River tight and then let go. She got into Miguel's car, and River shut the door.

"I'll be in touch tomorrow," River said to Miguel before he got going.

"You do that." Miguel gave her the thumbs-up and drove off.

"What do I do next?" Dale said, seemingly at a loss.

"Go home. Get some rest. You'll need to file a report about the incident, but perhaps we need to think about how much you need to tell Sheriff Andersen."

Dale shook his head. "This is crap timing. I was about to talk to Old Bill about the connections he had with the FBI."

River ran a hand over her face. "He may be fine to talk to tomorrow."

Dale nodded, got into his car, and left a moment later. River watched as his car disappeared in the distance. A hand grabbing her shoulder made her jump.

"The old man has been prepped. The surgeon operating on him

is very good. He's got a good chance of pulling through," Rosa said.

"I'm glad to hear that. At least it's a better result than what I got this morning."

Rosa gave River a kind smile. "I hope you're not going to keep delivering patients at this rate, or we're going to be quickly overwhelmed."

"Not the reputation I wanted to build for my return to Saint Ab."

"At least someone is doing something about the cartel."

Rosa yawned. She looked at her watch and said, "My shift is about to finish. I'll get ready, and we can go home together."

"I'll wait," River said.

River sat on her bike waiting. She no longer wanted to think about the events of the day. She needed a fresh mind to decide what she would do next. Instead, her thoughts drifted toward the past, but she found that she didn't want to go there, either. She then simply lifted her head toward the clear sky and started taking in the spectacle that had always mesmerized her—that of the stars and the void surrounding them. She recalled the skies of Africa and the Middle East. Her mother loved stargazing, and she'd taught River how to recognize the main constellations. River sighed. Wherever she'd be in Saint Ab, the past would come knocking.

A few moments later, Rosa walked out of the entrance doors again. She waved at River, and they both made their way to Luke's house.

River arrived at the same time as Rosa. She rode the bike slowly to avoid making too much noise and waking up the family. Rosa went to the kitchen, and although she looked tired, made a pot of ginger tea.

"I can't go to sleep just yet," Rosa said as she got a couple of mugs out of a cabinet. She placed them on the kitchen counter and returned to her tea making.

River pulled out one of the stools at the kitchen counter and sat down. "It's been a full-on day. That's for sure."

"You must have seen plenty of action when you were deployed," Rosa said, pouring River a cup.

"Somehow it feels different." River took a moment, thinking about why she felt that way. "I was trained to do my job when a special ops team was in theater. I knew what to expect. It was tough to be dropped in the middle of hostile terrain, surrounded by enemies who wanted nothing more than to kill you and the guys you were supposed to save, but it was teamwork, and everyone pulled in the same direction."

"You mean there was camaraderie?"

"That's right," River said before taking a sip. "Here we've got to be careful because the cartel has informants, even at the hospital. It feels very wrong, and that angers me."

Rosa nodded. "It angers me, too." She took a couple of sips and seemed to hesitate. "Luke and I have a different approach to what's happening in Saint Ab at the moment."

River wasn't entirely surprised, after witnessing their disagreement about Sheriff Andersen's involvement in drugs, but said nothing. Perhaps the disagreement was more substantial than she'd imagined.

"He doesn't see what I see on a regular basis. Addicts and teenagers who OD don't end up going to their doctors. They end up in the ER."

"Luke and I saw the effect of drugs in Africa when AIDS began to spread through needle sharing. It was terrifying, although we were too young then to fully understand."

Rosa sipped from her mug. "I sometimes wonder whether that was all too much for him—you know, traveling around all the time."

"He didn't like it as much as I did. But he never said anything to Mom or Dad. Maybe he didn't want to disappoint them." River again surprised herself. She'd never thought about it that way. He'd always been the perfect son as far as she could recall.

"He said you were fearless. Always ready for an adventure," Rosa said, stretching and stifling a yawn.

River didn't know what to say to this, either. She then yawned, and Rosa chuckled.

"Bedtime for both of us."

River picked up the mugs and put them in the dishwasher. She hugged Rosa and made her way to the spare bedroom. She hadn't unpacked her duffel bag yet, but she couldn't muster the energy to do so. She stripped down to her bra and underwear and slid between the sheets.

Africa

Her parents are seated at the dinner table when the radio buzzes—there are no phones in Rwanda, only radios and sometimes satellite phones. Her father moves to catch the call quickly. He looks anxious, and River wonders why. Even when her parents receive emergency calls, they don't seem fazed by them. Not that they don't care, but they are professionals who know what to do, and panic is not part of their MO.

Her father nods to her mother, indicating that she should join the call, and they both listen, sharing the handset as best they can. There is very little said on their side—yes; no; not sure. Her parents glance at her and Luke a few times. Luke keeps eating his food as though nothing's happening. River nudges him, but he frowns and keeps concentrating on his plate.

When the call ends, her parents return to the table. They take time to finish their dinner. River wants to ask a question. She wiggles on her chair. Her mother sees it and knows her daughter too well to grant her her wish: River is about to ask a question her mother doesn't want to answer.

"Finish your food and then bed," her mom says.

Luke does as he's told. River might have protested, but something is off, so she finishes her meal and goes to bed, too. Her mom and dad didn't come to say goodnight, and that keeps River awake.

She hears a car arriving, stopping in front of the house. A door slams shut. She hears voices. One of them is her father's. River can't hold back. She creeps out of bed and makes her way downstairs without being heard or seen.

A man she's never met before is in the living room with her parents. He hands over a briefcase that her father opens. He pulls some equipment out of it. River doesn't think it's medical. And then a gun. River takes fright and returns to her bed, incapable of falling asleep until the wee hours.

River sat up in bed with a start. She was covered in perspiration, her chest heaving. She hadn't thought about that odd moment in her parents' life for a long time. Even when she learned about their death, she hadn't connected the dots. Or perhaps she hadn't connected the dots then. She hadn't yet seen the note that Chuck Clery left on his desk. The note that mentioned her parents' names alongside the name of a man called Dr. Death—the most prominent arms dealer in central Africa and the feared leader of a group of mercenaries that wreaked havoc in the DRC.

River threw the covers off and went to the bathroom. She splashed her face with water and dried herself with a towel.

The piece of paper she'd picked up from Clery's office was in her duffel bag. She hesitated but then returned to her bed and tried to make herself comfortable again. She tossed and turned a few times, wondering how she was going to bring up the subject of wanting to see what had been sent to Luke from Africa. Luke wouldn't want to talk again about his perceived failure to pay a visit to his parents shortly before they were murdered. River could understand that. She, too, had spent a lot of time blaming herself for not having made peace with them.

The last time she'd seen them was when she told them that she was joining a newly formed rapid response team of medics who operated alongside special ops personnel. Her parents had been opposed to it, and River felt they'd refused to understand her calling. She still thought it had been the best decision she ever made. She enjoyed the way service aligned with duty, and it made her proud to be part of the unit she'd joined.

River turned over one more time and felt around the bedside table to find her cell phone. She checked the time. It was 6:47 a.m. She stretched. It was too late to go back to sleep, so she decided to give her running shoes a nice long workout. She needed exercise to clear her head of her dream and gauge how to ask Luke for what she needed from him.

The household was still asleep when River crept out the door. The sun was rising as she started her run, working her way through the neighborhood she once called her own. Every house looked well-tended and spacious, sporting either a small lawn or a rock garden as well as the inevitable two-car garage. She hadn't planned her run, so she just followed the streets as they struck her fancy.

She got into a solid rhythm quickly, and her attention shifted to her immediate surroundings. The sun was now a clear ball of fire, spreading hues of pinks and blues across the sky. The landscape around Saint Ab was spectacular—mountains of scorched red rocks, hardy green bushes that clung to the slopes, and then the desert, unforgiving yet vibrant. The places River had missed the most in her nomadic childhood were those that took her close to nature. She'd never spoken to her mom and dad about it, but she suspected that they, too, enjoyed the vastness of the outdoors. After all, her father had been brought up around these mountains.

River kept going for another forty minutes and found herself on a loop back to Luke's home. She slowed down as she was getting close and noticed in the distance that a car she didn't recognize was parked in front of the house. She jogged back to the front door and opened it to the smell of breakfast. Upon entering the dining area, she discovered that Harry Wilson was seated at the table.

Harry turned his head as soon as River entered, and he gave her a broad smile. Their unhappy encounter of the day before seemed a distant memory. Carmen was seated next to him, with Franklin eating his breakfast on the table, too. Her niece looked relaxed with Harry, the way a kid would with a favorite uncle.

"Here she is," Harry said, getting up to give her a hug.

River hugged him back briefly, uncertain about the change of attitude from yesterday. Carmen shrieked in delight and came to join the hug. Franklin observed from a distance, then crossed the table to give her a head butt and demand a scratch around the ears. River obliged and was rewarded with a loud purr. Luke appeared through the kitchen doorway and asked, "One or two eggs?"

"One, please," River said, "but give me ten minutes. I need a quick shower."

"Sure. I'll start cooking when you're ready."

River disappeared back into the guest room, threw her jogging clothes off, and took a quick shower. She towel-dried and went to select a fresh pair of jeans and a new sweatshirt she'd bought on her way to Utah. She liked the patterns in various shades of blue, which matched her eyes and reminded her of the sky she'd just admired on her run.

When she returned to the dining area, Carmen and Franklin had disappeared, no doubt so she could get ready for school. Luke got busy with River's egg. She sat down at the table and poured herself a cup of coffee. Harry pushed a plate full of pastries in front of her.

"They were baked fresh this morning. Were still warm when I brought them."

"Thanks, Harry. That's very kind of you."

"I do that regularly. It's good to come and see my goddaughter."

River hid her astonishment. She hadn't realized that Harry was Carmen's godfather. But then again, she hadn't been in touch with Luke much since his two children were born.

"I'm sorry if I was a little curt yesterday, but having to autopsy a teenager who shouldn't be on the slab always gets to me," Harry said, shaking his head.

"True—it can't be fun. I did do a couple of autopsies for the MP when I was deployed. I never liked it much. I don't mind dealing with the wounded, but opening the dead—I couldn't get used to it," River replied before taking a sip.

"Anyway, I know you mean well about this young woman, but the cartel is everywhere. It's risky to upset them," Harry said, lowering his voice.

River shrugged. "I realize that. Although I don't understand why Sheriff Andersen doesn't do more to stop them."

Harry pulled back a little. He swirled the rest of his coffee in his cup. "I'm sure you've heard, but Andersen isn't exactly clean himself."

River nodded. Luke appeared with a plate full of egg, tomatoes, mushrooms, bacon, and toast.

"That smells delicious," River said, picking up a fork.

Luke looked pleased. She hadn't noticed that he'd donned an apron that said BEST DAD EVER. She smiled at the sight, and Luke returned her smile. He consulted his watch and undid his apron, shouting as he leaned up into the stairwell.

"Carmen, we're going to be late."

River heard Carmen respond but couldn't make out what she said. Harry grinned.

"She's playing with her cat."

"He's very cute, even though he is an old boy."

Harry sighed. "I wish the same could be said of me."

They both chuckled, and Harry refilled his cup with more coffee. Luke appeared with Carmen following. She was wearing a bright pink puffer coat and a blue backpack covered with cartoon characters River didn't recognize. She gave a hug to Harry and skipped to River and gave her a hug, too.

Luke turned to Harry as he was leaving. "See you at the practice."

"I'll be there in a moment. Just finishing my coffee."

River heard the door slam shut and then the sound of Luke's car pulling away. Harry was watching her eat her breakfast, and his attention made her nervous.

"What are you gonna do today?" he asked after taking a sip of coffee.

River shrugged. "Not sure yet. I haven't been to some of the old favorite spots we used to go to with Mom and Dad. I thought I might visit Sand Hollow." River tucked into her egg and scooped up some yolk with her bread. "Or perhaps I'll take a ride to Devils Playground. Luke and I used to have fun around there."

A shadow moved across Harry's face. It seemed that as far as he was concerned, Devils Playground wasn't such a good idea.

"Sand Hollow reservoir has had a revamp. It's worth visiting since you haven't been there in ages."

River smiled. "Then Sand Hollow it will be."

Harry looked pleased with her answer, and he finished his cup in two long pulls.

"Got to go. My first patient is in ten minutes."

He wiped his lips with a napkin, stood up, and came to place a kiss on River's head. He turned away without waiting for her to respond. "Enjoy your day," he said as he left.

River waved from her chair. "I sure will."

She finished her breakfast and checked her watch. It was 8:17 a.m. Rosa was asleep upstairs. She wondered why the racket hadn't awakened her, but perhaps she was used to the morning activity in the house and could sleep through it. She might wake up in another couple of hours, though. River would then ask her to inquire about Old Bill at the hospital. This gave River enough time to go on a short reconnaissance mission to Devils Playground.

The ring of her cell phone startled her. She pulled it from her jeans pocket. Miguel was calling.

"They shot her. They took the girl," Miguel said, holding back tears.

"What? Who's been shot?" River stood up.

"Martha—they shot her. This morning. Got to her house. Her husband, Diego, was in the garage. By the time he got inside, they'd shot Martha and taken Dolores."

"Where are you?" River said as she ran back to the guest room to get her jacket and helmet.

"At the hospital. I got there as soon as I heard from Diego. They're operating as we speak."

"I'm on my way," River said. "Does Cristina know?"

"I haven't told her yet. She was still asleep when I got the news."

River put on her jacket, moving the phone from one hand to the other.

"We've got to find a way to protect her—and you and your wife. If they've gotten to Martha, they might put two and two together."

"I know, but I just can't think straight right now."

"And I'm sorry to mention it, but I'm gonna need that Glock. The one I forgot last night."

"It's in my car. I didn't take it inside the house because I parked in the garage."

River hung up and left. She straddled the bike, gunned the engine, and was on her way. The cartel men didn't yet know she was involved, but she would soon have to think about the consequences of their finding out—for her and her family.

Chapter 8

The room in which the girl had been bound, gagged, and blindfolded stank of the various chemicals that the lab next door used. Alfonso knew it was odd, but he rather liked the smell. He walked into the room alone despite Luis's insistence. He didn't want his father's boy to try to put a spin on what the girl had to say. The girl twitched as she heard the door open, and she whimpered.

Alfonso waited for a moment. She was only a teenager, and he wondered, out of curiosity rather than greed, how much men in Vegas would pay for her. Her father had assured him that the sex trade in Vegas was one of the best in the country. Alfonso didn't care about finding out. He would take his father's word for it.

He moved closer to the mattress on which the girl sat, and the girl recoiled even more. He grabbed his knife from inside his jacket pocket and flicked it open. Alfonso pulled the gag away from her mouth and said, "I'm going to cut it away. Don't scream, or I'll have to put it back."

He waited until the girl nodded. He then slid the blade underneath the cloth and with a sharp move severed it. The girl started coughing. Alfonso took out a bottle of water he'd put in his jacket pocket.

"I'm going to give you some water."

He opened the bottle and brought it to the girl's mouth. She felt with her lips around the opening of the bottle and started to drink in large gulps as he titled the bottle. She coughed again. Water dripped down her chin, and Alfonso stopped.

"You need to take it slowly."

He brought the bottle to her mouth again, and this time she drank without hurrying. He gave her half the bottle, then pulled away, grabbed a chair that lay against the wall, and came to straddle it in front of the girl.

"I'm going to ask you some questions." His voice was calm. "I know you have the answers, and I don't want to have to hurt you to get to them. Do you understand?"

The girl nodded slowly.

"What's your name?"

The girl was taken aback but then murmured, "Dolores."

"Do you remember who took you to the hospital?"

Dolores shook her head. "I had passed out by then."

"So a stranger found you and helped?"

Dolores shuddered, and Alfonso knew this wasn't the whole story. He kept going. "Do you remember the name of the woman who was at the hospital with Martha? I hear she's not a nurse there but that she's a medic."

"She didn't tell me who she was," Dolores said, her lips trembling.

Alfonso dragged his chair closer, still sitting on it. It made a screeching noise that told Dolores he was getting nearer to her.

"I heard one of the doctors call her River."

"Anything else? You must have spoken to Martha when you went home with her."

Dolores shook her head. "She said it was best if I knew as little as possible."

Alfonso waited. Dolores was nibbling her lips, nervous and yet courageous. He had to admire this young woman, who was doing her best not to betray her friends or the people who'd helped her. But he had a job to do, and his father was expecting him to deliver the girls, once they'd been cleaned up, to the other cartel men in Vegas. One of them would never be delivered, and that was bad enough. But more than one, and he couldn't predict how Señor

Cruz would react. And Luis would be waiting to seize the opportunity.

"I don't believe you, Dolores, and you must know that if I don't believe you, this is not a good thing, right?"

Dolores started crying silently, her shoulders shuddering as she did.

"I don't have the time, and the man waiting on the other side of that door will do what it takes to make you talk," Alfonso said, his voice more menacing.

"Martha was talking to someone she knew well. I couldn't hear everything because she walked away once she noticed I was listening, but I think River is related to one of the doctors at the hospital," Dolores blurted out.

Although Dolores couldn't see him, Alfonso nodded. "That's good."

He stood up and left the room. Dolores had started crying again, and he couldn't blame her. Her future was grim.

Luis was waiting outside, leaning against the hood of a black SUV that looked brand new. He stood up and came toward Alfonso.

"What do I do with her?"

"Keep her secure in one of the ranch rooms. I want her around for a while longer. We may still need her. Then take her to the mine when the other girls arrive."

"She's been to this place," Luis said, moving his head around.

"I'm not proposing we set her free," Alfonso shot back. "I said to keep her here under lock and key. She may be helpful if we catch the other girl, Cristina."

Luis shrugged and muttered something under his breath that Alfonso didn't catch. But he didn't need to hear it to know that it was unlikely to be a compliment.

Luis walked toward the shed, turning his back to Alfonso, but then Alfonso called him back.

"And Luis, I don't want to see any unnecessary bruises on the girl. She needs to be delivered in good condition to the Vegas Cruz men. Is that clear?"

He nodded and kept going. When he'd disappeared into the shed, Alfonso called Pablo.

"Can you check why Luis is driving a brand-new SUV and what happened to the old one?" Alfonso killed the call. He had an inkling, but he needed to be sure.

Miguel's old Ford was parked near the ER entrance, and its door was open. River slowed the bike to a halt. She spent a moment observing the car, fearing the worst. Someone had gone in and found the Glock.

River got off the bike and walked in a wide circle around the parking lot, trying to get a better view. She then walked between a couple of cars in order to get closer, moving quickly from one to the other. It would look suspicious to anyone observing her, but she couldn't think of any other way to get closer without putting herself in danger.

When she was a few yards away from the open door, she risked taking a better look. A man was slumped over the steering wheel. He was wearing a black T-shirt, and his hair was tied in a ponytail. River ran toward the car—Miguel had been hurt. She was about to slide a hand over his shoulder when the sound of a sob stopped her. Miguel was crying, and River's heart tightened. She then knew.

She removed her helmet and sat down on the ground, head and back resting against the side of the car. Martha hadn't made it out of the operating room alive. River put her hands over her face and tried to muffle her own tears. She took a moment to compose herself, then stood up slowly. Miguel must have heard her. He was now wiping his tears with the back of his hand.

"I'm so sorry, Miguel," River said as she squeezed his shoulder gently.

Miguel nodded but couldn't speak.

"What can I do to help?"

Miguel managed a few words. "Cristina, Jen—my wife—we need them safe."

River pushed back the tears and said, "I'll speak to Dale. Go home, and I'll meet you there."

Miguel nodded again, and River went back to her bike. She sat on the seat, taking it in—a teenage girl who only had been hoping for a better life, and a good person who had dedicated her life to helping others, were dead. This wouldn't go unpunished.

She took her phone out of her jacket pocket and called Dale.

"I heard," he simply said as soon as he answered.

"We need to make sure other people are safe," River said, not sure whether the cartel had the ability to listen to phone calls.

"Where are you?" Dale asked. His voice became fuzzy, and River gathered he must be in his car.

"At the hospital."

"I'm on my way. It's my day off, and I'm in a red pickup truck."

"Shouldn't we meet somewhere else?"

"Sorry, I should have told you. Old Bill is proving to be a handful for the nurses, and I'm gonna try to get him to listen to reason."

Good luck with that.

From what River had seen of Old Bill, she doubted he would pay attention to anyone who was forty years younger than he was—certainly not Dale.

When she finished her call, River scanned the parking lot. Miguel's old Ford wasn't there any longer. Dale arrived a few moments later, and she waited for him to park. She let him step out and surveyed the area once more. She still couldn't spot anything suspicious and made her way toward him.

Dale had changed into jeans and a blue-and-red plaid shirt. His hair looked as though it had just been trimmed. If she hadn't known, she would have pegged him as one of the helpers on a ranch outside Saint Ab—an attractive young cowboy. There was something kind in his demeanor that felt reassuring.

"What has Old Bill been saying?" River asked as he reached her.

"He wants to go home."

"With the blood he's lost, that's not a good idea," River said.

"Why don't you come in and say that to him yourself?"

River followed Dale. "Not sure it'll make much of a difference."

They entered the hospital building through the public entrance. Dale asked for Bill Barrick. They rode the elevator to the second floor. When they arrived in his room, Bill and a woman were having an argument they could hear through the open door. River raised an eyebrow. Old Bill didn't sound like someone who'd been shot only a few hours ago.

"I'm going home now if it's the last thing I do."

"You're not fit enough to go home, Mr. Barrick."

"Who says?"

"I say."

"I'm not taking orders from no one."

River and Dale walked in. Old Bill was sitting on his bed. He'd managed to put his pants on. His arm was bandaged, and a fresh shirt was draped over his shoulders. The nurse crossed her arms over her ample bosom. She didn't want to back down, either.

Bill glared at her and then switched his attention to River. She noticed a change in the old man's eyes, almost a plea, or perhaps he was trying to tell her something he didn't want to say in front of the nurse.

"What if Old Bill finds someone to look after him?" River said.

The nurse and Dale turned to look at River as one. The nurse seemed at her wits' end, and Dale seemed to think River was mad.

"I'm a medic. I worked in the armed forces."

The nurse threw her hands up and left the room.

"What about your—" Dale started, looking concerned.

River cut him short with a frown, and Old Bill nodded approvingly. She went to check the corridor and returned.

"Why are you so keen to go?" she asked Old Bill.

"They're going to come back," he said.

"You mean the *sicarios*?"

Old Bill nodded again.

River shook her head. "You're not serious about wanting to wait for them on your own there, are you?"

"Nah. I'm not that stupid," Old Bill said as he struggled to put on his shirt.

River walked to his bed and helped him put his free arm through the sleeve.

"Then why?"

"I need to take a few bits and pieces I want to keep before they come and ransack the place. I could ask Sheriff Andersen for some help. But he and I don't get on so well. Plus he's on the side of the crooked."

"Where are you gonna go after that?" Dale asked.

"There's this place in the mountains—" Old Bill stopped and waited. The nurse entered the room again and handed over a clipboard with a form.

"You've got to read and sign," she said.

Old Bill grabbed the board and signed at the bottom of the piece of paper. The nurse rolled her eyes and took the clipboard away, pointing a finger at River.

"And *you* bring him back to us if he starts feeling dizzy or develops a fever," she said. She shoved a couple of small bottles into River's hand along with an arm sling and disappeared.

Old Bill buttoned his shirt as best he could. River fitted him with the sling. Surprisingly, he didn't complain. He stood up slowly. River was expecting a little wobble, but it never came. He smiled to them and said, "Let's go home."

Dale walked in front to call for the elevator. River stayed close to Old Bill. An elevator arrived, and they took it to the first floor. Dale offered to get his pickup and drive to the front of the building, and Old Bill didn't object.

"Where is this place?" River murmured.

"It's a place I used to hunt from," Old Bill replied quietly.

"Can it fit more than one person?"

"Might do. Why?"

"Cristina isn't safe anymore, and Miguel's wife is now in the same situation."

"What happened?" Old Bill said.

"Let's talk later," River replied.

Dale walked through the doors and waited. They followed him to his truck. Old Bill paused and whistled. "Nice ride."

Dale opened the passenger door, and Old Bill got in. Dale got in, too, and asked, "Back to the ranch?"

"Yep," Old Bill said.

"I'll follow you with the bike," River said. She ran back to the place where she'd left her motorcycle, put her helmet on, started the bike, and caught up with Dale's pickup.

At Old Bill's ranch, the devastation of the shoot-out was apparent. The main house and the barn would need some serious repair. Old Bill stepped out and stood for a moment, taking it all in, then made a move toward the open front door. Dale and River followed.

Old Bill walked into his house and headed straight through to his bedroom. He came back with an old suitcase the likes of which River hadn't seen for a very long time.

"I need some help with the basics and a few things I don't want to lose," he said.

River came to stand next to him and gently put a hand on his thin shoulder.

"I'd like to know where we're going first," she said.

Dale nodded. "So would I."

"I know this cave," Old Bill said, losing a bit of his swagger.

River rolled her eyes. "You can't be serious. You need a place with running water and a fire to keep you warm."

"We're taking you back to the hospital. C'mon," Dale said, turning back toward his truck.

Old Bill lifted a hand and sat down on the only kitchen chair that hadn't been hit by bullets.

"Wait—it's not what you think. I built the cave to be a spotting point. My wife and I made it comfortable over the years."

River shook her head. "I'm sure it's comfortable when you're in your twenties and haven't just been shot."

Old Bill straightened up, looking miffed. "What's that supposed to mean? I was there last spring, and it was perfectly fine. Besides, it's well hidden, and no one is going to find us there."

Dale was about to reply, but River stopped him. "What are you suggesting?"

"You asked whether there was room for someone else. I suppose you're talking about Cristina and Jen. The place can house at least two more, but it'll need some attention and supplies."

"You mean you build a sort of house in this cave?" Dale said, incredulous.

"Me and my wife. Took us a long time."

"Who knows about it?" River asked.

"No one. I mean, we did it bit by bit, and people would have assumed we were buying things for the house here."

Dale scratched his head. "But why make it such a secret?"

River grinned. "'Cause Old Bill policeman here didn't ask for a permit."

"It's just a little cave." Old Bill shrugged.

River rubbed her hands together. "Tell us what you need, and we'll get you there with your supplies."

Dale was sent to the barn to gather large plastic containers for water and charged batteries for the generator. River gathered food and helped Old Bill with clothes, bedding, and rugs. He went around the house gathering a few items that must have mattered to him, including a framed photo of him and his wife on their wedding day. The color had faded, but the joy of the two people who smiled back at the onlooker was still evident. He picked up an old wooden box and a couple of books from a shelf. A laptop that looked ancient got added to the lot. He looked around and said, "That's it."

He then walked to a solid-looking cabinet in his bedroom. Drew a key from his key ring and opened the doors. A couple of rifles were hanging in there.

"I thought you only used shotguns," River said.

"This is extreme emergency stuff."

Dale walked in and whistled at what he saw. "Serious heat, right?"

"But with my arm in a sling, I'll be better off with my shotgun."

Dale and River gathered the weapons and ammunition. They loaded them into Dale's pickup, and the small convoy made its way up the mountain. It took them thirty-five minutes to reach the base of another ridge before Old Bill told them to stop. Old Bill and Dale got out of the truck. River stopped alongside it. The three of them went around a large boulder and down a gentle slope, and then both River and Dale paused in a wow moment.

A large dome of rock with two bay windows stood a few feet away from them. Old Bill was already at what looked like a front door of heavy glass. He turned around, and Dale got the message. He jogged to him and helped Old Bill with the stiff door. A strange smell wafted outside as Dale managed to open the door.

"Mix of charcoal and rock salt," Old Bill explained. "It's good against humidity."

River removed her helmet, and the three of them entered the main room. River and Dale took a moment to admire the space. The unevenness of the red sandstone forming the walls and ceiling made the room seem magical. Old Bill walked to an ancient woodstove that looked as though it'd been there for years and had been well used.

"We need to get a fire going, and then we'll change the generator batteries," Old Bill said, opening the grid in the front of the stove. "Dale, you'll find wood that's already chopped at the side of the house in the shed."

River picked up the generator, and she and Old Bill took it to a utility room and put the charged batteries in. The lights in the cave came on all at once, and River grinned.

"This is an amazing place you've got here," she said, looking around. "And how do you manage with water?"

"I installed a pump that accesses groundwater."

"Really adventurous and clever."

"It was my wife's dream. I didn't get it to start with, but she was right, as always." Old Bill sighed.

Dale was calling them. He had dropped logs and smaller pieces of wood on the floor in the main room and was waiting for instructions.

River and Old Bill joined him, and Old Bill started telling the young man what to do. Dale was doing a decent job at building a fire, and Old Bill turned toward River.

"What do you think?"

He wasn't asking about the cave. River walked outside and stood on the wide terrace that ran along the house. She turned to the far end of it. The ground fell steeply all along and below the terrace so that it hung over a precipice. It would be difficult to reach the place unless you were to go around the boulder and be immediately seen. She came back in.

"It's a pretty good situation you've got here if you're intent on holding a position."

"Tell Miguel to bring Cristina and Jen, then," Old Bill said.

Dale, who hadn't been paying attention, struck a match and lit the pieces of newspaper he'd been given by Old Bill. Flames sprang out and started licking the small pieces of wood. One piece caught, then another. Old Bill pushed the grid shut and nodded. "Well done."

River took her cell phone out of her jacket pocket and brought up one of the apps she enjoyed most—the compass. She memorized the coordinates of Old Bill's cave and said, "I'm going back to Saint Ab to tell Miguel he can bring Cristina and Jen here."

"And I'm going to keep Dale around here a little longer. I need some help," Old Bill said, pointing at his wounded arm.

"Are you sure the coordinates will be enough?" Dale asked.

"Yes," River said. "No one can miss your red pickup from a mile out."

Dale looked a little taken aback, and Old Bill came to his rescue.

"Nothing wrong with a nice red vehicle. That's what I say."

River waved her goodbyes and returned to her bike. If she rode due north and then east, she would reach Saint Ab before lunch.

River made good progress on rough terrain. She marveled at the thought that memories of the mountains were coming back and that it all looked familiar again. She stopped the bike as soon as she could see the houses of Saint Ab's outskirts in the distance. She called Miguel, and he answered immediately.

"I found a place," she simply said.

"Is it far?"

"Not really, but it's well hidden," River said. "Do you remember the place you and I spoke about the first time we met?"

"I do."

"Let meet there in twenty minutes rather than your home."

"We're ready to go. So we'll see you there."

River followed the outskirts of Saint Ab toward her rendezvous with Miguel and the other two women. She liked the cave for its remoteness and secrecy, but she hoped that the remoteness wouldn't work against them. Out there, they would be on their own with a wounded old man.

Chapter 9

River arrived first at the Red Benn Diner. She parked the bike and removed her helmet, then went into the diner and took a seat in the back of the place. Miguel arrived ten minutes later. He hadn't bothered with a ponytail, and his unruly black hair looked disheveled. His eyes were rimmed with red. He sat opposite River, and they both waited for one of the waitresses to take their order.

"What will it be for you?" a plump and smiley woman asked.

"Two coffees, please," River replied.

The woman took their order and disappeared toward the counter.

"I guess Jen and Cristina have stayed in your car," River murmured.

Miguel nodded. "Where is this place?"

River waited for the coffee to arrive, then she told Miguel about Old Bill's secret cave, and he looked relieved. "Even I haven't heard of it, and as a journalist I make it my business to know everything."

"I have the coordinates. Dale is up there helping Old Bill ensure that everything works. It's Dale's day off."

Miguel took a sip of coffee and then said, "He drove his red pickup?"

River smiled. "Can't miss it when you get there."

"Jen is going on her own with Cristina. She's going to rent a car outside Saint Ab, and then she'll drive up to the cave. I don't know whether my car has been flagged by the cartel."

"After that, we need to talk some more. We need to put a plan in place."

"I'm in, whatever you do," Miguel said.

River shook her head. "I said I needed help to put a plan together. I never spoke about the execution."

"I'm in," Miguel repeated as he grabbed River's forearm. "My sister is dead, and my family will never be free if we don't stand up to these thugs. They've been exploiting this city for far too long."

River pressed her fingers on his hand. She understood him more than he could ever imagine.

Miguel nodded in acknowledgment. He opened his jacket and pulled a packet from the inside pocket. He pushed it across the table toward River.

"This is what you've been asking for. Sorry for the delay in delivery," Miguel said. "There's one spare clip. I'll come up with more ammo when we next meet."

River picked up the packet and put it onto her lap. "I also think we need to start using burner phones. I'll get a couple, and we can set ourselves up."

"Let's meet again midafternoon," Miguel said as he pulled out his wallet to settle their bill. "And let's meet somewhere else. The Moon Room restaurant, in the center of town."

Miguel stood up and went to pay. River followed him and went outside to her bike. She resisted the desire to check on Cristina. She thought she hadn't been followed, but being cautious was now essential. She slid the wrapped gun into the bike's storage pod, then put her helmet on, throttled up, and hit the road back to Luke's home. It was lunchtime, and she wanted to speak to Rosa and Luke.

The aroma of cooking welcomed River when she opened the door. She was expecting to see Luke, but instead Rosa was already up and in the kitchen. River dropped her helmet and backpack to the floor. She'd slid the gun into it and covered it with her jacket.

"You're up already," River said as she walked into the kitchen.

Rosa turned around and came to give River a hug. "You heard about Martha?" she said, her arms still around River.

"I heard from Miguel," River said, giving Rosa a tight squeeze.

Rosa pulled away and wiped away a tear with the back of her hand. She turned back to the stove and stirred the food she'd been cooking in a large pan.

"Carmen is at a friends for lunch, and Luke is coming in later. It's his turn to spend the afternoon helping at the migrant center, so he'll stay a little longer at the doctor's practice to make up for it. He does that every week," Rosa said as she added peppers to the pan.

"Do you need some help?" River asked.

Rosa dropped the wooden spoon she was using onto a small plate and locked eyes with River. "What I need is someone who has the balls to face these douchebags."

River was startled by the intensity of Rosa's glare. She was ready for a fight, and River worried about where it might all lead.

"Mexican cartels are more powerful than most people think," River said.

Rosa shook her head. "You sound like your brother. Everybody knows that the cartels are powerful and ruthless. I've lived close to the border with Mexico my whole life. I have family in Mexico. But it doesn't mean that we give up."

"I'm sure Luke is worried about what might happen to you and the kids."

"I know he is. I also know losing your parents the way you both did was terrible," Rosa said. "But if we can't fight the cartels, at least we can try to kick out Sheriff Andersen."

River sat down at the kitchen counter. "I hope you don't mind my asking, but does Luke ever speak about Mom and Dad?"

Rosa covered the dish to let it simmer and came to sit next to River.

"Very little. And we met only a year or so before they passed," she said, her tone more mellow.

"So he never speaks about what happened in the DRC?"

"Only once, when we received a box with some of their belongings. I don't even know what was in it."

River's throat tightened, but she forced herself to ask, "Do you know whether he kept it?"

"It's in the attic. He sometimes goes up there and goes through it. He doesn't tell me, but I know because it's the only thing up there that has no dust on it."

River nodded. She couldn't understand why he hadn't mentioned that he'd kept some of their parents' belongings. Yes, she could have asked, but they'd barely spoken at the funeral or during the scattering of the ashes. After that, it had been years of silence punctuated by the odd message to let her know that he'd gotten married or that he'd become a father.

Rosa put her hand over River's shoulder. "You didn't know about the box?"

River shook her head. She didn't want to cry; Luke might arrive any moment.

"The attic isn't locked," Rosa said. "Now you know that, and you know where it is."

Rosa went back to check her cooking. She stirred the contents of the pan a few times and came back to sit next to River.

"You spoke to Miguel. What did he say?"

River paused. She needed to remind herself what Rosa knew and what she didn't know. "He was devastated about Martha and worried about Dolores."

"If this girl isn't found soon, she'll be on her way to Vegas."

River frowned. "What do you mean?"

"That's what these SOBs do. They use the girls as mules, and then they ship them to Vegas to fuel the sex industry. It's human trafficking."

"How come you know so much about it?" River asked.

"In the ER, we get the occasional girl who's escaped, like Dolores, but Luke also hears through Harry about the other ones who're not as lucky."

"Harry popped in this morning," River said.

Rosa raised an eyebrow but then added, "He usually gets to the office early. But then I suppose he wanted to come in and say hello to you."

"Actually, I saw him yesterday. I went to the morgue to talk to the coroner about the other girl, Teresa. Turns out the coroner is Harry. He wasn't that happy to see me there."

Rosa thought for a moment. "Harry has changed since he started this coroner job."

"Is Sheriff Andersen pushing him around?" River said.

"I wouldn't be surprised."

"But why not go over Andersen's head? Speak to the FBI?"

"I don't know," Rosa said. "What were you looking for when you went to the morgue?"

"I just wanted to know whether he wanted to speak to me as the person who found Teresa when she was still alive."

"And did he?"

"Not really."

Rosa went back to her pan and lifted the lid. A wonderful aroma of spices, onions, and tomatoes filled the air. She dipped a spoon into the sauce, blew on it as she brought it to her lips, and tasted the liquid. She gave it a nod of approval.

"I wonder whether it might be a good idea to check what Harry's keeping at the office."

River gave her a sidelong look. "And how would that be possible?"

"I don't know." Rosa shrugged innocently. "But if I were to keep documents that I didn't want anyone to find, I'll do it there. Both Harry and Luke are paranoid about confidentiality, so the office has top-of-the-line security systems."

"How would you go about getting in there, then?"

Again, the guiltless look in Rosa's eyes was almost convincing. "With Luke's keys, of course."

River gave Rosa a knowing grin. "And where would I find—"

The front door opening interrupted River. "Whatever it is you're cooking smells delicious," Luke shouted from the entryway.

Rosa gave River a nod. "Speak of the devil."

Luke entered the kitchen and went to kiss his wife and then River.

"I'll set the table," River said, disappearing into the dining area to give them space and think about what Rosa had just suggested.

Once the table was set, she summoned Rosa and Luke. Luke walked in carrying a dish brimming with food. Rosa followed with a pitcher of water and a tray of bread. Luke placed the dish at the center of the table and took off his jacket, which he draped around the back of a chair. The women sat down, too, and they made small talk for a while. River did her best to invent a reason for her trip to the mountains that didn't involve hiding Old Bill in his secret cave and sending Cristina and Jen there to keep them safe.

"It's strange how memories of the mountains come back," River said.

"Maybe we can find a place where we can set up camp, build a fire, and have a barbecue," Luke said.

Rosa smiled. "Jack is coming back from his school trip soon. I'd love that, and so would Carmen."

"And perhaps we could invite Harry. He really enjoyed seeing you again, Riv."

The two women exchanged a look, and River said, "It was lovely of him to pop in."

She must have sounded suitably happy, because Luke added, "I'll think about where we could go, then."

After everyone had finished, Rosa said, "I'll make coffee."

"My turn," Luke replied, planning a kiss Rosa's forehead.

Rosa smiled and watched Luke as he walked into the kitchen. She leaned back and mouthed to River, *Now.*

River delved into one of Luke's jacket pockets and found two key rings. She showed them to Rosa, who tilted her head to the right. River pocketed the office keys and replaced the other key ring where she'd found it.

Rosa cleared her throat, and River straightened up just in time for Luke to appear with three mugs.

"Are you still going to the Santa Clara migrant center today?" Rosa asked.

"As planned. Today is a little less busy at the practice, so I'll do my full half day there."

They drank their coffee, chatting about a possible barbecue place, and River noticed that Silver Rim and the Devils Playground were off the menu. Luke seemed to favor going due south, crossing into Arizona. River and Rosa didn't object. It kept Luke happy, and that was all that mattered for the time being.

River helped Rosa clear the table. Luke got ready and left the house so he could arrive at the Santa Clara center by two thirty.

"You'll need the code," Rosa said as soon as Luke left.

River hesitated, and Rosa picked up on it. "Remember: Luke said to me that you were the daring one. And I saw how concerned you were about Dolores at the hospital."

"As long as you don't get involved," River said. "It's okay if I take a risk, but it's not okay if you do. If Luke hears of this, he'll never forgive me."

Rosa planted her fists on her hips in mock anger. "I'm perfectly capable of getting into trouble *without* your help."

River rolled her eyes. "I haven't known you for long, but I gathered *that* much. Still, I'm more expendable than you are."

Rosa shook her head. "No one is expendable. Not you, not me, not these girls."

River leaned against the kitchen counter, thinking. She didn't want Rosa involved, but she didn't want her trying to fight the cartel on her own, either. "I could do with someone who finds out about a pattern of arrival of these girls into Saint Ab."

Rosa thought for a moment and said, "I'll see what I can gather from the ER records. I might be able to access the morgue records as well."

"Sounds good," River said.

She checked her watch. It was time to make her way to her meeting with Miguel. "What time does the practice close?" River asked.

"Six o'clock. But there's always someone there after hours. Harry will be doing some filing or other administrative stuff, probably until seven."

"How about the custodians?"

"Good point. They come in at six and leave at seven. Either Harry, Luke, or one of the nurses stays behind to let them out."

River nodded. "And what's the code?"

"Easy to remember. It's your mom's birthday."

River gave Rosa a quick hug before she picked up her jacket, helmet, and backpack. It had gotten a little heavier, thanks to Miguel's gun. She checked that her phone was in her jacket pocket and went out of the house. She got on the bike, started it, and was on her way to the Moon Room to meet Miguel.

River rode to the center of town. She spotted a shop that sold electronic goods and stopped there. She picked up a couple of burner phones, paid for them, and continued to the Moon Room. Miguel's car wasn't yet there. She walked in, scanned the place quickly, and chose a booth as far from the door as possible.

A waitress came to take her order. She asked for a sparkling water and two glasses, hoping this might prompt Miguel to turn up. The water arrived, and River poured herself a glass. She took the burner phones out of her backpack and set them up, then checked her watch. She'd been there for almost forty minutes, and Miguel hadn't arrived yet.

She thought about calling his cell but decided to call Dale instead. The call went to voicemail, but she didn't leave a message. He would see that she'd called and, she hoped, call her back.

Someone sat opposite her as she turned to slide her cell back in her backpack.

"Sorry I'm late," Miguel said. "We had to find the right place to rent a car, and then I needed to get some ammo for your gun." He sat down and poured himself a glass of water.

"Do you know whether Jen and Cristina have arrived?" River asked.

"I had a short text from Jen. No specifics. But we decided on a code, so yes, they're good."

River took a sip of her water and then said, "Good. Then we work on finding Dolores. You already told me a lot about the cartels, but is there anything else you might have forgotten?"

Miguel wasn't offended by the question. He thought for a moment.

"Can't say there is."

"Do you know how often these guys move girls across the border?"

"I don't. Martha said it was getting more frequent, but she never told me whether it was monthly or weekly." Miguel's face dropped as he mentioned his sister's name. He took a sip of water before continuing. "If we could access the ER records and the morgue, we might get somewhere."

"I'm working on that," River said. "How can we find out what routes the coyotes and the traffickers take?"

"We could start with where you found the dying girl."

"I think we need a good old-fashioned paper map."

Miguel managed a small smile and reached into his backpack.

"Something like this?" he said as he took out a folded piece of paper. He opened it up and spread it over the tabletop. River and he exchanged a quick fist bump.

Miguel pointed to a long canyon that started way beyond Silver Rim in the mountains and ended on the outskirts of Saint Ab. He then took a ballpoint pen out of his jacket and handed it to River.

River drew an X on the map. "From what I can recognize, this is where the truck that was carting the migrants stopped and lost the girls."

Miguel nodded. "That looks about right."

She then followed the canyon with her fingers through the mountains. She marked a couple of places and continued. "I can see that there is a way to get around the mountains and end up in the desert in a direct line to Vegas."

Miguel gave it some thought. "The coyotes bring the migrants across illegally. They make sure the girls offload the precursors near Saint Ab, somewhere in the canyon, because"—he stopped again and then snapped his fingers—"it's close to the lab. And then another lot of cartel boys moves the girls down to Vegas once they're chemical-free."

"Why Saint Ab?" River asked.

"It's on Interstate 15, and that's one of the main routes for drug distribution."

River pondered that, but then shook her head. "I wouldn't put the lab close to the route used to offload the precursors. The lab needs to be close enough for convenience but far enough away to avoid being discovered if the route is busted."

Miguel frowned. "Yeah. You might be right on that one."

"I spotted a construction site when I was scouting the canyon yesterday. I think that's worth a visit."

"Can you place it on the map?"

River moved the map around a few times and finally pointed to a place with her finger. "Around there, I think."

Miguel shook his head. "That place must be either ancient and forgotten about or extremely recent, because I can't remember anyone mentioning there was a building in the area."

"Still, we've got two targets," River said. "The place where the precursors are offloaded and the lab."

Miguel took a few sips of water and then said, "We're assuming they're keeping Dolores at one of these two places."

"True, but do you really think the cartel wants to spread out their men? Meaning that they have a lot of different sites to keep safe?"

"Three wouldn't be that many."

"But it's a cartel that's muscling in on the others. I'd keep my operation tight if I were them."

Miguel nodded. "Okay, I buy that. So shall we split the load?"

"I'm not sure that's a good idea. If we're lucky enough—or perhaps unlucky enough—to find where the cartel does its business, we're going to need to stick together. I don't know much about Mexican cartels apart from what I read in the news. But if they're anything like what we faced in Afghanistan, even the US military couldn't finish them off."

"That's true, and in Mexico it's also the army that fights these

SOBs. But here on the other side of the border, I'd like to try something I've never done before," Miguel said.

River grinned. "That sounds promising."

"I've got a friend who flies a helicopter. We sometimes work together when I do a piece for a local news channel."

"Do you want to survey the area with him?"

Miguel nodded. "I could cover a lot of ground and do what you did at Silver Rim canyon, but on a bigger scale."

River took a few more sips of her water. "Will that alert the cartel men that someone's looking for them?"

"Good point. I'll ask Felipe whether he's due to fly in the next couple of days, maybe to pick up sightseers for a tour of the canyon and desert around the area. He does that all the time."

"Perhaps we could split up after all," River said. "We don't have a lot of time, and Dolores will be on the next shipment to Vegas."

"If she's still alive," Miguel said with sadness.

"She is. Otherwise . . ." River's voice trailed off. She didn't know how to put it to Miguel without sounding brutal.

Miguel spared her. "I get it. She, too, would be at the morgue by now."

"Talk to your friend," River said. "If he's flying today, you should take the opportunity to join him. I'll get to the canyon and investigate the structure I saw."

Miguel took his cell from his jacket pocket and walked outside. River gathered her backpack and helmet, paid the bill, and left. Miguel was leaning against his battered old Ford, having what looked like an animated conversation. She waited until he finished and then rode the bike to his car.

Miguel gave her a thumbs-up. "We're in business. I just have enough time to get to the helipad."

"Let's circle back here in three hours' time," River said.

She was about to ride off but then turned to Miguel. "If I'm not back, call Dale. I might have bitten off more than I can chew."

Chapter 10

River no longer needed to consult the GPS on her cell phone. She knew where she was going. She rode the I-15 all the way to the place where she spotted the vultures yesterday. When she arrived, she slowed the bike down to a crawl and finally stopped. Everything was quiet, but she waited a moment to dismount. She then took her binoculars out of her backpack. Walked to the edge of the cliff and scanned the landscape.

She wasn't high enough to see the structure she'd noticed the day before and didn't want to lose time climbing to the top of the ridge again. She checked whether there was any sign of activity in the canyon. There was nothing on the horizon or along the canyon walls. River ran the binoculars along the trail she'd taken before and tried to find another way down, but there wasn't any obvious alternative.

She returned to the bike and made her way to the bottom of the ravine. Stones started to roll underneath her wheels again, but this time she was prepared. She rode on the footrests, body slightly back. When the large boulder approached, she used the gears to control the speed of the bike and slid past it comfortably. River accelerated slowly and then kept going until she reached the bottom of the canyon. The ground was sandy and gravelly, but she upped the pace until she reached the narrowest part of the gorge.

The space between the two walls of the gorge got closer, and River slowed down to a stop. She rested the bike on the kickstand and went to check the path farther ahead. Her fingers ran along some tire tracks in the dirt. A couple of vehicles had been there not long ago. The wind hadn't had time to disperse the dust, and the weather had remained dry. She stood up abruptly, suddenly felt exposed. She was stuck in a ravine that was narrowing, giving her less room to maneuver the bike, and she didn't know how far she'd need to go before she found an exit at the end of the ravine. Still, she needed to make progress until she found the structure she'd seen the day before.

River took her binoculars out again and surveyed the walls of the cliff. She could climb down them and leave the bike at the top of the rim rather than being stuck at the bottom. She took a couple of photos with her cell phone so she could find the location again. She straddled the bike once more and retraced her steps. She then followed the same bikers' trail she followed when she visited Old Bill's ranch, but this time she rode along the rim of the canyon until she recognized one of the rocks she photographed.

River stopped the bike again, dismounted, and approached the edge. She walked farther out but still couldn't see any structure. She kept going for three hundred yards or so, wondering whether she'd imagined it. She was about to return to the bike when she spotted what she'd been looking for.

Now that she was close to it, she understood why Miguel might not have known about it. It looked like an old mine cut from the walls of the ravine with an odd structure still hanging over the entrance. The planks of wood had broken down, and some had fallen to the ground. River returned to the bike and turned it around. If she needed a quick escape, this would help. She surveyed the approach to the cave, but a bend in the ravine prevented her from seeing all the way down the canyon.

The rock felt solid underneath her feet when River tested it. She took her Glock out of her backpack, stuffed it against her back, and started to climb down the stone face. There was a sort of staircase that seemed to have been carved into the rock, and River wondered whether this might have been done by the people who'd exploited the mine. It took only a short time to reach the ground below, and

River moved away from the cliff, lifting the visor of her helmet so she could see better.

She made her way to the entrance of the mine and stood there for a moment. She was on her own, it seemed, and she pushed forward inside the cave. The stench that met her when she entered the place told her what she needed to know. The girls had been given laxatives to empty their bowels so that the trafficker could recover the sacks of drugs or precursors.

She put her arm across her face to try to dampen the foul smell and used the flashlight on her cell phone to see better inside the mine. The place had been cleared of any mining equipment. Instead, chains with collars had been screwed to the walls, two or three sharing a single hook. It looked inhuman. River imagined the teenagers and young women chained to the wall until they were ready to deliver the contents of their stomachs and then be moved again all the way to Vegas. Animals might be treated better. She snapped several pictures of what she saw.

She pushed farther inside the cave and saw that a few blankets had been piled in a corner. There was very little otherwise. The place was deliberately left empty of anything that could identify the lab activity. The reek of the place became unbearable as she kept moving farther in, and River's stomach heaved. Something or someone might have died in the back of the mine.

River ran outside and took a couple of deep, cleansing breaths. She walked away from the opening and toward the planks that lay on the ground. Part of the structure was still standing, although barely. It must have been a large shed of some sort. A rusty wheel was still hanging in the air, fixed to a wooden frame that was threatening to collapse. She carried out her inspection and couldn't find anything that might help with the identification of the lab. She walked farther up the ravine just to be certain, but apart from a couple of boulders and the tracks she'd already identified, there was nothing else.

The distant sound of a vehicle approaching startled River. She hadn't paid attention to her surroundings because she'd been focused on the old shed and the tracks on the ground. She had strayed away from her escape route, and she wasn't sure she had time to get back to the carved steps and climb the side of the cliff before the car arrived. She looked around and ran back to the boulders she'd just spotted. She squeezed between the rock face and the largest one, hoping the car would stop at the cave.

From what she could make out, the car stopped close to her hiding place, and the driver switched off the ignition. She couldn't see the vehicle from her position but guessed it was an SUV by the sound of the engine. A door opened and was slammed shut. Then River heard a voice in the distance.

"Where are you?"

There was a pause and then the voice carried on.

"I don't have much time, either, but we need to talk."

River had heard the voice before, but she couldn't recall whom it belonged to. She crept closer to the edge of the boulder she was hiding behind and peeked. She might be able to hide behind the smaller of the two rocks if she removed her helmet. She slowly unclipped the strap and pulled it off. She slid her arm through the visor opening and crawled to the next boulder.

Another vehicle had just arrived. She gingerly lifted her head over the top of the rock and saw another SUV parked next to the one she'd heard arriving. The first man walked to the car and stopped in front of the driver's door. Sheriff Andersen hadn't bothered to change clothes, although he'd bothered to change vehicles. The window of the second SUV slowly dropped down, and Andersen said something to the person inside she couldn't understand. River craned her neck, but Andersen's large body shielded the open window, and she couldn't see who was inside.

She concentrated on the second SUV, a black Jeep Grand Cherokee. She'd seen quite a few of those around, so it wouldn't help ID the owner. Sheriff Andersen's voice rose suddenly, and River paid attention.

"She's got to be stopped," he said, arms now resting over the roof of the vehicle.

The reply that came from inside the Jeep took a moment. The

119

person who was replying seemed to need to justify why he'd failed to stop the woman he was supposed to stop. River hoped they were talking about her, but Rosa, Jen, and Cristina were good candidates, too.

Andersen and his interlocutor talked some more, and then the driver of the second car started the engine again, but instead of driving away he reversed the SUV inside the mine. Andersen followed and disappeared inside, too. River heard a car door open and slam shut. Perhaps she'd been right; someone had died in that cave and Andersen and his accomplice were disposing of the body.

River waited for a moment. There was silence. She couldn't hear Andersen's voice and surmised he must have gone deep into the mine. She estimated the distance between the boulder behind which she was hiding and Andersen's SUV, and then the distance from the SUV to the bottom of the steps that led to the top of the cliff. She needed to get away, and she'd rather take her chance now than risk being discovered and cornered behind the boulders.

River put her helmet back on. At least it would protect her identity if she was spotted. She took the Glock from behind her back, racked it noiselessly, and squat-walked to the edge of the last boulder that kept her hidden. There still wasn't a sound coming from the cave. So she ran low, gun at the ready, until she reached the back of Andersen's SUV. She squatted there for a few seconds, heart pounding.

Two voices could now be heard arguing inside the cave. River took the opportunity to run to the base of the steps she would need to climb to get to her bike. The voices got louder as River hit the cliff wall. She replaced the Glock against the small of her back and started scaling the rock face. The two men were now outside the cave, still arguing.

River couldn't concentrate on what they were saying. She needed to focus on her climb. Midway through, River slowed down because the rock had become more brittle, something she hadn't noticed on her way down. Her foot slipped, and a few pieces of rock rolled down the cliff. The two men stopped immediately. River accelerated her pace. It was too late to be subtle.

Andersen shouted, "Stop."

He followed a minute later with a gunshot that ricocheted next to River's head, sending some rock splinters against her helmet and arm. She made her final push as more bullets hit the rim of the cliff. She rolled on her side and stood up, then ran to the bike. Andersen was a heavy man, and his paunch would drag him down if he tried to follow her. She straddled the bike, gunned the engine, and left in a spray of gravel. She rode the bike close to the rim of the ravine and saw the Jeep Cherokee leaving at full speed, fleeing the scene. River pushed the bike a little harder, but the cliff edge veered to the right as the canyon started widening toward Silver Rim.

River kept going until she reached the trail that led to Old Bill's ranch. The Jeep was now only a dot in the distance, and she had no hope of catching it. But something attracted her attention now that she'd released her focus from the fleeing SUV. A plume of dark smoke was rising toward the sky with a faint glow at its base. Old Bill's ranch was on fire.

River winced. She hadn't noticed, but a rock shard had cut through her leather jacket and planted itself into her left arm. She gingerly pulled up her sleeve to survey the damage. She plucked the fragment out and bit her lip. It was bleeding, but it wasn't life-threatening. In the distance, the smoke kept billowing, and she needed to call the fire department.

She took her cell out of her jacket pocket and checked for reception. One bar flickered on and off. She'd have to take her chances. River dialed 911.

An operator replied immediately. "Nine one one, what's your emergency?"

"I'm near Silver Rim canyon, and Old Bill—I mean Bill Barrick's ranch is on fire."

The response came back garbled, but River thought she could make out the word "repeat."

"Bill Barrick's ranch is on fire," River shouted.

Again, more interference, but finally she heard something that told her the operator had gotten the message—"sending out."

River revved the engine again and rode hard toward Old Bill's place. When she arrived, the fire had spread to half the first floor. The gate that had been crashed open the evening before was lying shattered on the ground. River rode in, stopped the bike, and ran to the side of the property that the flames hadn't yet reached. She looked for a hose of some sort but couldn't see one. She ran to the barn and spotted what she was looking for. She turned the tap on and dragged the large hose toward the house.

The pressure was strong enough, and she tried to douse the part of the first floor that hadn't yet caught fire with water. But the inferno that was burning next to her made it impossible to get close enough for the water to reach inside the house. She kept going for several minutes, moving in and out, pulling back when sparks threatened to catch her clothes on fire.

She fought until the entire house was engulfed in flames, then she dropped to the ground. She removed her helmet and let it roll next to her. Her left arm was soaked in blood. She ran her other forearm across her face to wipe away the grime and the tears. All had been lost of a home Old Bill had built over the course of decades.

River stood up slowly. In the distance she could hear the sirens of the fire trucks. Sadness was replaced by anger. She walked toward the broken gate, holding her arm. The pain she hadn't succumbed to until now was taking its revenge. She slumped against one of the gateposts and rested against it.

River noticed that a piece of glass seemed to be protruding from the wood. She moved her fingers over it and then stopped abruptly. It wasn't a piece of glass; it was a lens. River stood back a little. Now she could see it. She pushed the wood around, and a panel slid open. A miniature camera was recording anything that happened between the gate and the house's front door. River couldn't help but smile. Once a copper, always a copper, and Old Bill had done his former profession proud.

The lights of two fire engines flashed in the distance. They would be here any minute. She grappled with the recording device and managed to unplug it without creating damage. She switched it off and pushed the camera into the inner pocket of her jacket. The pain in her left arm made her queasy, and she leaned once more against the gatepost.

The first fire engine arrived, and the fire chief got out first to survey the fire. He spotted River and rushed to her immediately. He didn't ask whether she was hurt but instead shouted to one of his men. "Randy. Emergency kit. We've got a casualty."

River blinked her thanks. Randy turned up with an emergency kit, the likes of which River had seen too many times.

"I'm Randy," the young man said. "What's your name?"

"I'm River . . . River Swift." She looked around and spotted an old stone bench she hadn't noticed the night before and said, "I'm a medic. I can tell you it's not bad, but the wound needs cleaning and a good bandage. Let's move to that bench over there."

Randy supported her until she got to the bench. River sat down heavily and slowly removed her jacket. Her T-shirt was bloodstained and torn where the rock fragment had penetrated the skin.

"What happened?" Randy asked.

"Was scaling down a rock face and got hit by falling rocks," River said.

Randy cocked an eyebrow. "Rock climbing dressed like this?"

River looked down at herself—jeans, biker's boots, and leather jacket. "I know. Not optimal."

"It must have been a hell of a rockfall to force a shard into your arm. You're lucky it's not worse."

"You can say that again," River said, watching as the young man started cleaning the wound and applying antiseptic cream. He was doing a good job of it, although the pain had increased a notch, and she couldn't help moaning from time to time.

River let Randy patch her up. She turned her attention to the fire crew. The second engine had arrived, and the men had already unfolded their main hose. They were dousing the house in water and trying to contain the fire so that it didn't spread to the barn.

"Quick pinch," Randy said as he gave River a shot.

"Hey. What's that?" she asked, her attention returning to her wound.

Randy seemed taken aback by her reaction. "Just a local anesthetic to make sure you can ride home without being in too much pain."

"Sorry," River said. "I like to know what I'm being given. Medics are the worst patients."

"It's lidocaine," Randy said. He showed the vial to River, and she nodded. It would do the trick for an hour or so.

"How long will it be before the fire's out?" she asked Randy.

Randy shook his head. "A couple of hours. It's too strong now to be stopped fast."

The chief called out to Randy. "You done?"

River stood up slowly. "Thanks a lot."

"You're welcome," Randy said, and then, turning to his chief, "I'm coming."

Randy's chief walked to River and said, "I hope there was no one in there."

"I don't think so. When I arrived, the fire had already claimed half the first floor. I tried with a hose from the barn."

"Not a chance unless you've got one of these big guys," he said pointing to the double jacket hoses that were in action around Old Bill's house.

River sighed. She pushed back the tears to ask, "Do you need me?"

"No. I got your name. You're Luke's sister, I guess. Just go to the police station to make a statement."

The crew chief turned around, back to the fire he and his men were trying to control. River shivered in shock. Saint Ab was a small town, and word circulated fast. If the fire chief knew she was Luke's sister, who else did? She picked up her jacket, cautiously slid into it, and went to collect her helmet. Randy was now fully kitted in his suit and walking toward one end of the house. River stopped him.

"Thanks again."

"Just doing my job," he said with a smile.

"What's the name of your chief?"

"Chief Watson. Teddy Watson."

River walked back to her bike and picked up the backpack she'd dumped next to it in a hurry. She checked the time—5:37 p.m. She was due to meet Miguel in half an hour. She thought about informing Old Bill about the disaster. But perhaps he knew already. If the camera had the capacity to transmit data over a radio frequency, he would have picked up images of the fire.

River retrieved the camera from her jacket pocket and inspected it. She thought she recognized it as an IP camera—an internet protocol camera, which transmitted over a network but also recorded on the device. If Old Bill checked his feed or the recorded footage regularly, he would know not only what had happened but also, crucially, who had set fire to his house.

She took the burner phone out of her backpack and called the only number she'd stored there—Miguel's.

"On my way," Miguel said when he picked up. "I'm in the car, and I think I've spotted something."

"On my side, I've got good news and bad news."

Miguel's cheer turned into a heavy silence.

"The good news is that I found the place where the cartel retrieves the drugs or the precursors. The bad news is that Old Bill's house is on fire. I'm there now. It's bad, but I don't think anyone was inside."

"Fuckers. I hope whoever they are burn in hell."

"At least there is a chance we're going to find out who did this."

"How?"

"Old Bill fitted a camera into one of the gateposts. It was still working less than an hour ago."

"So it recorded everything."

"It should have," River said. "It also means that Old Bill must know what's happened. I'm going to call him and ask him how I can get access to the footage."

"What do you want me to do?"

"Get a laptop. I'm not planning to go to the cave, so I'll try to make it back as fast as I can."

River dropped the burner back into her pack. There was no way she could shoulder the bag, her wound being too raw. So she stuffed it into the storage compartment of the bike, started the engine, and got going. The wound was tugging at her, but she'd be fine for an hour until she reached town.

She stopped ten minutes later and checked reception from her cell phone. It wasn't ideal, but she couldn't use her burner because she wanted Old Bill to know who was calling. She took a deep breath and braced herself. She was about to tell the old man he'd lost his house to a fire.

She searched for Old Bill's number, found it, and pressed the Call button. The phone rang, and a cranky voice said, "You almost got yourself killed tryin' to put that damn fire out."

"'Almost' is the operative word, though," River said, surprised—but then she got it. "You knew they would come back and that you'd catch them on camera."

The old man grunted. "Got a good picture of 'em. But I guess you know that since you took the camera out of its hidey-hole."

"Well, I didn't know for sure, and anyway I didn't want one of the firefighters to come across it and remove it."

"That was a good move on your part," Old Bill said.

"Do you know who these people are?"

"Never seen them before, but I guess they're the same people who came the night before and tried to kill us."

"Could I use the camera to download the footage and take a look myself? I saw two of them yesterday, and I think I'd recognize them."

"Sure. I'll send you the username and password."

"Thanks, Bill. I intend to catch these SOBs and bring them to justice."

"I know you will."

There was a short silence that felt a little awkward, and then River said, "And I'm sorry for the ranch."

"I know . . . lots of memories there. But I got the bit I cherished the most, and what matters at the end of the day is people. I'm keeping two nice girls safe. That's the important part."

River nodded as though Old Bill could see her and then said, "Look for a number you don't recognize next. I'm going to call you from a burner phone."

"All right," Old Bill said. "And River, remember—these guys are real pieces o' dirt."

"I gathered that."

River hung up and fired the bike again. She pushed it as hard as she could and hoped she wouldn't encounter a not-so-friendly patrol car. She needed to get back to Saint Ab before the analgesic stopped working altogether.

Chapter 11

River recognized Miguel's old Ford when she went to park her bike in the Moon Room lot. She spotted him as soon as she got in, tucked away in a booth at the back of the room. He'd opened a laptop and was looking at the screen when she sat opposite him.

"Got some news," she said.

Miguel lifted his head from the screen, and his face dropped. "What happened? You're hurt."

River looked at the rip in her jacket and smiled. "Just a scratch."

"It looks like more than a scratch."

"I'm good. A nice firefighter called Randy patched me up and gave me a painkiller."

"Should you've been riding the bike?"

River rolled her eyes. "Gee. Even my dad wouldn't have been that concerned." But then she stretched out a hand and squeezed Miguel's arm. "I'm sorry. I know you're worried, but I'm good at knowing how far my body can go."

Miguel nodded. "That's okay. I guess being a medic in the military isn't an easy task."

A young waitress arrived to take their order. They both asked for sodas and apple pie. She smiled and disappeared toward the kitchen.

Miguel pushed the laptop aside, picked out the map from his backpack, and spread it over the table. The pen mark River had made in the early afternoon stared at them. Miguel took the same pen out of his jacket pocket and wrote on the map OFFLOADING CENTER. He put it down on the table between him and River.

"It's an old mine. It looks like a cave from the outside, but when you get in, you can see it's deep," she said.

"Utah was a mining center in the eighteen hundreds. Copper, gold, and other metals. Still is today," Miguel said.

"But this mine was abandoned years ago. The parts I saw from the distance are remnants of a structure, a kind of shed. Just as well the cartel guys didn't think about removing it."

River stopped as the sodas and pie arrived. She tucked into her apple pie. She suddenly felt famished.

"I saw two men there," she said before taking a second mouthful. "One I recognized immediately. It was Andersen. The other one was familiar, but I'm not sure now. He drives a black Jeep Grand Cherokee."

"Lots of them around," Miguel said. "Is this little accident linked to your visit to the mine?" Miguel said, pointing at the rip in River's jacket.

River swallowed another mouthful and then said, "Sheriff Andersen is a crappy shot, but I'm not gonna complain. At least I had my helmet on so he couldn't see my face."

Miguel started on his pie and then pulled a face. "This isn't as good as my Jen's."

"Are they okay, Jen and Cristina?" River said. "Old Bill mentioned he was looking after them."

Miguel nodded. He cleared his throat and drank a little soda.

"Let's take a look at what Old Bill has on his surveillance footage," River said as she produced the camera from the inner pocket of her jacket. She took her cell out of another pocket.

Miguel pushed his plate and glass away and settled the laptop in front of him. He logged in and waited for instructions.

River turned the small device around in her fingers. "SurveyTech XPS," she said.

Miguel found the website and then the camera name. "Need a username and password."

River found a text from Old Bill on her cell, as promised. She read it in a low voice to Miguel, who typed it in. He waited a few moments and then pushed the laptop toward River. "You saw the guys, and I didn't," he said.

She pulled the laptop toward her and looked at the time stamp. The camera had been disabled at 4:16 p.m. She rewound the recording so it would start an hour before that time. There was nothing. She then pressed Play until she picked up two men walking toward Old Bill's house. She identified one of them as the man who had driven the SUV to Old Bill's ranch the previous night. The other man she hadn't seen before. They looked confident, with their muscles bulging under their shirts, and they had a swagger River didn't like.

So proud to set an old guy's house on fire.

River froze the image and zoomed in on the man she recognized. He had an unusual tattoo on his right upper arm. She zoomed in again and could identify some symbols that might be Mayan, and a face—maybe that of a god with his tongue in the form of a blade sticking out. It looked threatening and yet beautiful.

"Do you mind if I create a file and store some images on your laptop? I have a couple of good shots of these guys' faces, and there's a tattoo that could be distinctive."

"Go ahead," Miguel said. "But before you do, show me the tat."

River turned the screen toward Miguel. He enlarged it to study it better and then returned the laptop to River.

"It's a Cruz Cartel tattoo. I saw a similar one on a guy I interviewed a couple of years ago for a piece I was writing about the Mexican cartels' dominance."

She stored several images in a new folder she called SAINT AB VISIT. She then sent a copy to her own email address and returned the laptop to Miguel.

"We're now sure that the Cruz guys are expanding their influence on the US side of the border," River said.

"And we have some evidence to prove it," Miguel said with less enthusiasm than River would have expected.

"What's on your mind?"

"You saw Andersen, but he saw you, too. He's going to speak to the cartel guys, and they're going to clean the mine and hunt you down."

"I took some photos of the inside of the cave, so at least that's something, and remember: I had my helmet on."

Miguel thought for a moment and then said, "I suppose the helmet buys you some time. But when it comes to cleaning up the place, it's all going to depend on when the next lot of girls arrive. If they get here in the next couple of days, the men probably don't have time to find another cave that suits their purposes."

River took a sip of soda before she added, "You're right. I'm on borrowed time."

Miguel swirled his drink slowly in his glass. "Andersen is going to have every single one of his men on the lookout."

River finished her pie and pushed the plate aside. "Well, between the cartel and Andersen's men, I've suddenly become a very popular woman."

Miguel blanched. "But they don't know who you are, right?"

River shook her head. "Not yet, but I can't imagine it's going to take them much time if they really want to find out. I brought Teresa to the hospital, and I visited Dolores. I had a tiff with Andersen, and I went to the morgue asking questions."

"What are you going to do?" Miguel asked.

"It's simple. Either I get these guys, or they get me." River finished her coffee. "What happened on your helicopter ride?"

"Nothing new around Saint Ab," Miguel said, half thinking.

"I thought you said you had some news."

"Sorry. Let me explain. There is no new construction I could spot, so what this means is that the cartel is using an abandoned building."

"But there must be a ton of places like that."

Miguel went to his laptop. His fingers moved swiftly over the keyboard, and then he said. "I found a list of abandoned properties in the area that are too derelict to restore, and it's not that many. Saint Ab is becoming popular, what with its new golf course, and people buying old ranches in order to renovate them. But they're not interested in ruins that they have to demolish. This new crowd is looking for *authentic* buildings," Miguel said as he made air quotes with his fingers.

"And you say this leaves us with only a few of these ruins."

"Well, yes. If you consider that the lab must be relatively close to the mine you spotted."

Miguel took the pen they used before, brought the map closer to him, and made three X's. The third place Miguel marked drew River's attention—Devils Playground. He was about to comment on the merits of each place, but then River interrupted him.

"Tell me more about that one."

Miguel looked a little surprised. "I was gonna leave the best for last."

"I used to eat dessert before the main course when I was little—nothing's changed."

"This old ranch is at the bottom of the Devils Playground cliff but on a small elevation so that it's secure from the arroyo's flash flooding. It's just run-down enough not to attract the hordes of people wanting to renovate, but the ranch comprises a couple of buildings and a barn that can just about be used if you're not too picky about comfort."

River thought for a moment and then asked, "Are the buildings big?"

"Big enough. Why?"

"Could you fix up a few rooms inside the structure without anyone noticing from the outside?"

Miguel scratched his chin. "That's an interesting idea." He pulled the laptop toward him and used the keyboard, then nodded. "Big enough from the measurements I see here—four thousand square feet on a single floor. But the roof has come down on part of the main building, and the walls have collapsed on two sides."

"Still, a lab doesn't need that much space, and then part of the barn can be used for accommodation. Or they can use yet another building."

"The other two places I was about to mention are a little too far away. I don't see these guys wanting to leave the place unattended or even put guards on duty. The more movement you've got, the more noticeable you become."

"That's true," River said. "You said the ranch was on top of a small hill. Can you see it easily from the top of the cliff?"

Miguel used the keyboard once more. "Good question," he said. He found what he was looking for and then added, "I'd say it's hidden by a taller hill at the back."

River picked up the pen and circled the place. "I need to go take a look. It could be the place where they keep Dolores."

"*We* need to go take a look," Miguel said, correcting her, his index finger raised. "Besides, you're injured. You need backup."

River shook her head. "I just need another injection of lidocaine. I'll be as good as new."

Miguel gave her skeptical look. "I need a second opinion from another medic to believe that."

River brought a hand to her arm and winced. Perhaps Miguel was right. She couldn't go it alone this time.

"Okay. But we need to go tonight," River said as she was folding the map together. "We'll take your car. The bike is too noisy."

Miguel took the map and stuffed it into his backpack. "I reckon these guys will be cooking drugs well into the night."

"Then we should go when there's still activity at the lab. At least whatever noise we make will be less obvious."

"What time should I pick you up from Luke's house?"

River blinked. She hadn't heard anyone call her grandparents' home Luke's house yet. "Ten o'clock. Everybody will be in bed by then."

Miguel didn't look as though he was ready to leave.

"Something else on your mind?"

"You haven't mentioned Dale. I guess you haven't heard from him."

"I haven't, but Old Bill sounded fine when I called him. I'm sure he made good use of Dale to secure the cave and make sure they have all they need up there."

Miguel nodded and closed his laptop slowly. He was right, River thought. Dale should have called, and if he didn't soon, she would try to get hold of him again.

She stood up, and a wave of pain shot through her arm, making her pause for a moment. River then nodded to a concerned Miguel. Leaving the Moon Room and still feeling out of sorts, River got to her bike as Miguel went to pay the bill. She took a deep breath and managed to get her helmet on with one hand. She started the engine and eased the bike into traffic. She needed to get back now before Luke came home from the migrant center. With any luck, Rosa could help.

The garage doors were open when River arrived. Rosa's Chevrolet Equinox was in the garage, but Luke's own SUV wasn't there yet. She steered the bike into the garage, leaving enough room for Luke to drive in when he arrived. She wouldn't ride the bike until the following day. She removed her helmet cautiously using her injured arm, opened the bike's storage compartment, and removed her backpack.

She fished her keys out and walked to the door. She opened it slowly and sneaked inside. She could hear cartoons playing on the TV in the living room and gathered that Carmen must be watching with Franklin in attendance. River walked noiselessly past the room and went into the kitchen. Rosa wasn't there, so River took the stairs to the second floor. As she arrived on the landing, Rosa came out of the bathroom, her hair wrapped in a towel.

The smile on Rosa's face vanished as soon as she noticed that River wasn't holding herself straight. River put a finger over her lips and indicated that they should go into the bathroom.

"What happened?" Rosa immediately asked as soon as they were in.

"It's a long story, but a shard of rock got lodged in my arm."

River peeled off her jacket and shirt to expose Randy's bandage. Rosa opened her mouth and put a hand over it to muffle a small cry.

"I'm not sure whether you heard, but Old Bill's ranch caught fire, and I tried to stop it."

Rosa shook her head as she started to undo the bandage slowly. "I hadn't heard, but at least your wound was dressed professionally."

"A very nice firefighter called Randy."

Rosa lifted her eyes for a moment and smiled. "A lovely guy."

She undid the bandage completely. River pressed her lips together and winced.

"Did he give you something for the pain?"

"A shot of lidocaine."

Rosa nodded in approval. "You need to try to rest your arm."

"Perhaps tonight, but I've got to be able to use the bike tomorrow."

"Learn anything new about Dolores?" Rosa asked as she opened a well-stocked medicine cabinet.

She selected more disinfectant, antibiotic cream, and a bandage. Rosa indicated that River should sit on a small stool, then she put the medication on a long counter next to one of the sinks. She returned to the cabinet and came back with a syringe and a small vial.

River followed Rosa's moves, wondering how she could avoid talking about the mine and her encounter with Sheriff Andersen. Rosa started treating her wound and then said, "It's not fire that caused this wound. More like a piece of rock dislodged by a shot."

River slumped against the wall behind the stool. "Look, I don't want to get you into trouble."

"Too late," Rosa said. "I've been nosing around the ER database and the morgue records. I think I've noticed a pattern. Girls are delivered twice a week, I believe. Not always on the same day, but two or three days apart."

River frowned. "That's very precise."

"I spent the whole day on this, going back two years. There is a pattern. I'm sure of it."

"We have one more day, two at the most, to figure it out when the next lot of girls is arriving and find Dolores," River said, moaning in pain.

Rosa kept working on River, tending the wound, wrapping the bandage around her arm, and then preparing a shot of lidocaine. She held the syringe up and waited a moment.

"This is blackmail," River said, shaking her head.

"Yep. So what about Dolores?"

River relented. "I have an idea but nothing concrete yet. I promise I'll tell you as soon as I know."

Rosa was still holding the syringe up. "And Harry's office?"

"I haven't forgotten," River grumbled. "Early hours of the morning."

Rosa leaned close to River, chose a spot she'd cleaned, and gave her the injection. River felt herself relax instantly. It wasn't so much the medication acting immediately as the knowledge that it soon would.

"You're good for a few hours," Rosa said. "I'll make sure Carmen doesn't jump on you and reopen the wound."

River closed her eyes and nodded. "She's a lovely kid."

"She is," Rosa said, "but then she's my kid, so I'm biased. I think she's very fond of you. I could see that right from the start."

"And I hope I can spend some time with Jack when he returns from his trip."

"You have a fan in him—way before he even met you." Rosa grinned at the thought.

"A fan?" River asked, surprised. "But he doesn't know me."

"No, but he's been told you were a medic with the air force, and—"

There was a distant sound, and River straightened up. "When is Luke due back?"

"Any moment now." Rosa said. "And just so you know, he leaves for the practice after dropping Carmen at school. So you need to get his keys into his jacket pocket before 8:00 a.m. Otherwise, he'll notice they're missing."

"Understood. I'll make sure they're back by then. I don't want to attract his or Harry's attention."

Rosa nodded and took River's jacket and bloodstained shirt. "I'll clean this up. Let me find something else for you to wear."

She disappeared and returned with a blue-and-green checkered shirt that made River's blue eyes stand out. River put it on quickly and asked, "Has Luke arrived?"

"You probably have a few minutes."

River went downstairs. The TV was still on, and River stepped past the room quietly and then went into the spare bedroom. She took her clothes off and managed a quick shower without wetting the bandage. She changed her jeans, put Rosa's shirt on, bundled the rest of her dirty clothes, and returned to the main house. Rosa was waiting for her outside the kitchen door. She grabbed the clothes and disappeared into the utility room.

River walked into the kitchen just as the front door opened and Luke shouted, "I'm home."

Carmen sprang from the sofa and ran to her dad, shouting, *"Daddy!"* Franklin followed her but then sat—miffed, it seemed, that he no longer was the center of attention. River smiled at the scene. Luke was tossing Carmen in the air, trying and failing to imitate the sound of an airplane. And then a memory flashed in River's mind— River and Luke's father coming back from one of his missions to yet another underresourced part of the country in which the family had settled, walking into their accommodation, shouting "I'm home," and then tossing both River and Luke in turn in the air, humming the same funny sound.

Carmen turned around and ran toward River. Rosa walked out of the kitchen, grabbed her daughter by the waist, and murmured something in her ear while kissing her cheek. Carmen nodded and walked toward River, measuring every step. When she reached her, she put her arms gently around River's waist. River closed her arms around her and started rocking slowly.

Luke walked into the kitchen and put his arm around Rosa's waist. "Has everyone had a good day?"

Carmen turned around and said, "River has had a tumble."

Luke's eyebrows shot up. "With the bike? Are you okay?"

He let go of Rosa and got to his sister in two long steps.

"I'm fine," River said before she smiled. "I was the first person to notice that Old Bill's home had caught fire. I called the fire department and tried to help. Got a little more than I bargained for."

"I hope he wasn't in there," Luke said.

"I don't think so."

"I dressed River's arm when she arrived. It'll be fine tomorrow," Rosa said.

Luke looked reassured, and River was glad the conversation could move on.

"How about we order pizza?" River said. "I'm buying."

Carmen's head started to bob in agreement. Luke pulled a drawer open, took a menu out, and said, "Thanks, Sis. That's a great idea."

He laid the menu on the counter, and everybody gathered around it. Carmen was the first to make up her mind. "I know what I want without looking at it."

Luke followed. "Me, too."

River and Rosa read the entire menu and then nodded. "Decided," they said almost in unison.

Luke took his cell out of his pocket and dialed the pizza place. He gave the order—one pepperoni pizza, one cheese pizza with extra mushrooms, one vegetable and beef pizza, and one chicken pizza with double jalapeños. River gave Luke her credit card number, which she knew by heart. That drew a smile from Luke. River had always had a prodigious memory.

River and Carmen disappeared to set the table. Rosa and Luke prepared a salad, and when they were done, the doorbell rang, and Rosa went to open the door. The aroma of pizza wafted into the dining room. Rosa parked the pizza boxes at the end of the table. Luke brought in the salad. Carmen jumped on her seat, and Franklin jumped on the seat next to her. Rosa opened the boxes, and everyone helped themselves, including Carmen. It looked fun and easy, and River wondered whether she, too, could settle down one day with a partner and kids.

The image of her ex-fiancé, Jason Wayne, floated in front of her eyes. They two were sharing a pizza and a beer, having a fun and intimate moment. But then she'd decided to walk away. They'd spoken about marriage, and she thought she wanted to tie the knot until the moment came to make arrangements for the wedding. And then she'd fled to Alaska—to her friend Karen's small town and Inupiat way of life. River shook her head. Not the time to reminisce.

Luke must have sensed her shift in mood. He'd stopped eating and was looking at her with concern and something she hadn't seen much before—remorse. He averted his gaze as soon as she noticed, but River could see it in his face. Her presence was a constant reminder of what they had with their parents as kids, of his guilt about not visiting them one last time. Perhaps it was also a reminder of the worst regret of all—not telling River about the box in the attic.

She forced herself to eat more pizza and helped herself to some salad. But her mind returned to the attic. There was something important in that box. Something she needed to know about. The conversation shifted again to the planned barbecue. She joined in and tried to let go of her resentment. She'd keep Luke happy for the time being, then she'd find out what was in the box.

The evening dragged on a little. The lidocaine Rosa had given her made River a little drowsy. Fortunately, Carmen and her cat provided plenty of entertainment, and everyone laughed. At 8:00 p.m., Luke took Carmen and Franklin to bed.

Rosa started clearing the dishes and stopped River from helping. "How are you feeling?"

"I'll be fine," River reassured her.

Luke came down after reading Carmen a story, and they sat around the table; Luke with a cup of hot lemon water and Rosa and River with coffee. They talked a little more about the barbecue, and then Rosa yawned and said, "I'm tired. Time to go to bed."

She stood up and squeezed Luke's shoulder. River stood up, too, bade then good night, and retired to her bedroom. She had half an hour to spare before Miguel turned up. She sat down on the bed and fought the urge to lie down.

River pulled her cell phone from her back pocket and dialed Dale's number. The call went to voicemail. She waited a couple of minutes and then tried again with the same result. River tapped the phone a few times against her lips. Perhaps Dale was still at the cave. She'd try again when she returned from her reconnaissance with Miguel; by then Dale should be back.

Her duffel bag lay open after she'd taken out a few pieces of clothing she thought needed to be hung up—a simple light-blue dress and a white shirt with a fancy pattern on the front, perfect to dress up a pair of jeans. She got up and rummaged through the bag and found what she was looking for: a heavy dark-blue pullover. She put it on, carefully sliding her damaged arm into the sleeve, and then slowly pulling it over her head. She took a belt-bag out of the bag. She put her cell phone into it, an extra clip for her Glock, and the keys to the house. She slid the gun into the waistband of her pants and pulled the sweater over it. She was sure it wouldn't show if Luke or Rosa met her in the house, although she doubted Rosa would object.

River left her room and stood outside in the courtyard for a moment. The house was dark, and there wasn't any sound. She got to the kitchen door, entered, and stood still again. The household was asleep. She walked to the front door, opened it carefully, and closed it behind her without a sound. She found a spot by the garage wall where she could observe the street without being noticed and waited for Miguel.

The sound of a car attracted River's attention, but when it rounded the corner, she could see it wasn't Miguel's battered car but a black Jeep Grand Cherokee like the one she'd seen at the cave. River pushed herself against the wall and held her breath. The car slowed down but didn't stop. It carried on, and River let her breath go.

Another car rounded the corner, but this time River recognized Miguel's old Ford. She waited for him to stop, then got out of the shadows and jogged to the passenger side. She opened the door and slid in.

"Saw a Jeep Cherokee drive past," River said as Miguel took off.

"It's only 10:00 p.m.," Miguel said. "People are still driving home."

"I know—paranoia. But that's what kept me alive when I was deployed."

Miguel nodded slowly, thinking. "How would they know you live at your brother's?"

"Everyone knows I live at Luke's now that I'm back in town."

"You're saying that the cartel knows you're there?"

"We discussed this. It doesn't take a genius to put two and two together and actually make four."

"What do you want to do?"

River was torn. Should she leave Luke and his family on their own tonight? Yet they needed to find Dolores.

"We need to find out where the lab is. Then we can get rid of these guys for good," River said. "Let go to the Devils Playground."

Chapter 12

The sky was clear, and the temperature would be dropping a little more still. Alfonso zipped up his fleece and waited for Pablo to arrive. He sat on one of the flat rocks that surrounded the old ranch. The place had been a find, and the real estate agent who'd been asked to market the property was easy to persuade that he should forget it ever existed when he was offered money and shown a gun.

Alfonso took in the spectacle of the night. As a child he'd enjoyed stargazing and had gotten good at identifying the galaxies and prominent stars of the Milky Way. His mother had even bought him a book about astronomy. But his father hadn't approved, and the book one day disappeared. Alfonso took a deep breath—his mother, too, had disappeared one day and had never been heard from again.

The sound of someone approaching refocused him. He turned around to check who was getting close. Pablo lifted his hand in greeting and said, "Hola. Soy yo."

"Hola," Alfonso said. "What have you found?"

Pablo came to sit down next to Alfonso and sighed. "This isn't good."

Alfonso said nothing and just waited.

"There is another girl out there missing from the last consignment. I checked the number of girls who crossed the border using the tunnel and then with the guys in Vegas. Including the dead girl, there were three missing, not two. I'm certain."

"You have a name?" Alfonso asked as he clenched his fist.

"Cristina Velasquez. She was traveling with the other two."

Alfonso nodded. He could explode now and confront Luis, but Luis would find an excuse, knowing that Alfonso's father, the head of the Cruz Cartel, would back him up.

"What else?" Alfonso said, leaning forward, his forearms resting on his thighs.

"Luis got involved in a shoot-out at one of the ranches near Silver Rim. A man was badly wounded, and Luis's SUV was trashed."

"He was trying to get the girl back, I presume, and then he failed," Alfonso said.

"That's what it looks like. He won't talk about it, and even his men are silent about the whole story. I managed to get one of them to speak, but it wasn't easy."

Both men fell silent.

"We've known each other a long time," Pablo said.

Alfonso nodded. "If you want to tell me what's on your mind, go ahead."

"You need to get rid of Luis."

Alfonso straightened up. "I know that. And you know why it's difficult. Since the death of Javier, Father has not been the same, and Luis reminds him of my older brother."

"I'm not talking about removing him from the operation. I'm talking about getting rid of him . . . permanently."

Alfonso turned his head toward Pablo and scrutinized his friend's face. He'd known Pablo all his life—he was the son of one of his mother's maids. His father, to be fair, never objected to the friendship. But his father didn't understand that that friendship had morphed into something much stronger, something Alfonso could hardly admit to himself. He'd become something a Cruz Cartel man couldn't be.

"How could I explain to Father that I let Luis be hurt, let alone be killed?"

"You don't need to do it," Pablo said. He broke his eye contact with Alfonso. "I can do it."

Alfonso felt himself go cold. "I won't let you go on a suicide mission to get rid of this idiot. I need you with me."

He took a moment to calm down and added, "There must be another way . . . there must."

Pablo shook his head and said, "Perhaps—but know that the first one remains an option."

Alfonso waited again, his mind blank at the thought of losing Pablo. He stood up, walked a few steps, and said, "What about the identity of the woman who found the dead girl?"

"It was harder than I thought. For some reason, people were not willing to talk. But I've got a name: River Swift."

"Why the hesitation?" Alfonso asked.

"She's the sister of a popular doctor in Saint Ab, and she was in the military—a medic, too."

"Andersen's got to earn his money. We pay him enough, so he can damn well find out who stands in our way."

"Andersen delivered at the end. And he has a grudge against the woman, it seems. It might become helpful when the time comes."

"What sort of grudge?" Alfonso said.

"She challenged him at the police station. She wanted a proper inquiry into the girl's death."

"He thinks she's trouble," Alfonso said.

"He thinks she's going to try to find out what happened herself."

"It's not finding out what happened that's the problem," Alfonso said. "It's finding the evidence of what happened that ultimately matters."

He returned to the flat rock and sat down again. "The drugs' cooking is going well, and we'll be done with our next batch tonight. I'm very close to finding a way to create fentanyl precursors out of unlisted and unregulated chemicals."

Pablo seemed to be waiting for Alfonso to finish his train of thought.

"So I'm not ready to move the lab yet. I'm too close, and the next batch of girls is arriving the day after tomorrow. We also need the mine, at least for one more shipment."

Alfonso stood up again, restless, and nodded toward the dilapidated ranch that hid the lab and his team of chemists. "If you find more evidence she's getting close to our operation, we'll have to"—Alfonso hesitated but then concluded—"terminate her."

The terrain had gotten too hazardous for them to continue with the car. Miguel found a couple of boulders that provided cover and parked the old Ford behind it. They both stepped out of the vehicle.

"We don't want to alert anyone who might be at the Devils Playground ranch that we're coming," River said. "Our headlights will be obvious for miles. Stopping now is the right move, even if we have a long walk ahead."

Miguel nodded. "The old beater sounds as though it's on its last legs, and that's not very discreet, either."

River looked around to get her bearings. The night was clear, and the moon provided a good amount of visibility. Miguel slung a backpack over his shoulders and started walking toward the hills at the bottom of the gorge.

"What have you got in your pack?"

"A camera," Miguel said without turning around. "It's a Canon EOS 2000D. A good piece of equipment for night photography, and it's light. I also brought some binoculars."

"I didn't think about that," River said, falling in step with Miguel. "I was about to use my cell to take pictures."

"That's my job. I hope I can write a piece about this whole story with good photos to support it . . . in memory of Martha."

River let out a little sigh. She, too, understood the need to make sense of a senseless killing. She, too, was on a quest, although hers would have to wait a little longer to come to fruition.

They walked in silence for a while, hugging the side of the hills to avoid detection, and stopping from time to time to listen for sounds. River's arm had started to feel sensitive again, and she hoped the analgesic would last long enough to complete the mission. Miguel suddenly lifted his hand and stopped. He turned around and murmured, "We're almost there."

He took the binoculars out of his backpack, surveyed the landscape, and resumed the walk at a much slower pace. They rounded the corner of one of the hills and then stopped again. The ranch was now visible in the distance. River took in the terrain and found a deep crevasse slashed into the earth to the left. She softly pressed Miguel's shoulder and showed him the crack. They ran low toward it and slid into it. Miguel stretched on his belly, his arms resting over the rim of crevasse. He brought the binoculars to his eyes once more and scanned the ranch layout.

"We've hit the jackpot, I think."

"Can you see people?" River asked.

"I can make out two men . . . not sure whether they have guns," Miguel said. "Shit. Yes, they do."

"What did you expect?" River mumbled.

"I can see a little light coming out of one of the buildings," Miguel said. "Someone has gone in. The light has disappeared."

"Just as we thought. They've built a structure to house the lab inside the building and made sure it can't be seen from a distance or from above."

"They must be cooking the drug as we speak," Miguel said.

"How many buildings can you see?"

"Two that are very close to each other. There may be more, but if there are they must be on the other side of the hill."

"I guess they need a place to house the chemists they use to cook the fentanyl," River said. "Can you see anything in the other building?"

"Completely dark," Miguel said, adjusting the binoculars.

River slid alongside Miguel and presented her hand, wiggling her fingers. Miguel handed over the binoculars, and she started to scan the area, too.

"The men are concentrated on the side of the first building, where they're cooking the drug."

Miguel frowned. "What do you have in mind?"

"Dolores could be in the other building. The one that's under a lower level of surveillance."

"But at this stage we are only assuming the building that's better guarded is where the drug is."

River dropped the binoculars. "That's true."

She picked the binoculars up again and scoured the landscape. "Let's go to the building on the far left and see how close we can get."

She returned the binoculars to Miguel, who put them away, and they both slowly crouched. This time, it was River who got in front. They ran low from one boulder to the next, until none were left to hide their progress. They were now only a hundred yards or so away from the building they'd targeted.

"It's very exposed," River murmured as she sneaked a peek. "Too risky for the two of us."

"You're not going to get rid of me that easily," Miguel whispered a little too loudly.

One of the guards stopped. River and Miguel retreated swiftly behind the boulder and froze. They waited for a few very slow minutes, but then River chanced taking a look again. The guards had resumed their rounds. She counted the seconds that elapsed between their changes of position and slid back next to Miguel.

"The only way it's gonna work is if I crawl the next hundred yards," River whispered. "You take plenty of pictures of the place and the men we can see."

"How is that going to help?"

"We're gathering evidence to convince people like the feds, aren't we?"

Miguel nodded, but River could see he wasn't happy.

"Look, I know you want to do more, but it's not worth both of us being caught. And if I find Dolores, I'll need to extract her without anybody noticing. We're not having a shoot-out."

"Okay," Miguel grumbled.

River checked that her Glock was still secure in the waistband of her pants. She lay on her belly and waited for the man the closest to her position to move away. She had a couple of minutes before a guard reached the point around the building that was closest to her. She started her belly crawl, slow and hardly visible. River cursed inwardly as her arm started to complain. She gritted her teeth and moved steadily toward the second building.

She was halfway through when an athletic-looking man came to sit on one of the flat rocks that surrounded the building she was aiming for. She flattened completely against the ground and waited, not daring to make a move. Another man arrived. She could hear two voices. They started a conversation that was conducted in a low tone. River waited until she felt they were focused on their discussion and risked rising her head. She'd lost track of the guards' movements and had to wait to catch up with the count again.

As soon as she had reacquired the count, she crawled forward, hoping she could catch some of the men's conversation. She reached the first of series of flat stones that spread along the ground and led to the front of the building. She listened hard and managed to catch a few words.

Cristina Velasquez...
Identity of the woman...
And then... *River Swift.*

Her mind scrambled with the revelation. The Cruz Cartel knew her name. She strained to listen, but the men's voices had dropped again. Her heart started racing in her chest. If they knew who she was, she had to assume they knew where she lived. Now Luke and his family were in danger.

She hesitated. Should she stop and go back? No, her father had taught her this: In danger, the way forward is sometimes the only way.

It took a moment for her to realize that the two men had moved on. She didn't know where they'd gone, so she crawled slowly until she reached the largest of the flat rocks. River came to a crouch and scanned her surroundings. The guards were still doing their rounds, but they grew farther away as she'd gotten closer to the second, more distant building. She instinctively brought her hand to her wounded arm. It felt warm, tender, and wet to the touch. She must have re-opened her wound.

Shit. Have to get a grip.

She resumed her progress and got to the old building's dilapidated wall. She strained to hear a sound, but all was quiet. She cautiously walked beside the planks that had once been a wall and came to an opening. As predicted, a few tents had been erected in the center of the building, no doubt providing a makeshift dorm for the cartel's chemists. River followed the perimeter and came to a low structure that had been newly erected—she could tell by the smell of young wood and wood dust.

River hugged the wall of the new space and found a door. The place was silent, so she gave the door a try. It wasn't locked. She heard voices in the distance and retreated hastily behind the broken wall; her body flattened against it. Two men walked into the room speaking Spanish. She couldn't understand all they said, but one seemed to be complaining that he was tired. She heard them open the door, and their voices faded away until they reappeared. Then someone closed the door with a bang, and the voices receded in the distance.

One of the guards called after them in Spanish, and this time River understood that they were asked to hurry. They were cooking a fresh batch of fentanyl. River waited for the guard and the two men to move away. Then she made her way back to the door, which she hoped would still be unlocked. She pushed the handle, and the door opened without resistance.

The place was dark, and she hesitated. She could sense that the room was full—full of newly baked drugs, by the smell of it. She stretched out her arms forward and felt around with her right foot. She hit a large bundle and stopped. Her eyes got used to the darkness. She could make out bags of pills. She scanned the room and spotted a space at the far end where a mattress had been put on the ground. A form was lying on it—Dolores.

River held back. She wanted to get to the girl but couldn't take the risk of startling her in case she cried out. River moved slowly toward her, hoping she'd be able to place her hand on the teenager's mouth before she woke up.

River was only a yard or so away when she stopped. Something didn't feel right. She fought the desire to accelerate the pace. She resumed her progress, and when she reached the bed, she understood. It was empty. The blankets had been dumped in a hurry, and from a distance, they resembled a human shape.

Now, River didn't know whether Dolores had somehow managed to escape, or whether she'd already been taken away and driven by the cartel men to the mine in Silver Rim canyon.

River bit her lip. Whatever the reason, she was too late. She backtracked and went out of the room, closed the door, and slid along the walls of the old building. She considered finding a way to destroy the fentanyl pills but thought better of it. It would achieve nothing but a short-lived revenge.

River used all her military training to patiently wend her way back to the spot where she'd left Miguel. She just wanted to be out of the place because she felt doubly cheated—unable to torch it and unable to rescue Dolores. Her arm was starting to throb, and every move on the ground sent searing pain into it.

When she finally reached the boulder where Miguel was hiding, she curled against it and rested her head against her knees. She slid her hand underneath her wounded arm and took a moment to recover from the pain. She looked around as the soreness subsided. Miguel was nowhere to be seen. She let her head fall against the rock. He couldn't have been caught; surely she would have heard the commotion. She softly called his name—nothing.

And then she heard shuffling to her right, and Miguel appeared. His face dropped when he saw she was alone.

"She's gone," River murmured. "I don't know whether she's escaped or whether they've taken her to the mine already."

Miguel dropped to the ground next to River, his camera loose in his hands. "You don't think they . . ." he whispered.

The word Miguel wanted to utter seemed too hard.

"I don't know, but I think she's still alive. She's valuable to them. She didn't see the cartel men, only the coyote."

Miguel shook his head. "What do we think we're doing? We must be mad."

River stopped him by squeezing his arm. They needed to get back.

Miguel nodded, and they got up and retraced their steps. They remained silent until they reached the car.

"What do we think we're doing?" Miguel repeated. "Just the two of us against the Cruz Cartel and half the Saint Ab Police."

River opened the car door, got in, and said as Miguel was starting the engine, "I say we're doing fine. In two days, we've discovered the cartel's lab and the transit point for the girls."

Miguel drove slowly toward one of the better-used trails. "But who are we going to contact? We can't just call the feds out of the blue. The cartel has got people working for them everywhere. I thought Dale was on our side, but you've not mentioned him once. I assume he's not returned your calls, so perhaps he, too, has decided it's too dangerous to fight the cartel."

River didn't know how to reply to that. She had tried Dale a couple of times and had assumed that Old Bill was keeping him busy at the cave, but she had to admit the prolonged silence was starting to make her uncomfortable.

And now that the cartel knew who she was, she was even more in doubt. Her name could have come from several people, but the fact that she was a cause for concern could only have come from a couple of them. Miguel cast an eye toward her, waiting for a response.

"I'll try Dale again tomorrow morning," she said, no longer certain that she'd been right to trust him in the first place.

"I say we pay him a visit now," Miguel said, hands clenched on the wheel.

River thought for a moment and then nodded. "You're right. There's not much point in delaying. Let's find out why he hasn't replied. Where does he live?"

"He's got a place in Saint Ab Middleton, not very far from the police station."

"Something else on your mind?" River asked.

"He knows where Jen, Cristina, and Old Bill are," Miguel said. "I might be unfair to Dale, but I'd rather be sure."

"You're right. Let's go," River said.

Miguel picked up speed. The moonlight was still good, and he kept his headlights off. Both fell silent, Miguel concentrating on the road and River on what she'd learned at the lab. One thing had become painfully obvious. They were just too thin on the ground, given that the cartel men and their contacts were everywhere.

River touched her arm gingerly. It was hot, and the pain had become constant, a regular stabbing feeling she knew would only intensify with the passing of time. River checked her watch—11:46 p.m. She hoped Dale would be home and that she then could get back to Luke's place to tend to her wound. Her night wasn't over yet. She still needed to pay a visit to Luke and Harry's practice to glean whatever information she could find and return Luke's office keys before 8:00 a.m.

Chapter 13

Miguel parked the old Ford at the entrance to the cul-de-sac on which Dale lived. He and River agreed to walk the rest of the way, checking for vehicles that looked out of place in this quiet neighborhood. River had a fleeting sense of paranoia, but having her name mentioned by one of the cartel's men justified it, she thought. They got out of the car, and River scanned the area. She touched her back, checking that the Glock was still in place.

"Nothing suspicious," River said in a low voice. "Let's go and find Dale."

They entered the long lane that led to the cul-de-sac itself and walked toward Dale's house, but halfway there they froze. Instead of Dale's red pickup, a black SUV was parked next to the sidewalk. The vehicle sat low on its chassis, indicating that the frame had been reinforced. River slid her arm through Miguel's and pushed him along.

"Let's play happy couple and walk past them," she said.

She and Miguel started to chat nonsense about food and drinks. They both staggered, feigning drunkenness. River threw her head back in laughter and cast an eye toward the SUV. The windows were tinted, but she could have sworn she saw movement inside.

"What do we do now?" Miguel murmured as they reached the center of the cul-de-sac.

"Let go to the house next to Dale's and look as though we've forgotten our keys."

They turned right and walked up to the house. Miguel started searching his pockets, and River stood next to him, swaying to keep the drunken pretense up. There was no light in Dale's house. The place didn't have a garage, so the pickup would have been parked outside his door.

Miguel stopped his search for the nonexistent keys and murmured, "Let's have an argument about the keys and go back to the car."

River gave a slight nod and shouted, slurring her words, "It's always the same shit with you. You never know where the fucking keys are."

"You could have taken a set, too," Miguel shouted back. "Why is it always my fault?"

River shrugged and started walking back to Miguel's car, shouting, "Bet you they're in the car."

Miguel staggered after her, and they traded insults until they were back to Miguel's old Ford. They got in, then Miguel started the engine and took off as fast as he could. River glanced in the rearview mirror to see that a man had gotten out of the waiting SUV and was standing in the road, watching as they left.

River puffed out a breath and said, "Man. That was close."

"What about Dale?" Miguel said, glancing in the rearview mirror as well. He took a few turns to get out of Middleton. River shifted her attention to the side-view mirror.

"Shit. They're trying to find us," she said.

"Are you sure?"

"I saw a set of lights across the top of the street we just turned off of. If we hadn't, they would be on top of us by now."

"You're probably right," Miguel replied. "What's the chance of having a car on the same road as us at this time of the morning in Saint Ab?"

"None," River said. "A good call to have kept the headlights off, too."

"I've done a lot of waiting, watching, and following for my

journalistic investigations. I sorta know how to stay discreet," Miguel said with a final check in his rearview mirror.

River took her phone out of her jacket pocket. "I've got to try Dale again. He needs to know these guys are outside his house."

Miguel put a hand out and stopped her. "Hang on. Sorry to be harsh, but we don't know why they were waiting for him."

"You mean he could be in on it, and they wanted a word?" River said. "Why not give him a call?"

"Maybe he hasn't delivered what they expected, and they need to rough him up a bit."

River thought about it.

What was it he might be asked to deliver?

She snapped her fingers, realizing Dale was on the up and up. "You're right. He hasn't delivered."

She picked up her phone again and dialed Dale's number. Miguel frowned, but he must have sensed she was on to something because he didn't interrupt her. Dale's phone rang a few times and went to voicemail. River killed the call and tried again with the same result. This time she left a message.

"Call me back as soon as you get this message. But whatever you do, don't go back to your place."

Miguel shook his head. "Why did you call him?"

"I don't know for sure whether Dale is on it or not. But I think the cartel's men are making the rounds of all the police officers they think they can shake. Plus, Dale has been seen helping me out. They're going to ask him questions and find out whether they can get answers out of him."

Miguel turned toward River. "Jen, Cristina, and Old Bill may no longer be safe, then."

"We don't know that yet," River said, although she understood Miguel's anxiety. His sister was dead and his wife in hiding.

"I've got to call Jen," Miguel said.

He slowed the car to a crawl and took his cell phone out of his pants pocket. It was River's turn to stop him.

"Are you confident your phone hasn't been compromised?"

Miguel looked at his phone with a mix of anger and fear.

"I'll use the burner phone we both use. She won't recognize the number, but she might still pick up, and if not, I'll leave a message for her to call back."

River nodded, and Miguel replaced his phone in his pants pocket and took the burner out of another pocket. He dialed Jen's number and waited. She didn't pick up, and he left a message.

"It's Miguel. Call me back at this number as soon as you get this."

Miguel accelerated and resumed the drive to Luke's house. They arrived ten minutes later, and Miguel stopped a street away.

"I'll call you if I hear from Dale, and please call me as soon as you hear from Jen."

Miguel frowned. "What's next?"

"We need to assume we're no longer safe," River said. "The cartel knows who I am. I heard one of the men say my name at the Devils Playground."

Miguel slammed the wheel with his fist and said, "If I don't hear from Jen in the next fifteen minutes, I'm going to Old Bill's cave. I still have the coordinates."

"What if you're followed?"

"The roads are empty at this time of the morning. I'll know whether someone is on my tail."

River ran a hand over her face and said, "Okay. But let me know what you decide. And if you decide to go to Old Bill's cave, we'll need to agree on regular updates to make sure that security for you and the others isn't compromised."

"Fine," Miguel said.

"One more thing," River added after opening the car door. "We need a place to hole up, too. Somewhere conspicuous where we can just blend in."

"You mean instead of going back home?" Miguel asked.

"That's right. We need to disappear before they decide to do to us what they're supposed to do to Dale."

"I know a place," Miguel said.

River closed the door of the old Ford softly and walked the rest of the way to Luke's home. She cracked open the front door and listened, but the house was dead silent. She stepped in and tiptoed to the kitchen and then to the guest bedroom. She went in without turning the lights on and stood in the middle of the room for a moment.

Her arm was now throbbing with pain, and she felt a little lightheaded. Removing the Glock from behind her back and laying it on the bedside table, she walked to the bathroom. River picked up the tumbler she used when brushing her teeth, filled it with water from the tap, and drank it in a few long pulls. The medicine cabinet, which hung over the sink, had been restocked, and she silently thanked Rosa. She'd loaded it with medical supplies and a couple of shots of lidocaine.

River touched her arm gingerly and sighed. Her T-shirt was wet underneath the thick pullover she'd put on earlier. She cautiously peeled the sweater off. A deep red patch had started to spread on the sleeve of her shirt. She removed it carefully—the sleeve of the good arm first and then the sleeve of the wounded arm. Blood had seeped through the bandage before staining the T-shirt, but on further examination, it wasn't as bad as it looked.

She chose supplies from the cabinet, laid them next to the sink, and started to remove the dirty bandage. She bit her lip when it came to exposing the wound and dabbing disinfectant on it. She was right. The deeper part of the gash had reopened a little, but the rest looked as though it was already healing. She bandaged her arm again, doing a good enough job one-handed. River then injected herself with a dose of lidocaine close to the injury.

River threw the mess into the small bathroom trash can, making a mental note to get rid of it in the morning. She returned to the bedroom, chose another T-shirt, and slowly put it on. She set the alarm on her phone, giving herself a three-hour rest. Then she'd leave the house and visit Luke and Harry's medical practice.

The alarm woke River up with a jolt. She struggled with the heaviness of sleep. The lidocaine didn't help on that score. Turning on the side of her good arm, she felt slumber rolling over her like a wave. She forced herself to sit up, grabbed the bottle of water sitting on the bedside table, and took a few sips. She picked up the Glock, checked the weapon, and then slid it in the waistband of her pants, against her back. She opened the bedside-table drawer, took Luke's keys out, and stuffed them in her pants pocket.

She picked up her cell phone and then froze. Miguel hadn't called. She checked her text messages and breathed a sigh of relief.

Jen, Cristina, and Old Bill fine.

River stood up, chose a thick hoodie from inside her duffel bag, and made her way again to the kitchen. It was still pitch-dark, and a few clouds had gathered in the sky, obscuring the waning moon. She opened the door quietly and listened. The family was still asleep. She made her way to the front door, stopping a few times as the old house creaked and ticked.

She stepped out, closed the door softly behind her, and walked to Luke's practice. The roads were deserted apart from the odd cat who scuttled away as she walked past. She kept going for around ten minutes and then stopped in the shadow of a pine tree as she came to the intersection where the building she was looking for stood. She stayed hidden for a few minutes, observing the place. It was silent and quiet. River crossed the street and walked to the side of the practice, where she found the staff entrance. She used her brother's keys to get in. The screeching of an alarm filled the place with a deafening sound. She reached the panel in a couple of strides and entered her mother's birthday on the keypad, hoping Rosa was right. The alarm stopped, and River returned to the door to secure it shut.

Her brother's practice was exactly as she'd imagined it would be—neat, welcoming, and spacious. She used the flashlight on her her cell phone to guide her past the reception area toward the individual examining rooms. Harry's name was the first one she came across—Dr. H. Wilson. River stopped in front of the door and checked her watch: 5:12 a.m. The practice opened at 8:00 a.m. She had time to go through his office in search of information. She pressed the door handle down and pushed, but the door resisted—locked.

Shit. Should have thought of that.

She stayed in front of it for a few seconds and then went to the next examination room—Luke's room. She pushed the handle and tried to get in, but it, too, was locked. She frowned and then took Luke's key ring out of her pocket. She'd noticed it was holding more than the two keys needed to open the staff entrance door. She tried one. It didn't work, and neither did the second, but the third key opened Luke's office. She locked the door and went to Harry's office. She used the last key, and the door opened.

She couldn't help but smile. Her brother had always been obsessed with making sure he could enter any room of the house when they were children and adolescents. He couldn't bear the thought of being locked out. She remembered arguing with Luke about it during their teens. Her bedroom was a sanctuary, and no one was allowed in—especially her overly serious brother.

River entered Harry's office and ran the beam of the flashlight across the place. The desk stood in one corner of the room with a couple of chairs positioned in front of it. Filing cabinets ran across one of the office walls, and a curtain ran across the other wall, no doubt hiding an examination table.

She approached the cabinets and tried one at random. It was locked. She thought about it for a moment and shrugged. If these were patients' files, then Harry's assistant—or Luke, in an emergency—would have access to them. It was unlikely that Harry would file any compromising information in them.

Harry's desk looked a little more promising. She walked to it and sat in his chair. A large frame holding an assortment of photos stood prominently next to Harry's computer—kids growing up and enjoying themselves on vacation. River resisted the desire to look at them more closely and returned to her quest. The drawers were unlocked apart from the one at the bottom. She opened the others, looking for something she could use to force the bottom drawer open. There was nothing that seemed helpful. She tapped her fingers a few times on the arm of the chair and then stood up.

She stepped out of Harry's office and walked farther along the corridor and found what she was looking for—the kitchen. She discovered a drawer containing kitchen knives and selected a small sturdy blade. She went back to Harry's office, closed the door, and sat again in his chair. She then pushed the knife into the small gap between the top of the drawer and the desk itself. She pressed hard, but it didn't budge. She tried again, and this time she felt a slight shift. She'd found the weakness in the lock. She kept pushing and shoving until she heard a loud crack. The lock toppled inside the drawer, and she yanked the drawer open.

It contained only a few items . . . including a fat roll of $20 bills. River estimated it must total more than $1,000. She found a small book that looked like the type of notebook in which her mother used to write patients' notes on the go. But when River opened it, it didn't contain written notes but columns of names and numbers, together with dates.

River took her phone out and started to take pictures, beginning at the end of the book. She stopped halfway through, replaced the notebook in the drawer, and ran her fingers deep inside it. She felt a small metal box and pulled it out. It rattled as she opened it, and she found three USB flash drives inside. She put two of them in her pocket and stuck the last one inside Harry's computer port.

The screen woke up, and a picture of Harry and his two sons popped up on the screen. The three of them looked happy, and the man who smiled in the picture seemed so very different from the man who'd invited himself for breakfast yesterday. She looked around for a place where Harry might have left his password. She lifted his BEST DAD mug, opened the drawers that had been left unlocked, and finally lifted the keyboard—nothing.

She thought for a moment and then picked up the picture frame. She turned it around, flipped the two holding pins, and removed the back—and there it was. Harry's password: drugD . . . D44. River frowned, and then she understood. As an additional precaution, Harry had only written part of the password. River memorized it and reassembled the frame. She was about to reactivate the screen to test the password when a sound stopped her in her tracks. The alarm of the staff entrance had been activated. Someone was coming in.

She moved away from Harry's desk, looking around for a place to hide. She pulled aside the curtain that hid the examination table, closed it again and crouched next to a tall cabinet that held medical supplies.

River's heart was beating hard in her chest, and she held her breath for a short moment. She checked her watch—6:34 a.m.—and wondered who was coming in so early to the office. The alarm had stopped, and then she heard nothing. She waited, stood up, ready to dive down again if Harry entered his office, but nothing happened. She walked quietly to the door and cracked it open. Someone was preparing coffee by the smell of it, and that someone was humming a song. It was a female voice singing a country song River didn't recognize.

The song grew louder. River closed the door and retreated behind the curtain again. Then the door of Harry's office opened, and light flooded the room. River dove behind the examination table, making herself as small as she could. The woman was still humming her song, unlocking one cabinet and then another, perhaps looking for files. She moved to the far end of Harry's office, probably his desk. River cursed silently. She'd left the USB drive in the computer port and the knife on the desk.

The singing stopped abruptly, and River shrank even further. She imagined the woman looking at the knife and the desk drawer . . . and then at the USB drive, realizing Harry's desk had been broken into. Could she escape without being seen? She slid the hood of her sweater over her face and braced herself.

But then the singing resumed. The woman went to the door. Switched off the lights and walked out. River slumped against the wall for a moment. She stood up again, slowly, and dashed to Harry's desk. The woman had simply taken the knife away but left the USB drive where it was. River grabbed it, pocketed it, and moved swiftly to the door.

She opened it a crack and listened. The woman had gone into the reception area. River checked her watch again—6:52 a.m. She checked the rest of the corridor and spotted the ladies' room. Perhaps she could find a way out from there. She dashed out of Harry's office and reached the bathroom. The place was small, with only two stalls and an equally small window that led to the outside. River walked to it and tried to open it. It slid open only halfway. She tried to push it open more, but it felt jammed.

River gave it another shove, and it budged a little. She kept working on it with small pushes, trying to be as quiet as possible, and it finally opened fully. River heaved herself through it. Pain shot through her arm, and she muffled a cry. She finally rolled outside, landing feet first, and stayed low for a moment. She gingerly touched her arm, but the pain had subsided, and she hoped the wound hadn't opened yet again. She stood up and, unnoticed, started to walk back to Luke's home.

When she turned the corner of Luke's street, the lights were on in the house. River checked again that the wound hadn't seeped blood onto her hoodie. When she opened the door, she found Luke awake and talking to Rosa. He half turned when River arrived in the kitchen, an anxious look on his face.

"Impossible. I had them in my pocket in my good jacket, and I didn't take that jacket to the migrant clinic yesterday," Luke said, hands in his pockets as though looking for something.

Rosa cast an eye toward River, worried.

River understood. "What happened? You lost something?"

"The keys to the practice," Luke said, his voice trembling, upset. "I *never* lose anything."

River looked suitably amazed and then said, "I found these in the small flower bed next to the garage. Are they what you're looking for?"

She dangled Luke's keys in front of him and smiled. He jumped forward, snatched the keys from her, and gave her a relieved smile.

He grabbed her in his arms and squeezed. River's jaw clenched, and she closed her eyes, the pain soaring through her body. She worried, too, that he might find the Glock nestled against her back. She tried to return the hug in a way that felt natural but couldn't quite manage it. Luke pulled back, looking a little embarrassed. They hadn't embraced each other since she'd arrived.

"Thank you," he said. "I can't believe I didn't notice I dropped them."

Rosa walked to Luke and put a hand on his cheek. "As you say, you never lose anything, so why would you check?"

Carmen then called from the second floor, and Luke dashed upstairs to lend her a hand.

River slumped on one of the stools at the kitchen counter and whispered, "That was close."

Rosa shook her head and poured a glass of water that she handed to River. "You can say that again. And I'm sorry about your arm. I can't believe you didn't scream your lungs out."

River simply nodded, took the glass, and sipped some of the water. They heard a storm of footsteps coming down the stairs. Carmen appeared with Franklin in tow a few seconds later. She squealed when she saw River and came to ask for a hug with her arms outstretched. River smiled at her niece and wrapped her good arm around Carmen's small frame, cuddling her.

Luke appeared in the door frame, his coat on, ready to go. Carmen let go of River and knelt to give her cat a final hug and instructions: "You be a good boy today, and I'll be back real soon."

She gave her mother a cuddle, too, and skipped to the door. Luke kissed his wife goodbye, gave River a smile, and disappeared down the hallway. Both women waited for a moment before they spoke. Then Rosa asked, "What happened?"

River gave her a quick summary of her visit to the clinic. Rosa listened to River, focused.

"Do you think Harry will notice the drawer has been broken into?"

"He will," River said, "but he won't call the police. Well, at least officially, if what's on these USB drives is evidence of drug dealing."

"But he'll call his pal Sheriff Andersen," Rosa said.

River took a couple of sips of water, thinking. "I don't know if he will. It depends whether he trusts Andersen. Would you tell this guy you've lost some vital information? I wouldn't, because I wouldn't want the cartel's bosses to be made aware."

Rosa puckered her lips. "That's a valid point—but Harry will want to get that information back."

"That's true," River said. "And I hope Luke won't talk about losing his keys and my finding them. Otherwise, he might suspect."

Rosa smiled. "Luke will never admit losing his keys—ever."

"That gives me more time to decide what's my next move will be, which might well be to relocate myself out of this house," River said.

Rosa raised an eyebrow, and River laid a hand over Rosa's arm. "It's getting too dangerous for me to stay here. I'll find an excuse, like spending a couple of days in the mountains. Luke and I used to do that a lot with our parents."

"We'll miss you," Rosa said with genuine kindness. "But more important, you must be careful."

River looked around the kitchen. "When I first spoke to Luke, I wasn't sure what it would feel like coming back, but it's been lovely. You made it easy for me, so thank you."

Rosa nodded. "And thank you for helping us with the cartel."

"I haven't achieved anything yet."

"But you're working on it, and that's more than a lot of people are doing in this town."

River's cell buzzed in her pocket, interrupting the conversation. She took it out and checked the caller—Dale, at last.

River mouthed *Sorry* to Rosa and went into the backyard.

"Where have you been?"

"And very nice to hear from you, too," he said stiffly.

"Sorry . . . Good morning. You got my message, I guess," River said.

"Yes," Dale replied, sounding happier. "Thanks for letting me know about the *sicarios*. I heard that they've visited some of the officers of the Saint Ab Police Station. They don't even seem to care whether they're seen or not."

"Where were you when you heard?"

"I spent yesterday making sure Old Bill and the two ladies who arrived later were comfortable," Dale said with enthusiasm. "It's one thing to help Old Bill, but with Jen and Cristina around, I had to make sure everything was perfect."

River smiled—*friendly Jen and fiery Cristina*.

"Did you spend the night there?"

"No," Dale said a little on the defensive. "I drove to Salt Lake City."

"And?" River tried to be patient.

"I told you. Old Bill used to be a copper, and he's kept in touch with old pals—feds."

"Retired?"

"Yeah, but still well connected."

"Names?" River asked.

"Not on the phone," Dale said, sounding strained.

"We need to meet. Where are you now?"

"I stopped in a motel outside Saint Ab and crashed for a few hours," Dale said. "We could meet at the Red Benn Diner."

"Not a good idea. Too predictable," River replied, thinking. "Do you know the Moon Room restaurant?"

Dale hesitated and then said, "Downtown. I know the one."

"Meet you there in an hour's time."

River killed the call and walked back into the kitchen.

Time to ask Rosa to make sure Luke buys my mountain-hike story. I'm moving out today.

Chapter 14

River and Rosa spoke again about River's need to move out for a few days. Rosa agreed to break the news to Luke before River reappeared at lunchtime. River then retreated to the guest room, took a quick shower, and selected fresh clothes—cargo pants and a long-sleeved black T-shirt. She was glad to see that her bandage was clean, so no need to change it yet.

Rosa had very kindly cleaned her leather jacket, and River was glad to be wearing it again. The dent the rock splinter had made seemed to give it extra credibility as a tough biker's garment, and this made River smile.

She took her laptop, which she hadn't used yet, out of her duffel bag and slid it into her backpack. She fished the USB drives out of her dirty pants and stuffed them in with the laptop. She walked out of her bedroom and to the kitchen. Rosa was there, waiting for her.

"Thanks for everything," River said.

Rosa pushed a small parcel toward River. "Just in case."

River didn't need to open it to know that it was lidocaine and other medical supplies. "I won't use it unless I must. I'm riding the bike again."

Rosa nodded. "I'm on my day off. You need anything, you call me."

"I will," River said as she put the small packet into her backpack.

She walked out of the house and into the garage. She pushed the door open, stowed the backpack in the back of the bike, straddled the seat, and started the engine. She rode out just as Rosa appeared at the front door. She waved River away, indicating that she would take care of the garage door. River waved back, and she made her way to the Moon Room restaurant.

The roads were getting busy, so River slowed down; she didn't want to make herself noticeable and get stopped by a police officer. Moon Room was starting to empty when she arrived. She parked the bike as close as she could to the main entrance, took her backpack out of the storage compartment, and entered the restaurant. There was a table at the far end of a long window where she settled and waited for one of the waitresses to take her order.

In the meantime, she slipped her laptop out of her pack and booted it up. She found the first USB drive and inserted it inside the laptop's port. A folder with several files materialized on the screen. When she chose one at random tried to open it, access was denied. She needed a password.

River remembered the partial password she'd spotted on the back of the frame on Harry's desk. Then she recalled a trick her dad had taught her when she needed to memorize a password: Choose a keyword and construct a password around it.

It looked to her as though the first and last letters of that center keyword were *D* and *D*. It was a start, but she didn't have the rest of the word. She sagged back in her chair. A pretty waitress turned up, cheerful, and seemed to pick up on River's mood.

"What can I get you that's gonna lift your spirits, miss?"

River attempted a smile and said, "Coffee—black—and a piece of apple pie, please."

She hadn't had time for breakfast at Luke's, so she might as well indulge in a dessert that reminded her of home. River arrived three days ago, and she wouldn't have felt at home in her grandparents' house had it not been for Rosa. The decor had changed completely after she and Luke had made it their own. And River had hardly ventured upstairs, where her and Luke's bedrooms used to be.

Staying in the guest room had made it feel like a visit to any other place, or perhaps she hadn't wanted to remember the happy days with the family all gathered together, having a good time.

Her cell phone chimed.

On my way, stopped to buy supplies.

She wondered what that meant. Doubt lingered for a moment, but she pushed it away. She had to go with her instincts, and her gut told her she could trust Dale.

The pie and coffee arrived.

"Anything else?" the waitress asked.

River shook her head and smiled back. She wolfed down half her pie and grunted. She hadn't realized how hungry she was. She took a couple of sips of coffee and returned to her conundrum—Harry's password.

River opened a blank page in Word and typed the partial password: drugD . . . D44. She liked a riddle, but she didn't have much time to solve this one. She thought about the context. Perhaps this was an association of ideas. What did Harry associate with drugs? River sipped more of her coffee and came up with a couple of words: *dread, dependency, damaged*. She called the folder up onscreen again and tried the three words. They all returned "incorrect password."

She finished her piece of pie, still trying to find an angle that would help her figure out the password. She heard the buzz of a phone, turned her cell phone over, and realized it was her burner phone. She scrambled to get to her backpack in time and just caught Miguel's call before it went to voicemail.

"I found a place," he said. "It's in North Saint Ab. That's where the community center for homeless people is, and there are some cheap mobile homes for rent in the area. You can rent by the week, so I paid for a week in cash."

"Did you use your debit card to get the cash?" River asked, worried about leaving a trail.

"No. I got some cash out yesterday, enough to last us awhile."

"I'm at the Moon Room," River said, "waiting for Dale."

Miguel remained silent, and River could sense the concern. "I know what you think, but he has a good excuse for his absence."

"He left Old Bill's place early in the evening," Miguel said, doubtful.

"And drove to Salt Lake City to speak to some former colleagues of Old Bill. Feds—retired agents."

"Did you get their names?"

"Dale thought it'd be better not to speak on the phone."

Another long silence from Miguel made her feel a little foolish.

"I know, but on the other hand you and I have agreed to use burners for that reason. Not to speak about sensitive information on our cells," she said.

"Do you want me around?" Miguel asked.

"No." River shook her head as though he could see her. "If I've made a mistake, I'd rather be the only one to pay for it."

"Are you sure?"

"Absolutely," River said. "If you haven't heard from me in a couple of hours, then you need to get to Old Bill's cave and move everyone out."

"I still think I should come your way," Miguel grunted.

"You've got better things to do—like going through the pictures you took of the lab and its surroundings last night," River said.

"I've already started, and I've got some pretty good ones of the Devils Playground in the background. No one will be able to deny that this is where the lab is—or even was, if the cartel decides to burn the place to the ground."

River snapped her fingers. "You genius," she said. "That's exactly what I was looking for."

"Not sure I get it," Miguel said slowly.

"Never mind. I'll explain when we next meet."

River hung up, woke up the screen of her computer, and entered the password: drugDevilsplaygrounD44. She hit the Return key, and as if by magic, she was in.

The files were organized in alphabetical order, and Sheriff

Andersen's name was right at the top of the list. River opened the file and started reading. Andersen's life had been captured in great detail, from his two failed marriages and his problems with his kids to his recreational use of cocaine. Then there was information about his financial situation—the money he owed to various people, including the cartel, as well as some old gambling debts. Although River disliked Andersen, having the man's life torn open in front of her with so little left hidden made her uncomfortable. Then she noticed a word right at the bottom of the file: *in*. She thought about it for a moment and decided it meant that Andersen had been recruited successfully by the cartel.

She checked her watch. She still had a few minutes to go down the list and check for names she might recognize before Dale arrived. The name Officer Phil Bright rang a bell. She opened that file, and again the life was revealed in full, from Officer Bright's many arrests for grievous bodily harm to his wife's affairs with other men—many of them. Officer Bright was partial to a little white powder, too. River checked the letters at the bottom of the file: *in*.

River closed Bright's file and scrolled further down the list until she came to a name that made her heart stop—Officer Dale Jackson. She opened the file with a trembling finger, wondering whether she should call Miguel and ask for backup. But to her great relief, Dale's file was slim. It contained little, by way of evidence, that Dale was a corrupt or even a corruptible cop. It was derogatory about his intellectual capabilities, though, and this annoyed River. Dale wasn't a brash "dude," and that was all. She checked the bottom of the file: *testing*.

River took a sip of coffee. She would have liked the file to say *no* or *n/a*. *Testing* wasn't as conclusive as she wanted it to be. She closed Dale's file and carried on scrolling down the list of names, most of which she didn't recognize. There were two judges, a few more doctors and nurses. River cast an eye over the entire list. Just as she was about to close the session, she stopped abruptly. The name Dr. Luke Swift was on the list. She was about to open the file when a shadow fell over her laptop.

"I'm sorry it's taken a little longer than I expected," Dale said, standing on the other side of the table.

River took a few seconds but then lifted her head and said, "That's fine."

Dale's face fell, and she realized she'd sounded more dismissive than welcoming. "I'm sorry, Dale. I've had a bit of a shock. I'll tell you more about it, but why don't you get breakfast first?"

Dale nodded and waved at the waitress. The same friendly woman who'd served River came to take his order—bacon, two eggs sunny side up, hash browns, and waffles with syrup.

River watched him as he was ordering his food. A nice young man, polite and friendly, perhaps a little shy with pretty girls, but again, her gut told her Dale was one of the good guys. She went back to her laptop, opened one of the files, and turned the device so that Dale could see the screen when he sat down. Dale's eyes lingered a little too long on the waitress as she went back to place his order, and River thought she detected an almost imperceptible sigh as he sat in front of River and the screen.

"Read this," she said to him, pointing to the screen, "and let me know what you think."

Dale smiled at River and leaned forward to read what she asked him to. His eyes widened, and then he looked at River, a rush of pink rising to his cheeks. He opened his mouth, but nothing came out. Then he coughed and managed, "I never. I mean . . . I didn't know they were after me."

River crossed her arms over her chest. "But you see my dilemma, right?" She didn't want to give in so easily, even though Dale now looked miserable and upset.

Dale's food arrived. He nodded absent-mindedly to the waitress and ignored his plate, mug, and the pot of coffee left on the side.

"I don't know how I can convince you," Dale said, running a hand through his hair.

"You need to convince Miguel, too."

Dale nodded. "With Jen and Cristina involved, he needs to be real careful. I get it."

"Perhaps you can start by telling me about your trip to Salt Lake City."

"Okay," Dale said, eager to share his findings. "I met one of Old Bill's buddies from when he was still on the force here in Saint Ab. The guy's called John Lewis. I met him just outside Salt Lake at his home, because by the time I arrived it was late, almost midnight. I'd called him as I left, around 7:00 p.m., to tell him I was on my way. He didn't seem to mind."

River poured herself more coffee and said, "So this guy John seems to believe there is a case to be made if he agreed to see you."

"I think that's true, although . . ." Dale hesitated and then added in a low voice, "He did say he was getting bored with retirement and needed something he could sink his teeth into."

"That's not so encouraging," River mumbled.

"But then he agreed to call someone else. Someone who's still in the game, a guy called Loren Askew."

"Did he?"

Dale nodded. "He did, and that's when things got more interesting. I got the feeling that Askew knows about Sheriff Andersen and that they've been trying to nail him for a while."

"Why do you say that?"

Dale shrugged. "Lewis and I had a call with him even though it was past midnight by then. The way Askew asked real sharp questions about the sheriff—who he was hanging around with, his lifestyle, who he didn't investigate—made me think he knew a lot about him."

"That's more like it. But I don't see why they can't get someone on the case if they're already suspicious," River said.

"At the end, when I told them all I knew, they said I should keep it to myself and that they would be in touch," Dale said. "So I gathered that they're concerned about this leaking back to Andersen."

"Or they're trying to make sure Andersen's ass is covered, and this is why you had company last night at your home."

Dale's face colored again. He hadn't thought about that, it seemed. River pushed the plate of food Dale ordered in front of him and said,

"It's gonna get cold. You need to have something before we go to our next meeting."

Dale took a sip of coffee and started on his breakfast, but River could tell his heart wasn't in it. His short hair still looked a little ruffled, and his soft brown eyes drooped a little, giving his face a dreamy look. She couldn't believe that Dale would betray anyone.

Then her stomach jolted at the thought that Luke's name was also on the list.

River pulled the laptop back and scrolled down the list again. She found Luke's name and hesitated. Dale picked up on this and asked, "More things about me? I swear I didn't know—"

River shook her head. "Nothing to do with you, Dale. I, for one, believe you."

Dale's face broke into a smile. "You've made my day."

River clicked on Luke's name and started reading. First, the file listed Luke's qualifications. It looked as though he'd specialized in addiction. Then a story reporting his use of cannabis at college made River smile. It wasn't like him, but perhaps he'd tested boundaries. The part that surprised River the most was the extensive report concerning her parents' death. It didn't tell her anything she didn't know, but the details of their execution at the hand of rebels in the DRC had chills running down her spine. Someone had gone to a lot of trouble to find out what happened. Questions started to buzz around in her mind until she felt a light touch on her arm.

"Are you okay?" Dale said, removing his hand quickly.

She lifted her eyes to meet Dale's and said, "My brother's name is on the list, too."

Dale shook his head. "Impossible. Your brother is the best doctor I've ever met. He wouldn't get involved with these scumbags."

The force of Dale's conviction made River feel a little better. She finished reading the file, which mentioned Rosa and the kids. This part was scary, too, and at the end of the file there was the word she didn't want to read: *testing*.

Dale had pushed his empty plate aside and was drinking his

coffee slowly. He had a frown of concern on his face, and River said, "Seems like you and Luke are in the same boat."

"But what does it tell us about the person you got that from?"

Another blow to River. How could her father's best friend have done such a thing? Perhaps he, too, had been blackmailed.

"I need more time to go through all the evidence we've gathered and then decide whether we can trust Old Bill's contacts. Let's get out of here. Miguel has found us a safe place in North Saint Ab."

River closed her laptop, stuffed it in her backpack, and stood up, but Dale hesitated.

"C'mon," River said, jerking her head toward the door.

Dale rose slowly. "Do you think Miguel will want me around? I'm happy to take some time off so that he doesn't think I'm back at the station talking to Andersen."

"If he wants me around, he'll want you around," River said, pushing him gently toward the door.

Dale broke into a winsome smile. River hadn't thought about it until then, but he could be an attractive guy if he put himself forward a little more.

They walked out of the diner. River took her burner from her jacket pocket and dialed Miguel.

"I'm on my way," she said as soon as he answered.

"I'll text you the address."

Miguel didn't mention Dale, and she wondered if he thought she was coming on her own. She tried to recall what North Saint Ab looked like and realized she kind of remembered where to go. It had always been a poor area, one that most people avoided—unless you were her parents. River turned around to see Dale standing next to a car she didn't recognize.

"What happened to your pickup?"

"I figured it was too visible. So I rented a car for a couple of days."

River gave Dale a thumbs-up. "Well done, Robin."

Dale frowned, got it, and then nodded. "I'll follow you, Batman. I mean Batgirl."

River grinned, put her helmet on, and gunned the bike. She eased the Yamaha Super Ténéré onto the road and rode slowly until she was sure Dale was following her. She then revved the engine and forgot about the speed limit. She doubted there would be a lot of police cars patrolling the area around the community center.

She slowed down when she came to an intersection. Dale stopped his car alongside her, rolled down the widow, and asked, "Where to?"

"The community center."

"I know. Right and then left," he said.

River took the lead again. A few minutes later they both stopped in front of the center. She didn't need to check Miguel's text for the address of the mobile home park. It was right at the back of the center. She rode the bike straight to the gate and parked. Dale followed and did the same. River removed her helmet and dialed Miguel's number again.

"We're here," she simply said.

Miguel must have registered the use of *we*. Both fell silent for a moment, and then Miguel grunted, "On my way."

Dale got out of his car but stayed back. River took the backpack out of the storage compartment of her bike and scanned the area for Miguel. He unexpectedly arrived from another side of the trailer park and surprised them both when he stood next to River. He didn't look happy, but his face softened a little when he saw Dale waiting next to his rented car.

"Where's your red beater?" Miguel asked.

"Thought it was too obvious, so I rented this one instead."

"We'd better get to the trailer. We don't want to hang around for too long here," Miguel said, and then addressed Dale. "Leave the car here; we'll come back for it later."

Dale hesitated and then said as he walked toward River and Miguel, "I've got supplies I'd rather not lose."

Miguel raised an eyebrow, and Dale walked to the trunk of the rental. He opened it slowly as Miguel and River reached him.

"My apologies, señor. I got you wrong from the start," Miguel said.

"I didn't ask you what you meant by 'supplies' when you said you were late because of getting them, but I now see what you mean."

Apart from three sets of body armor the likes of which she'd seen Navy SEALs and other Special Forces wear, Dale had gathered an impressive range of weapons—Glocks, SIGs, M4s, AR-15s. He'd made sure there was plenty of ammunition to go around, too.

There was a box that River thought she recognized. She pointed at it, and Dale confirmed her suspicions. "Night-vision goggles. We don't know when these cartel guys are going to come for us. They've missed me once, and I'm sure the next time they won't."

"Dare I ask where you got this stuff?" River asked, wondering where in Saint Ab you could find military-grade supplies.

"Not in Saint Ab, if that's what you're wondering," Dale said. "But I made a call on my way to Salt Lake City the night before and got a friend to help, ex-military. He pointed me in the right direction."

Dale closed the trunk as a couple of men stopped to watch them. Miguel didn't say anything but hopped into Dale's car. River got on her bike, and this time she followed Dale as Miguel guided him to their trailer.

The place felt deserted, with an occasional stray dog crossing the road. Trash had been left to rot next to a building that looked like a shed. The mobile home Miguel had rented was at the end of a long road and looked forlorn and unloved. The paint was peeling, and the windows hadn't been washed for a long while. It looked suitably unwelcoming—the perfect place to hide for a few days.

The reek of mold startled River when Miguel opened the door, but at least it was warm inside.

"I got us some food and coffee. We can hunker down here for a while."

River walked to the living room—kitchen combo and dropped her backpack and helmet next to a dining table that had seen better days.

"Just what we need for what we gotta do," she said.

The two men looked at each other and nodded.

River met their eyes. "Hatch a plan and then go after the cartel."

Chapter 15

Miguel, Dale, and River returned to Dale's car and off-loaded the weapons he'd gathered as discreetly as they could. Then they got organized. Miguel spread the map on which he and River had marked the locations of the Cruz Cartel's hidden mine and lab over the table. River booted up her laptop, and Dale went to the kitchen to prepare a pot of coffee.

"Isn't Sheriff Andersen going to wonder where you are?" River asked before taking out one of the USB drives from her backpack.

"I told them I wasn't well and needed to take some time off," Dale replied.

"Don't you think he's going to become suspicious?" Miguel asked.

Dale shrugged. "I guess that time has come and gone. The cartel guys didn't find me yesterday, and Andersen knows I've spoken to River, so I ain't gonna have a job when I go back to the station. But that's okay. Didn't like working with those guys anyway."

"You probably don't even want to go back to the police station at all," Miguel said, searching the cabinets for mugs. He found some, looked inside and grimaced, then went to the sink to wash them.

"Unless it's Andersen who doesn't make it to the police station," River said as she turned her laptop around toward the two men approaching the dining table.

Dale found a free spot where he could lay the coffeepot, and Miguel placed three mugs next to it. He poured some coffee into the mugs before leaning forward to read. Dale had already started and was shaking his head in disbelief.

"I never," he repeated a few times.

Miguel went through Andersen's file and didn't comment until he'd finished it.

"Scumbag, Martha always said." The three of them fell silent for a moment.

River took a mug and sipped at her coffee. There was a lot to go through, and they needed to focus on their next step. But she couldn't begrudge Miguel his feelings about his sister. It was almost impossible to believe that she'd been murdered only yesterday.

"The files are split between people who are with the cartel and people they are testing. Just so you know, my brother is on that list with an indication that they're testing him."

River heard an intake of breath from Miguel. Dale shook his head, still in disbelief, and she felt a little better. They couldn't imagine her brother being one of the Cruz people.

"Where did you find the information?" Miguel asked as he took a seat next to her at the table.

He'd turned the laptop toward himself and started scrolling down the file, his face expressing surprise or validation depending on the names he came across. Dale sat next to him and said, "Yes. Where did you get this intel from?"

River thought about the man whose name she was about to reveal and shook her head. "Harry Wilson."

Miguel and Dale looked up from the computer, both shocked, although she felt Dale was perhaps less so. Miguel sat back and said, "I should have known. He was appointed coroner by Andersen a few years back."

"Still, it's one thing to be put under pressure by Andersen, but this"—Dale said, pointing at the computer—"this is very organized and must have taken a lot of time to compile."

"Years," Miguel added.

River had a sudden thought: What was on the other USB drives?

And what about the notebook pages she'd captured on her cell phone?

"This isn't the only USB drive," she said, reaching under the table to get her backpack. "There are two more and a notebook with records of payments, too."

Miguel stood up and went to the back of the trailer. He came back with his own laptop, sat down again, and booted up the device. River handed him one of the other USB drives she'd fished out of her backpack. She unlocked her phone, gave her phone to Dale and said to them, "The password is drugDevilsplaygrounD44, and in my photo library you'll find images of the notebook. I think we should go through the evidence we've gathered and then decide what we do next."

River scribbled the password on a piece of paper and handed it over. Both men nodded and went about their task. She removed the first USB drive from her computer port and replaced it with the other. The screen filled with a request for a password. She typed in the one she'd just given to Miguel, hoping Harry hadn't been smart enough to create a different password for each drive.

She pressed the Enter key, and files displayed across the screen. Bingo. *The soul of the diligent shall be made rich.* River couldn't recall exactly, but she thought that came from Proverbs 13:4.

But she clicked on the first file, and her heart sank. She knew what all of them were going to display: the names, photos, and salient attributes of the girls who were taken across the border.

River ran her fingers through her hair and forced herself to read the file she'd just opened. She looked at the date: 02-02-2024—a month or more ago. The name next to the date was Dolores Morales, from Guatemala. River recognized the smiling face of the teenager she'd met at the hospital and failed to find at the lab. She was described as a person who'd be easy to subdue and who would then cooperate. Her family had gone into debt after her father had fallen ill and couldn't earn a living. She needed to get across the border into the States to find a job and had been told the usual lie—that she'd become legal as soon as she was working for an American employer.

Miguel was the first one to break the silence.

"I can't believe it," he said pushing his laptop away. "Either Harry has been in the game for a long time, or he's taken over from someone else, because the list of drug movements across the border goes back ten years."

"The information River took photos of doesn't go back that far. It's only four years old, but there are a lot of details about who's been paid what by the cartel in Saint Ab," Dale said, lifting his head from River's phone.

"I'm lost for words," River said, her voice trembling in anger. "Harry used to be my father's best friend."

Miguel shook his head. "People change, sometimes before our very eyes, and we can't see it."

Dale sat back. "I think we're all in shock. The sheriff is a jerk involved with the Cruz Cartel, and then Harry, plus all the other people on this list we should have trusted—judges, police officers, and so on—but we've got a lot of evidence now. We've got to get it to the feds."

River and Miguel agreed, and then River said, "Do we trust the two guys you met, though?"

"Only one way to find out," Dale said. "I've not told them about you two. So I call John Lewis, tell him I've got some hard evidence, and offer to meet him. And then we see whether he comes to the meeting alone."

River frowned. "We use you as bait?"

Dale shrugged. "Why not?"

Miguel stood up again, restless. "What about Dolores?"

Dale turned to River, surprised.

"We found the lab where the cartel cooks the drugs," River said. "I got close enough to see that they'd kept someone in one of the barns, but she wasn't there anymore."

"Who do we prioritize?" Miguel asked.

Dale pushed his chair away from the table. "Don't we need more manpower to help free Dolores?"

"You're probably right," River said, "but we may not have that luxury. The next batch of girls is due to arrive tomorrow. I guess they'll be getting her to join them on their way to Vegas."

"Dale's got a point, though," Miguel grumbled.

"Okay, I get it. The three of us can't take on the Cruz men. We need these feds guys to be genuine."

"Then let's try to meet them this afternoon," Dale said. "I'll get in touch with John and tell him we've got lots of evidence we want to share."

Everyone went quiet for a moment and then River said, "Do it. I need to get back home for lunch, otherwise Luke is going to get worried or annoyed, and I don't want him to talk to Harry about it. Let me know what John the ex-fed says using Miguel's burner phone, then we can organize a welcome party."

"You got it," Dale said.

"And find a way to keep the USB drives secure. I'm not sure keeping them on us is a good idea."

Both men nodded.

River stood up, took her helmet and backpack, and returned to the bike. She slid the backpack in the storage compartment, put her helmet on, and started the engine. She rode the bike out of the park slowly. The place felt deserted, or perhaps people were keeping to themselves. She thought she noticed movement at a window, but when she looked closely, she couldn't spot anyone.

The ride to Luke's home took less than half an hour. She slowed down before rounding the corner of Luke's street and stopped altogether when she saw the car that was stopped in front of her brother's house.

A black Jeep Grand Cherokee was parked outside, and River was certain it was the car that fled from the mine as Sheriff Andersen tried to gun her down. River moved her hand to her back. The Glock was still there. She parked the bike a few houses away from Luke's and made her way there, walking as close as she could to the low fences that surrounded the other properties.

She arrived at the front door and listened for a moment. She could hear voices; they weren't raised and didn't sound anxious. River opened the door very slowly. The door creaked a little, and River stopped, but no one seemed to have noticed. She closed it and moved forward, her hand on the butt of her Glock. She was waiting in the corridor to identify the voices, ready to shoot. Luke walked into the hallway from the kitchen and stopped.

"I didn't hear you come in."

River straightened up and gave him a quick smile.

"I didn't want to interrupt, since you have a guest."

Luke frowned and then smiled. "It's okay. It only Harry popping in for lunch."

River tried to look enthusiastic but knew she hadn't succeeded, and Luke looked surprised. He turned around. She quickly slid the Glock into her inner jacket pocket, took the jacket off, and hung it on one of the coat hooks in the hall. When she entered the dining room, Harry was already sitting at the table next to Carmen. He was talking to her about a book that was open in front of her. The girl lifted her head and ran to River as soon as she saw her. River weathered the shock and laughed.

"Aunt River," Carmen shouted.

"And this is my lovely girl, Carmen," River said, hugging her with her good arm.

River had managed to prevent Carmen from hitting her wounded arm, and her gesture didn't go unnoticed. Harry looked at her with a coldness she'd never seen before. Yet she smiled and said, "Lovely to see you again, Harry."

His face returned to his former amiability. "Likewise, River. I hear you're planning a day or so in the mountains."

Rosa had done a good job at preparing Luke, who must have discussed the matter with Harry. The plan had been to organize a barbecue over the weekend, and perhaps Rosa had presented the idea as a form of reconnaissance.

"I'm getting used to the place again," River said, sweeping the room with her hand as though it were the outdoors. "And we used to do that all the time in the old days."

Harry nodded. She couldn't decide whether he was convinced or had seen through her story.

"Whereabouts are you planning to go?"

River hadn't thought of a credible lie, and she fumbled a bit. "Probably toward Arizona, Beaver Dam—somewhere like that."

Luke wiggled his nose. "That's a little dry and dusty around there. How about trying Apple Valley?"

"Why not?" River said, still cradling Carmen. The little girl didn't seem in a hurry to return to Harry's side, and the thought of this sex trafficker sitting next to her niece made her sick. "I can't recall the name of the place we used to go to. I'd like to check whether it's changed since we last were there."

"It has, and for the better," Luke said. "I didn't think about it, but it could be the ideal place for a barbecue. What do you think, Harry?"

Harry nodded at Luke. "I enjoy it there. It's much greener than Beaver Dam. I could give you the name of a nice B&B you could stay at," he added, turning his attention to River again. She felt the weight of Harry's stare and responded with another smile—more confident this time. She had to protect her family from this monster until she could expose the truth.

Rosa emerged from the kitchen and went to greet River. She gave River a look that meant she wanted to talk.

"Carmen, sweetheart, why don't you go and wash your hands with Daddy?" Rosa said.

Carmen gave River a tight squeeze, and Luke got up, and then they both ran to the small washroom off the hallway, Luke making some monster growls while chasing Carmen.

"I need some help with the food," Rosa said, directing her request to River. "And Harry, would you mind setting the table, please?"

She grinned at Harry. He stood up with a military salute and went to the sideboard in the dining room that held dishes and flatware. River followed Rosa into the kitchen, and they both walked to the stove.

"What did you find?" Rosa murmured. "I couldn't ask this morning but was dying to."

"It's bad," River replied quietly. It wasn't the time to disclose everything to Rosa—just enough to keep Carmen safe.

Rosa's face dropped. "He's involved," she said, her voice dipping even lower.

River nodded and added in a whisper, "And suspicious."

Rosa closed her eyes for an instant. She then turned off the heat from under a pan of chicken in a tomato-and-olive sauce and looked through a cabinet for a serving dish. River heard that Luke and Carmen were back in the dining room, and they stopped talking. They both busied themselves with the food, and Rosa took the hot dish to the table. River followed behind, carrying a large green salad and a basket of bread.

Carmen was already sitting with Franklin snuggled on a small stool next to her.

"Aunt River, you're next to me," she said with determination and a toothy smile.

River took her seat next to her, and Harry slid next to River. She tried not to show her disappointment, instead concentrating on helping her niece with her napkin. River straightened up and realized that her wounded arm was on Harry's side. She would have to be extra careful in her every move.

Rosa served everyone the main course, and the other dishes circulated. The conversation turned around Apple Valley and the Mojave River, which flowed intermittently near it. They spoke about Jack's return from his school trip to Washington, DC. River couldn't help but give Harry a couple of sidelong glances. She hoped he wouldn't notice.

Harry was surprisingly relaxed for a man whose office had been raided. Perhaps he wasn't suspicious of her but rather still annoyed by her visit to the morgue. He seemed to truly enjoy the idea of the barbecue everyone was talking about.

When they finished their meal, Rosa stood up and said, "Anyone for some ice cream?"

Carmen's arm shot up first. "Vanilla and chocolate, please, Mom."

Everyone nodded. River was about to stand up to help clear the plates, but Harry stood up before she did.

"Let me do this," he said, resting a hand on her shoulder and then squeezing hard.

River couldn't help stiffening. She clenched her teeth to stop herself from screaming.

Rosa called Harry immediately. "Do you mind helping with the ice cream as well?" Harry turned to Rosa with a mixture of surprise and anger. River stood up in an attempt to refocus Harry's attention, but it was too late. She could see it on his face. He'd gotten confirmation not only that River was the person who'd fled from the Silver Rim mine but also that Rosa knew of her wound.

Rosa tilted her head toward the kitchen, undeterred, and River joined in clearing the plates. Luke was already in the kitchen with Carmen, scooping ice cream into bowls and letting Carmen lick the serving spoon after he was done. Harry said nothing until all plates were cleared. River could feel the tension and rage in his body—raised shoulders, hands shaking ever so slightly, and a deep frown that made sharp creases on his forehead.

Harry sat next to Luke, wolfed down his dessert, and made an excuse about needing to run back to the practice. River ate her ice cream a little more slowly but was also eager to leave the house. Then Luke put on his coat and went back to work. Carmen was going to a fair organized by her school that afternoon, and he promised he would return home as soon as he could.

Both women waited until the only sound they could hear was Carmen humming as she settled in to read her book.

"Harry knows it's me, and he's now suspecting you," River said to Rosa. "I'm so sorry this is happening."

"He is a douchebag," Rosa said, banging pots and pans into the sink in anger. "I should have pushed harder when I had my suspicions. But Luke won't have it."

"He was our father's closest friend," River said. "I now think it's been much harder than I imagined for Luke to cope with our parents' death."

Rosa stopped her angry cleaning up and stood, a fist planted on her waist. "I get it, but he's got to wake up. This is now putting Carmen and even Jack in danger."

"You, too, Rosa," River said. "It's not only your kids."

Rosa shook her head. "We don't even own a gun. Luke is adamant that he won't have one in the house."

"Can you shoot?" River asked.

"This is Utah, Riv. Of course I can, although I haven't done it for a while."

River hesitated. She was setting herself on a collision course with her brother, bringing the cartel closer to his home—although with Harry it was already there—and now providing Rosa with a gun. River walked to the coatrack and returned with her jacket. She took out the Glock from inside it and laid it on the kitchen counter. Rosa opened her eyes wide and then smiled.

"You're a dark horse, Riv," she said. "I like it."

River smiled back but grew serious. "I have a spare clip in my duffel bag. But are you sure you want this? If you have a gun, you need to be sure that you're going to use it—no hesitation, because hesitation will kill you."

"If Harry comes in and threatens my kids, I'll have *no* hesitation," Rosa said.

She met River's eyes for a moment, and River knew she would do whatever it took to protect Carmen and Jack. Rosa extended her hand toward the gun, but River stopped her from touching it.

"Despite what I said, I want you to promise that this is a last resort. Don't go and shoot Harry unless you know he's a threat. I'm working on bringing him to justice, so don't think that he won't pay for what he's done."

Rosa sighed and then said, "I promise I won't shoot the SOB if he walks into my house and is no threat to us."

River nodded and released the gun. Rosa picked it up, released the clip, pushed it back into the butt, and then checked the safety catches.

"I'll hide it someplace where I can access it easily but away from Carmen and Luke."

River gave Rosa a hug. "You need me, you call me. I won't have my phone on all the time, but I'll check it regularly."

River went to the guest bedroom and picked up a couple of sweatshirts, socks, and underwear as well as her toothbrush, all of which she stuffed in a plastic bag. She returned to the kitchen, hugged Rosa one more time, and left the house. She placed her clothes in the storage compartment of the bike, kick-started the engine, and made her way back to North Saint Ab's mobile home park.

Chapter 16

Dale and Miguel were poring over the map Miguel had bought when River walked into the mobile home.

"They've agreed to meet me," Dale said as soon as he saw her.

"Where?" River asked after removing her helmet.

"In the canyon where we found the first girl," Dale replied. "I talked it over with Miguel and we thought it gave you two the right setup to have my back."

"I'm sure they'll know they're exposed," River said.

Miguel nodded. "That's the interesting part. They'll be arriving in an hour's time. If they're going to call for reinforcement of some sort, it'll be there already if it's local."

River stepped closer to the table to consider the map. "Are you suggesting we become the surprise party to the surprise party?"

"Something like that," Miguel said as he pointed at the map. "You know this hilltop. You were there the other day. That's where the cartel guys almost found you. This is the highest point in the surrounding landscape."

"We don't get there first, but we find a position from which we can see who's already arrived," Dale said. He took a pen that was lying on the table and marked a place that was close to the top of the ravine. "That place is ideal for surveillance."

"But what about down there, in the ravine?" River asked.

"It's two of us," Miguel said pointing at River and then himself.

"We clear the top first, and then I get down there by another route. It's a steep descent, but I've done this several times. Whoever is at the bottom of the ravine won't see me coming."

"What do these guys look like? Just so we know it's them," River asked as she turned toward Dale.

"John Lewis is a small guy, thin, close-cropped white beard. His pal Loren Askew is a black guy, a big man with a slight limp in his left leg."

Miguel nodded, and they both turned to River for her reaction. She stayed silent for a moment. Her mind drifted to Rosa and Carmen, and she shivered.

"Something wrong?" Miguel asked.

River leaned against the table. "Harry came to lunch at Luke's. I knew he might be suspicious of me, but what I discovered was that he was the man driving the black Jeep Grand Cherokee at the mine shootout. I saw it parked in front of my brother's house."

Miguel interrupted, thunder in his eyes. "We're going to get this motherfucker."

"That's only the bad news," River said. "The *very* bad news is that he grabbed my left arm, and he knew then that I was wounded."

"So he knows you know," Dale said. "I mean, he knows it's probably you who broke into his office."

River bit her lip. "And that puts Carmen and Rosa in danger."

The three of them took a moment to consider the information.

"How about we move them to Old Bill's cave?" Miguel said.

"What about the meeting with the feds?" Dale said. "We won't have time to go back to Saint Ab, take them to Old Bill, and meet these guys at Silver Rim. Although . . . perhaps I could meet them on my own."

"No way," River said. "This is too risky. Thanks for offering, though."

River struggled to find a solution that worked. She felt torn between the desire to take Carmen and Rosa to safety and the need to meet with Old Bill's fed contacts. Without them, the evidence she and Miguel had gathered amounted to nothing.

"Look," she said checking the time on her watch. "Carmen and Rosa are at home, and Rosa has my Glock."

The men looked at each other, then Dale said, "Do you think she'll use it?"

"If her daughter is threatened, I have no doubt, but I'd rather not test my assumption," River said.

No one wanted to make a decision until Dale finally said, "Let's get to the canyon and *then* take Carmen and Rosa to safety. If that's the wrong choice, let it be on my head."

River squeezed Dale's shoulder in a thank-you gesture. Miguel walked to the back of the mobile home.

"The weapons Dale brought with him are in the bedroom on the left," he said over his shoulder.

River and Dale followed. The three of them looked at the choices they had. River went for a Glock and a couple of spare clips. Dale went for a SIG and one of the M4 carbines and with a box of ammunition. Miguel chose a Glock, too, and an AR-15.

"Are you going to the meeting with your rifle?" River asked.

Dale shook his head. "I'll find a spot where I can hide it from the feds. If all hell breaks loose, I'll get to it and hope I can remember how to use it well enough to protect myself."

Miguel was about to pick up a couple of boxes of 5.56 NATO and stopped. "Have they called to check on you from the police station?"

"Zilch. Radio silence. Not even to ask when I'll be back."

"Right," Miguel said. "They must know you're on the team, too."

Dale shrugged. "I guess. I never liked Andersen in the first place, so it's gonna be okay when I get the sack."

They all left the bedroom and made their way to the dining area.

"I'll take the bike and follow you," River said. "I'll park it away from the road but before we get to Silver Rim. Its engine is less discreet than that of a car."

"I'll give you a ride to the observation point," Miguel said.

River slipped the Glock against her back, tucked the spare clips into a pocket of her cargo pants, and picked up her helmet. She was the first to leave the trailer. Miguel and Dale followed. She saw them holding their jackets over their chosen rifles. She wasn't sure it made them less conspicuous, but then again guns weren't that unusual in the neighborhood. She started the bike and eased it onto the road that led to the trailer-park entrance.

The place was still eerily quiet. River came to the main road and didn't wait for Dale and Miguel to catch up with her. She needed to give herself space and a good head start. She reached the outskirts of Saint Ab within minutes and pushed for speed. The road rose as she made her way to the mountain and to Silver Rim, and she was enjoying the ride.

It was good to concentrate on the drive and push away the worry that was weighing on her. She hadn't intended to bring trouble to herself or to her brother's family. Luke had always been a calm, reserved boy, and he used to tell her that *she* was trouble.

She recognized the entrance to the path that led to the Silver Rim canyon and slowed down. She turned into it and found a place to park her bike away from the trail. She used the raised terrain and a couple of boulders to hide it, then retrieved her backpack from the storage compartment, retraced her steps, and waited for Miguel to arrive.

The old Ford appeared in the distance, and she stuck her thumb out in a hitchhiker's pose. The car stopped, and Miguel lowered the window on the passenger side.

"Looking for a ride to spy on a couple of feds, by any chance?"

"How did you guess?"

She opened the door and got in. Miguel drove for another ten minutes and then inched the car down a narrow path that ended up at the edge of the cliff. A few rocks stuck out and formed a sort of platform from which it was easy to survey the canyon. River took her binoculars out of her backpack and adjusted them so she could zoom in. Miguel took a pair of binoculars from his own backpack, but instead of turning his attention to the rim he looked toward the bottom of the canyon.

"I'm checking on Dale's progress."

"And?" River asked.

"Can't see him yet."

"I presume he went down there on foot."

"Right—it would have taken much too long to drive around."

"What about the feds? Could they have driven around to the bottom of the canyon?"

"Unlikely," Miguel said, still scrutinizing the landscape below. "They would be caught if someone was positioning guns above their heads."

"Unless they have backup there already."

"Do you see anything?"

River scanned the surrounding hilltop slowly and then said, "Nothing I can spot, and I know there's no room to hide up there unless you want to dangle from the edge into the precipice."

"And then the ridge recedes to the right. That means no sight line into the part of the canyon Dale and these guys are meeting in."

They fell silent, each concentrating on their task.

"Come on, Dale, where are you?" Miguel grunted.

"Still nothing on my side," River said. "Could the two feds have intercepted him before he reached the bottom?"

"It would have to have happened on the road—I think. Dale was just behind me, but then he parked his car before I got to you."

"To take another path down? But what if—"

"There he is," Miguel interrupted, relief clear in his voice.

"Is he carrying his rifle?"

"No. He must have taken the time to find the right place to hide it," Miguel said. "I'm going to climb down and make sure I'm close enough to him before the feds arrive."

Miguel returned to the car and took out the rifle and the ammunition. He stuck the SIG inside his belt and closed the trunk. He slung the rifle belt across his front, and the ammunition went into his hunting-jacket pockets.

"I've got the burner phone with me," he said, shaking the device so that River took note. She dropped the binoculars for a moment and nodded.

"Mine is in my jacket pocket. I'll text you if I see anything, although we won't have much reception, if any, down there."

"Got it," Miguel said.

He turned toward the left, where the shrubs looked dense and seemed to obscure the view. He pushed them aside, and they closed back around him, whipping against the rock with a sharp slap. River returned to her observation. She didn't like it when things were so calm. She'd experienced it in combat zones—the pressure of waiting for the inevitable outburst of violence, waiting for the call to extract a wounded operative during the golden hour.

River shivered. She didn't want to go back there, even in her mind. She'd enjoyed her time in the military, but she had left hoping for a new life with her then boyfriend. It hadn't worked out that way, and she now knew she'd never return to being a medic in battle.

River blinked a couple of times to dispel images from the past. She needed to focus on her task. She returned to her observation of the hilltop above the canyon. The light grew a little dimmer suddenly, and she looked up. Some heavy clouds had obscured the sun, and it sent a chill through the air. She didn't think it would rain, though, so nothing to worry about when it came to floods in the ravine.

Her burner phone buzzed, and she checked the text. Miguel must have stopped where he still had a signal.

> **One of the feds guys is on the way, walking toward Dale.**

> **Which one?**

> **Loren, the black guy.**

> **Looking for white-bearded John.**

River widened her scan of the landscape around the canyon rim and the trail that led to the ravine. She still couldn't see anyone. Yet they must have arrived from somewhere. She thought about what Miguel had said earlier—on the other side of the cliff, the rim dropped down. Perhaps the two men had found a way to the canyon from there. They wouldn't have been noticed from the side on which River sat. She texted Miguel again.

Still nothing.

Loren is about to reach Dale.

River scanned her side of the cliff once more—nothing.

Going to check the other side of the hilltop.

No! Stay put.

These two guys arrived from somewhere we couldn't see. I'm going.

River ignored Miguel's next text. She slung the binoculars around her neck and made her way silently toward the Silver Rim ridge. She progressed slowly, in small increments, making sure she wasn't observed or followed. She ran across the path that led to the final climb and hid behind the boulders she used previously to conceal her bike.

Miguel hadn't texted her again. Dale and Loren must have met, so Miguel had probably moved closer and lost reception. River checked her surroundings one last time. She was sure she was alone. She dashed along the rock face in the final ascent to the cliff top and flattened to the ground as soon as she reached it. The thin soil around her smelled dry and metallic. She waited there for a moment and then slid to the edge of the stone ridge where she'd hung the night before, waiting for the cartel men to leave.

She grabbed her binoculars and brought them to her eyes. She could now see Dale and Loren facing each other in the distance. She slowly scanned the slope that led from the right side of the cliff to the bottom of the canyon. River could see why no one wanted to go down that route. The path was edged with thick shrubs that made it impossible to secure, and boulders provided places to lie in wait. She meticulously checked the path a few times until she noticed a glimmer among the greenery. The sun had pierced the clouds for a moment, and its rays had reflected off an object.

River tried to get a better view, but the shrubbery was too dense. She turned her attention to the path she needed to take to reach the cluster of bushes she wanted to investigate. It was steep and rocky. It would take a while to climb down without being noticed. She glanced back at Dale and Loren. The conversation looked animated, but she couldn't tell whether it was friendly.

She slid back down the slope she'd climbed and reached its bottom. She walked around and spotted what must be the trail the feds had taken. When she got there, she crouched and decided on the best approach. She chose a section of the path that meant climbing down rocks. She would be exposed for a moment, but she couldn't see any other way. She started her descent, moving as fast as she could without dislodging rocks and making sound.

She stopped once she reached vegetation, and the rock face eased into a trail. She flattened her body against the rock, slowed her breathing, and waited. Nothing moved, yet the glint of metal she thought she saw reappeared. She slid farther down toward the path and stopped again. She must be only yards away. She was about to take the Glock from behind her back when the racking of a gun froze her on the spot.

"Don't make a sudden move or I shoot," a voice said from behind.

It sounded craggy and ill-tempered. River instinctively put her hands in the air and said, "What's the problem?"

"The problem," the voice repeated with sarcasm, "is that you're sneaking around and getting involved with stuff you shouldn't get involved with."

"I'm just out for a walk," River said, trying to look surprised and scared.

The man who emerged from behind a boulder wasn't John Lewis. He was younger, with dark hair, blue eyes, and a bad scar over his right eye.

"This isn't the usual path to the canyon," the man said.

His SIG was aimed at her in a way that was meant to threaten, and his demeanor was menacing enough. She took a step back and felt shrubs preventing her from going any farther. He stepped slowly toward her, appraising her.

"I just like to get away from the beaten path," River said. "I don't see what the issue is."

The man stepped a little closer. She stepped back a little more herself. The branches of the shrub stuck into her like needles.

"Stop moving," the man ordered.

River held her hands even higher. "What are you gonna do?" she said.

"Just want to check you for a weapon," the man said as he was almost upon her.

No, you won't.

In one sudden move, River dove to the ground, and the branches of the shrub lashed out and struck the man in the face. His head whipped back, and he muffled a cry. River gave him a sweeping low kick, and he lost his balance, crashing heavily to the ground. She rolled away from him and stood up in one go as she was taking her Glock out. She trained it on the man and said through gritted teeth, "Drop your gun or you'll be the one to come down."

The man dropped his gun slowly to the ground and then raised his hands. "Shooting a federal agent isn't a good idea."

"Depends whether that fed is crooked or not," River shot back.

"What?" the man said with what felt like genuine surprise.

"Don't move, I said."

"But—"

"I'm the one with the gun. I ask the questions," River interrupted. "Where is John Lewis?"

The man's surprise grew, and he hesitated.

"If you think I'm not gonna shoot you, think twice," River said, her anger rising. "I was trained in combat zones, so this little setup of yours isn't gonna faze me."

"John is in the canyon, keeping an eye on Loren."

"Why should I believe you? For all I know you could have killed John already and are planning to finish off Loren and Dale. Or perhaps Loren is bent, and you and he have killed John."

The man shook his head vigorously. "No. You're getting this all wrong. I'm a fed, all right, and John is my father."

"Why did get you involved, then?"

"Because this drug story is hot and involves a lot of people, very senior people. You can't be too cautious."

"So you see my problem with your story . . ." River said, expecting him to supply his name.

"Gary," he said.

River took a step back. "Okay, Gary. This is what we're gonna do. Kick your gun to me—gently—or you're finished."

Gary looked around for the gun, slid his foot next to it, and kicked it toward River. She bent down slowly to pick it up, her Glock still trained on Gary.

"Do you have a pair of handcuffs with you?"

Gary was about to protest, but River cut him short.

"If you even think about pulling a fast one on me, I'll gun you down. Two innocent women have already lost their lives. So I won't hesitate."

Her voice must have conveyed enough anger and determination for Gary to take the cuffs out of his pocket and hold them out with his right hand.

"Slip one cuff on your right wrist and close it."

Gary shook his head. "You're making a big mistake."

"We'll see about that."

Gary did as he was told. Now the cuffs hung from his wrist.

"Step to the side toward the tree to your left and get your arms around it, then close the cuffs on your left wrist, nice and slow. You know where I'm coming from now, right?"

Gary did as he was told.

River walked to the tree that Gary was handcuffed to. With her Glock still pointed at him, she tested the cuffs. They were in place and wouldn't budge. She pulled away and thought for a moment. She slid the Glock against her back again, then kicked off her shoes, took her socks off, and tied them together, forming a long piece of cloth.

"I'm gonna used these to gag you," she said, getting close to Gary again.

He turned as much as he could to face her, and the look of horror on his face almost made River laugh.

"They're clean—I promise."

"You *are* insane," Gary said, pulling away from her as much as he could.

"It's either my socks or the butt of my Glock to your head," she said.

Gary gave her a murderous look but stopped moving. River tied the socks around Gary's mouth. She could feel him recoiling when she secured the knot, but she didn't want him to alert John once she was on her way.

She stepped away from him to consider her handiwork. It would do until she reached his father, near the bottom of the canyon. River resumed her descent. She hadn't received a text from Miguel, but then she remembered that reception was bad in the gorge.

River moved as fast and as quietly as she could. She stopped a few times to make sure she wasn't missing the elder Lewis, but then she saw him. He, too, had binoculars and was using them to survey the scene. She couldn't see any rifle by his side, but the dark puffer jacket he was wearing could be concealing a gun.

The large rocks John Lewis was hiding behind created a semicircle that seemed to block any passage around him. River understood. Anyone wanting to get to the bottom of the ravine would have to walk past him. She veered to the right and managed to squeeze behind the rock that jutted out the farthest. She took her Glock out, hesitated, but then shouted, while racking her gun loudly, "Hands over your head where I can see them, Agent Lewis."

Lewis's back stiffened, and she saw him hesitate.

"I won't ask twice," she shouted.

He raised his hands slowly. But there was something much more controlled in his manner—more experience, she felt.

"Okay," he said. "To whom am I speaking, since you know my name?"

"That'll come later, when I'm sure I can trust you."

Again, the same *Whaaat?* reaction she'd seen in Gary.

"Your son Gary seems to think I should trust you because you're both feds even if you're retired. I need some convincing."

This time she got an angry response, and Lewis jerked his head toward her. "What have you done to him? Because if—"

River interrupted. "He's tied to a tree with his own cuffs. He's unharmed."

Lewis's shoulders relaxed, but his head remained half turned, trying to size River up out of the corner of his eye. He couldn't see very much of her, though. Her entire body was concealed behind the boulder, and she'd rested the arm holding her Glock on top of the rock, head low to ensure shouting accuracy. Lewis was thinking. She could feel it, and she waited for him to speak.

"I get it," he said. "Trust is in short supply."

"Yup, and at the moment you're the one who needs to do the convincing."

River saw the flicker of a smile on Lewis's face.

"I'm gonna turn around and take my gun out and drop it to the ground. I'll then handcuff myself and we can talk."

Lewis waited for River's instructions. "Do you wear an ankle holster?"

Lewis shook his head. "I'll show you."

"Okay, turn around."

Lewis came to face River and did what he said he would—dropped his SIG, lifted the bottom of his pants to show he wasn't hiding anything, and handcuffed himself. He then sat on the ground, folded his legs in front of him, and rested his elbows on his knees, relaxed.

"I think we want the same thing," Lewis said. "Dismantle the Cruz Cartel."

"What's preventing you from doing it?" River asked, although she was almost certain of the answer.

"Lack of evidence and the network of corruption that prevails in high-ranking officials throughout the state."

"You mean like Sheriff Andersen?"

Lewis gave her a quick smile. "Andersen is worse than a fish—slippery and cold. But there are others. We have a list but only weak proof of a link with the cartel."

"You're a friend of Old Bill?" River asked. Lewis could still be spinning a story, and if she wasn't careful, she would find out only when it was too late.

He nodded. "Been friends with him for more than thirty years." His face brightened at the thought. "And you know what? He was old even then."

They both chuckled. River grew serious again, still not moving from her protected position. "It still doesn't mean anything."

"That's true." Lewis dropped his head back against the rock. "Someone is going to have to take a chance, I guess, because we don't have much time."

"Why not?"

"There's a consignment of girls arriving tomorrow. I expect the cartel boys will be using the same places and routes to transport them because it's too late to change anything now. But after that they'll be packing up, and we're gonna lose their trail again."

"How do you know? I mean that the girls are arriving tomorrow."

"We've established a pattern with the help of law enforcement in Mexico. We know when the girls arrive from elsewhere in Latin America and then are sent across. We just don't know what the route is when they reach Utah."

River straightened up and walked away from the boulder behind which she was hiding.

"Mind if I keep your gun?" she asked.

Lewis shook his head. River hesitated once more, but Lewis was right—they had very little time, and she needed to decide whom to trust fast.

"I'm going to keep your gun. You walk in front of me. Any funny business, and I'll shoot, even if it means shooting you in the back."

Lewis shrugged. "I guess I'll have to be okay with that. The cuff keys are in my jacket pocket, by the way."

"Go ahead."

Lewis got hold of the keys and freed himself quickly. He stood up and waited.

River gave a nod toward the path that led to the place where Dale and Agent Askew were meeting.

"Let's go and get to the meeting. We'll uncuff Gary later."

"Fine by me," Lewis said. "He should have been more on his guard."

"Tough love?" River asked.

"Tough love keeps you alive."

Chapter 17

"Luis has brought a young kid to the lab," Pablo said as he entered Alfonso's room, breathless.

Alfonso had used one of the barns to house more of his chemists and decided to stay on-site for the duration of the operation. He was at his computer, reviewing the latest results from the samples his team of chemists had cooked. He stood up slowly, a frown replacing a contented look on his face. The lab results were promising.

"A kid? For what?" Alfonso didn't want to imagine what Luis had in mind. Whatever it was, it wouldn't happen at the lab.

Pablo looked dumbfounded. "He says she's a hostage."

"Hijo de puta," Alfonso said, slamming his fist on the table.

He walked past Pablo, who tried in vain to slow him down.

"What are you gonna do?"

"Find out what this SOB is up to and then send him back to Mexico," Alfonso said. He no longer cared whether his father was going to object. Luis was going back to Nogales—alive, perhaps, but preferably dead.

Alfonso started to run, with Pablo running alongside him. "Where are they?"

"He stuck her in the room where we kept the other girl."

Alfonso slowed down as he arrived at the cluster of dilapidated buildings that formed the lab, the warehouse, and an area containing sleeping pods for the chemists. Some of Luis's men were stationed at the entrance, and he felt questioning stares fall on him as he arrived.

Luis didn't like him, and he couldn't help sharing his feelings with his men.

Alfonso ignored the attitude and snapped his fingers in an impatient gesture. The men moved away, and he entered the place, moving swiftly to the room that had been used as a makeshift cell for Dolores. He stood outside for a moment. He could hear someone sobbing softly. Alfonso laid a hand on the door and leaned against it. He quietly opened it and steeled himself.

The girl was sitting on a couple of burlap sacks that had been sloppily thrown to the floor. One of her wrists was tied to a pipe that ran along the wall. She'd been wearing a mask, but it had fallen from her face, and she was now rubbing her eyes with her free hand. The light in the room was dim, but there was enough for Alfonso to see that the sleeve of her T-shirt was wet. The girl turned her face suddenly in his direction. Startled by his entrance, she started to wail, clinging to the wall in terror.

Alfonso held a hand forward in an appeasing gesture. "I'm not going to hurt you. I promise. I just want to talk to you."

She couldn't stop her loud sobs, and Alfonso crouched, waiting for her to calm a little. "I just want to know what your name is. I'm not getting any closer. I'm here, not moving."

The girl made an effort to speak, but her voice didn't obey. After a moment she managed to stutter, "Car-men." She wiped her nose on the back of her small hand.

Alfonso nodded and said, "I'm Al."

The girl didn't move. He could feel the terror—a trapped little animal who didn't know how to escape. Alfonso sat down where he'd crouched.

"As long as I'm here, no one is going to hurt you, okay?"

Carmen gave him a slow nod.

"What's your last name?"

She hesitated and murmured, "Swift."

Alfonso made a fist. He now knew what Luis's plan was. Too lazy or stubborn to do as he'd been told, he'd found it easier to abduct a kid and trade her for the woman he was supposed to take care of.

"I'm going to get a little closer and cut off the rope," Alfonso said. "Is that okay?"

He stood up very slowly, and Carmen recoiled. He waited a moment and added, "I've got a knife in my pocket. I'm going to take it out to cut the rope, okay?"

Alfonso could feel her anxious eyes on him. He deliberately moved slowly as he stood up, and when he got to her, he bent down and asked, "May I take your wrist to cut the string?"

Carmen seemed to be transfixed by the presence of the tall man hovering above her. Alfonso delicately took her wrist and cut the cable. Her arm dropped like a lump, and she whimpered. She rubbed it with her other hand and waited; her face lifted toward him. Alfonso could now see that she was a pretty little girl, with large brown eyes and a heart-shaped face. He wanted to ask the terrible question that burned on his lips, but he didn't know how. Instead, he smiled at her and held his hand out to help her stand up. She hesitated but grabbed it and rose from the floor slowly.

"Let's get out of here," Alfonso said.

Carmen kept her hand in his, and Alfonso led the way. They walked out of the room and found themselves in the dilapidated barn. Two chemists had just walked in, dressed in white coveralls that sheathed their body and heads. Their face masks were hanging around their necks, and they were stacking bags in a corner of the shed. Carmen retreated behind Alfonso, and he instinctively put a hand over her head.

The two men looked curious but didn't ask who the girl was. Instead, the older man said, "We're ready for the transfer of the next cargo tomorrow. The last batch is cooking."

Alfonso nodded his agreement. He waited until the men had left and then walked in the opposite direction. Outside, Pablo was waiting for him. Luis's men had retreated to the far end of the yard, smoking and chatting among themselves.

"Where is that SOB?" Alfonso asked, Carmen still clinging to his hand.

"I hear he's around," Pablo muttered. He wasn't happy, either, that Luis had brought a very young girl to the lab.

"Bring me that shit stain. I want a word," Alfonso said. It was time he tested his own resolve to break free from what his father dictated he must do.

Pablo frowned. He hung back, deciding, it seemed, whether he should try to talk Alfonso out of it, but then nodded and made his way to the far end of the yard, where Luis's men were gathered. He'd just reached them when Luis rounded the corner of the barn.

Alfonso turned to Carmen and said, with a smile he hoped would pacify the girl, "Go back inside. I need to talk to this man."

Carmen held on to his hand, looking in Luis's direction in fear, but then reluctantly let go and hid inside the barn, close to the door frame.

Luis noticed her and grinned before he shouted, "What do you think of my gift? We'll get this other bitch to surrender or else—"

Alfonso lunged at Luis with his fists clenched. He ran partway, landed both feet on the ground in an attack position, and threw his left fist in an uppercut that hit Luis just under the chin. The sound of teeth shattering made a sickening sound. Luis staggered but managed to avoid the full force of Alfonso's second punch. Luis threw his entire weight into a tackle, and both men rolled to the ground. Alfonso landed on his back, and the fall winded him. Luis assaulted his sides with a series of repeated punches.

Luis's men had formed a loose circle around the two combatants, and they and Pablo were cheering their respective bosses. Then Alfonso delivered a near-lethal head butt to Luis. The man's nose exploded, and he shrieked. Alfonso hurled his opponent away from him and stood up. He delivered a kick into Luis's stomach and then took a few steps back, his scalp dripping blood. He resumed a fighting stance, ready for more.

The flash of a blade made Pablo shout and start toward Luis, but one of Luis's men stopped him. Alfonso sucked in his belly just in time to avoid the knife. He used Luis's momentum, lifted his own arm up following Luis's and then drove the hand holding the blade deep into the man's left thigh, where it got stuck in the bone. Luis's eyes bulged, and he collapsed. His mouth opened, but his cry never came. The blood spurting out of his inner thigh formed a pool that spilled underneath him.

The man who'd stopped Pablo knelt next to Luis and pressed on his leg, but Luis's face had turned pale. His breathing had become uneven, and he brought his hands to his throat, as though they could help him find his breath.

Carmen was bunched into a ball inside the barn, eyes shut tight and hands over her ears. Alfonso walked to her. He checked his hands and wiped the specks of blood away on a handkerchief, which he always carried with him. He gently lifted her from the ground and took her in his arms. He shielded her from the scene and headed toward the other building.

None of Luis's men knew how to keep their boss alive. It was now a matter of a minute or so at the most before he died. Pablo caught up with him and stopped him.

"What are you going to tell your father?" he asked.

"The truth," Alfonso said as he stopped. "And get rid of the body. I don't want it brought back to Nogales."

The sun was getting low, and the gorge was plunged into half-light. River and Lewis walked together toward Dale and Askew. Dale was the first to notice them, and his body seemed to relax. Askew was talking to him, and he stopped and turned around to check what had attracted Dale's attention.

He stiffened and turned to Dale, his hand creeping toward his gun. Dale tensed at his reaction, and he, too, felt for his gun. Lewis and River recognized the danger, and they both shouted, "It's okay. We're okay."

Lewis and River accelerated their pace to a jog so they could reach the other men and defuse the tension. Askew gave Lewis a quizzical look, and Lewis nodded. "We've decided to trust each other."

"What?" Askew said. "With your own gun pointed at your back?"

Lewis turned to River and shrugged. "She hasn't gunned me down yet."

River shrugged back. "I guess I won't now."

"Where is Gary?" Askew asked, relaxing a fraction.

"A rookie mistake," Lewis grumbled.

"He's tied to a tree with his own cuffs and my socks in his mouth," River added.

Lewis roared with laughter, and Askew looked horrified.

River raised a finger. "The socks were clean."

Lewis's laugh stopped dead, and his hand instinctively went to the place where his gun should be. Dale did the same.

"Someone's up there," Askew said, his hand on his gun, too.

River waved and gave the thumbs-up. "Someone has been up there for a while."

They waited a moment, and Miguel appeared from behind a boulder a hundred yards from where they were all standing. He had slung his rifle over his shoulder and was walking fast toward them. River introduced him to the other agent and former agent.

"So we're a happy family, are we?" Miguel said with a hint of doubt in his voice.

"We're good on my side," Lewis said, "although my son is still stuck somewhere on the path to the ravine with some socks in his mouth."

Lewis spoke with authority, and she gathered he must be the informal head of his team. Dale and Miguel looked at her. She guessed she must the head of their team.

"How about we go somewhere nearby, and you tell us what you know?" River suggested.

Lewis thought for a minute and then nodded. "Deal."

They started walking up the path toward Miguel's car. Lewis murmured, "Even with this team, taking on the cartel won't be easy. It's the army that deals with them in Mexico, and it's a never-ending battle."

"I gathered that," River said, "but we can start with our own American citizens—the ones who sold us short to make a profit and who couldn't care less how much pain and death they cause around them. Those traitors are the worst."

Lewis nodded, and they kept going in silence until they reached the top of the cliff.

"Our vehicle is not very far from here," Lewis said. "Perhaps you can give us a lift. And then I'll go and free my boy."

"You can go in my car," Dale said.

"I've got a bike," River said. "I'll follow Miguel."

A buzz inside her jacket told her that her phone must have picked up enough of a signal to receive a message, and then a series of texts started beeping, one after the other. Her throat tightened, and she rushed to retrieve the device. Rosa was trying to contact her, and her messages were the same.

Carmen has gone missing. Help.

River stuck her fingers in her hair and let out a cry. The four men around her froze. It wasn't hard to imagine that something bad had happened.

"My niece is missing," River said.

Miguel was the first to react. "From where?"

"From school. There was a sort of fair there, and she was going with friends," River said, checking her watch—5:01 p.m. She then shook her head. "Rosa must have tried to pick her up after the event finished."

But then she realized she didn't know and might be making the wrong assumption. "I've gotta go, now."

"We'll be at the Moon Room," Dale said. "Call us as soon as you know something—or sooner, if you need us."

Miguel and River rushed to Miguel's car. They drove in silence until they reached the place where River had hidden her bike.

River couldn't speak, but she squeezed Miguel's shoulder and ran out of the car to find the bike. She straddled it and was off. Grit flew from her rear wheel when she hit the path. Stopping to call would cost her precious time. She needed to get back and speak to Rosa.

She pushed the bike as hard as she could. The Yamaha responded, and she could feel the pressure of the air building against her leather jacket. The needle of the speedometer was creeping dangerously close to one hundred miles an hour. She was weaving her way through traffic without regard for her own safety. Something terrible had happened, and she couldn't shake the overwhelming feeling that it was her fault.

Rosa's car was parked in front of the house when River arrived. She left the bike next to it, took her helmet off, and removed her backpack from the storage compartment of the bike. She slid the Glock into the pack and went inside. Rosa was on the phone. She was speaking to someone in Spanish. River couldn't understand, but she could hear the urgency in Rosa's voice.

When River arrived in the kitchen, Rosa swirled around, and the change in her face devastated River. Fear was etched on it, and her eyes were wide open, as though the shock of not finding Carmen was playing in front of them in a loop. River worried for an instant that Rosa wouldn't want to see her, but instead she ended the call and collapsed in River's arms.

"They've taken her," she said. She started crying, big heavy sobs that lifted her chest in an uneven rhythm.

River wrapped her arms around her and started to rock Rosa slowly. The rage that rose in her chest was as intense as Rosa's despair.

Rosa pushed herself away from River and wiped her eyes on the sleeve of her pullover.

"This is what I received," she said as she showed the text to River.

No police or she dies—instructions to follow.

River checked the time stamp of the message: 4:38 p.m.

"Luke is on his way," Rosa said. "He was visiting an elderly patient outside Saint Ab when I called him."

"Who were you talking to just now, if I may ask?"

"Carmen's school principal. She's asking the staff who helped at the fair whether anyone has seen anything."

River frowned. "You better tell me what happened, and I'm sorry you have to revisit this, but—"

Rosa interrupted her. "It's okay. You need to know if you're to help."

Rosa pulled a kitchen stool close to her and flopped onto it. River chose the stool next to hers.

"The fair happens once a year. There are activities for the kids. Then they play games, have snacks. Mothers bake cakes in turn, bring knickknacks to sell for charity," Rosa said. "I went to join her and her friends at four o'clock, and she wasn't in the main hall, or the restroom, or the cloakroom or anywhere."

Rosa stopped abruptly. Her eyes welled, and River took her hand in hers.

"We looked everywhere," Rosa managed in a wobbly voice. "We just couldn't find her."

"What about her raincoat and backpack?"

"Gone as well."

River thought for a moment. "Does the school have cameras?"

"Not inside, but outside, yes. We looked with the principal and didn't see her leave," Rosa said. "And before you ask, we've told Carmen a million times about not trusting anyone she doesn't know."

Rosa bit her lip, not able to continue.

"I think Carmen is a clued-in kid," River said. "She wouldn't follow a stranger."

Rosa frowned. She hadn't had time to consider this, and the realization seemed to transmute fear into fury. "You think someone who knew her—oh, my God. This is evil. Some SOB who knows the family has done this."

"Hang on," River said. "I'm just saying it's a strong possibility."

"But no," Rosa said, shaking her head and squeezing River's hand hard. "That's the only explanation. The person knew her schedule well, was trusted enough for Carmen to go with him." Rosa was trembling as she said, "Who?"

River could feel the anger rise in her again. "Whoever that person is must know the school pretty well if they avoided the security cameras outside and the staff inside."

They both fell silent for a moment, and then one single name came to River's mind. Her stomach twisted at the thought.

How could he?

The look on Rosa's face told River that she had come up with her own name, too. She didn't have time to share it before the front door was thrown open and Luke ran inside the house. His face was ashen, and he looked as though he would start crying any moment. He pulled Rosa from the stool and squeezed her in his arms.

River slipped from her stool and stepped away to give them space. The name she'd come up with was buzzing in her head. It fit too well, but if she was right, she knew exactly what he wanted in exchange for Carmen.

Rosa let go of Luke gently and then said, "I received another message."

She showed him the text referring to no police involvement and the arrival of further instructions. Luke asked, "Do they want money? Is that it?"

Rosa glanced briefly at River and then shook her head. "We don't know. We have to wait."

"But is it a good idea to keep the police out?" Luke said.

"That's what they said to do. And anyway, do you trust Sheriff Andersen?" Rosa said.

Luke threw his arms in the air. "You're obsessed with Andersen's being involved with drug cartels, but you don't know for sure."

Rosa turned to River and said, "Talk to your brother. This denial of his has gone too far. Just tell him."

Now both Luke and Rosa were looking at River with a rare intensity. She gave a brief sigh and said, "Okay. I think I need to come clean."

Luke crossed his arms over his chest, and River felt her anger rise instantly. She'd seen him adopt the same posture so many times when they were kids. He, the big brother who was so much wiser, questioning her, the younger sibling who had no clue about the world. It never used to end well, and River doubted today would be any different. Some things never change.

"I was on the bike yesterday, exploring the canyon on the Silver Rim side, when I came across a mine. I don't think anybody knows it's there."

River's mouth had run dry, and she ran her tongue quickly over her lips. Luke hadn't moved, and his eyes were now boring into her.

"Then I heard cars approaching. I didn't know who it was, so I got worried, and I hid."

Still no movement from Luke.

"It was Sheriff Andersen and another car," River continued. She wasn't prepared to say it was almost certainly Harry Wilson—one bombshell at a time. "When I tried to leave the site without being noticed, he shot me. I'm glad he's a crap shot, but that's where I damaged my jacket. A rock splinter got me in the arm."

River showed the hole in the arm of her leather jacket as proof of what she was saying. Luke barely looked at it and said, "And what were you doing there anyway? What were you looking for?"

The coldness with which Luke asked the question sent a chill down River's spine, and she recalled that on Harry Wilson's USB drive her brother's name had come up as "testing." But it was Rosa who responded instead. She thumped the kitchen counter with such force that the cutlery in the canister jumped in a metallic crunch.

"Enough," she shouted. "Your stubbornness is going to kill people. It may even have killed innocents already, but I'll be damned if it kills Carmen."

Rosa's face was like thunder as she lashed out at Luke. "River has done what no one else has dared do to keep us all safe, and this isn't the time to be pointing fingers. This is the time to be strong. And it isn't only Andersen who's rotten to the core; it's also your good pal

Harry Wilson. This motherfucker who comes to our home, eats food at our table, and plays with our kids—"

The sound of a text on Rosa's phone stopped her dead. She dashed to her cell and read the message. The device fell out of her hands onto the counter as she raised her hands to her mouth. She looked at River with desperate eyes.

River picked up the phone and read.

River Swift and what she's stolen from us in exchange for your daughter.

Chapter 18

Luke snatched the phone from River and read the text as well. The anger in his eyes transformed into hatred. River Swift had come back into his life to wreak havoc.

"You can't help it, can you?" Luke screamed. "It's all about you and your great ideas about what's right, never thinking about the impact on others around you. You're a selfish cow, River. You always were. You've never had a second thought about what it meant for the family to do things your own way. And now you come *here*, in *my* house, and start hurting *my family*, too."

Rosa's face dropped, and River took a deep breath.

Here we go again. The good boy against the bad girl.

"It's always the same story with you, Luke. You can't cope with the pressure of bad things happening, and you take it out on me," River replied as coolly as she could. "And in any case, if you'd been honest with me after our parents died and told me that you have a box containing some of their personal effects, I might have not come down here to find out."

"What?" Luke stammered, looking at Rosa accusingly.

"That's right. I've seen the box in the attic. You should have remembered that this place used to be my house, too," River said, her voice rising. "And just so we're clear, since you seem to be in a mood to bring up the past, I learned that Mom and Dad were murdered, and I intend to find out why. You won't want to know, since it would disturb your well-ordered world. But don't worry: Once I check the box contents and take what's mine, you won't see me again."

River felt out of breath, the anger and resentment draining her. "Now, for the time being, I'll concentrate on finding Carmen. I don't care if it costs me my life."

The sound of another text hitting Rosa's cell stopped Luke from responding. He read it aloud.

> **Devils Playground arroyo, near the Ledge, one hour, River on her own. We'll know if she isn't.**

The anger that was suffocating the room dissipated instantly. The focus returned to Carmen, but Luke's sidelong glance at River told her it wasn't the end of the matter between the two of them.

"What are you going to do?" Rosa said, her voice trembling.

"If you read the text again," River said, "it doesn't tell you how they will free Carmen. So you need to establish this by sending a text back."

Luke was about to object, but Rosa grabbed the cell from his hands and stepped back. There was a tense moment when she dared him, in a silent duel, to take the device away from her, but Luke retreated. Rosa typed a text and waited for a reply, phone in hand. The cell pinged, and she read the reply aloud.

> **Once we've checked that the goods are there, we'll release Carmen near the Sand Mount.**

"The Sand Mount is the next big landmark after the Ledge," Rosa said, anticipating River's question.

"How far are they from each other?"

"Quarter of a mile, perhaps a little less," Rosa said.

River thought about it for a minute. She couldn't tell Rosa and Luke that she didn't buy the idea Carmen would be freed. If, in fact, the man who abducted her was Harry; he wouldn't want Carmen to live. The thought made her sick to her stomach.

"Whatever you do, we're coming with you," Luke said, breaking the silence.

River shook her head. "I understand why you would want to, but I can't protect you two and Carmen as well."

"This isn't negotiable," Luke replied, his voice rising again.

"You have another child who needs his parents," River said, holding her ground. "What happens if there's a shoot-out?"

Rosa stuck her head in her hands and shouted, "The clock is ticking. We need to do what's best for our kids."

Luke looked at her. "But someone needs to be there to collect Carmen if they—"

"Kill me," River said. "I know, and you're right. I have someone trustworthy in mind."

"Who?" Rosa and Luke asked in unison.

River hesitated, but she had to give a name, or they wouldn't agree to stay behind.

"Dale Jackson."

Luke frowned.

"The young police officer who helped with the girl who was found in the Silver Rim canyon," Rosa explained.

"I thought all police officers were corrupt," Luke spat.

"He's the exception." Rosa forced a small smile. "I think he's a good choice."

River looked at her watch and then said, "I must go. I'll call you as soon as I have news—or Dale will."

She didn't need to elaborate. She grabbed her backpack and her helmet and went out of the house. As she was straddling her bike, she allowed herself a moment of despair.

What if I can't save Carmen?

She held back the tears. Failure wasn't an option, just as it wasn't when she was sent to retrieve wounded operatives in theater—there, too, it was a matter of life and death. River picked up her burner phone from within her jacket and rang Miguel.

"What's happening?" Miguel simply said as he answered her call.

"Me and the evidence we have in exchange for Carmen," she simply said.

There was a short silence and then, "Where and when?"

"The Devils Playground arroyo, next to the Ledge. Forty-five minutes."

"They'll shoot you dead from the cliff," Miguel said angrily.

"But you guys won't let that happen, will you?" River replied.

Another short silence. "What have you got in mind?"

"This is what we're going to do." River said. She wasn't ready to give up on life. She had a score to settle on behalf of her parents.

The bedroom was plunged into half-light. Carmen was huddled on Alfonso's bed. He put a blanket around her and gave her a fresh water bottle. She took a few angry sips and curled up in the blanket. Alfonso went back to his desk chair, satisfied that the young girl was okay for the time being.

But what am I going to do?

Pablo had gone back to the barn to help get rid of Luis's body. Alfonso could count on his own men, but Luis's men would now be angry. The death of their leader meant that they had dropped a few notches down in the pecking order within the Cruz Cartel. And no one liked to be downgraded, especially gun-toting men eager to use their weapons.

A knock at the door startled him. His hand moved toward the drawer where he kept a SIG, but the door opened, and Pablo entered.

"Is it done?" Alfonso asked.

"Not quite. We've wrapped up the body in plastic bags. I've kept Luis's men away, but they'll know sooner or later that his body isn't going back to Mexico."

"I'll deal with that when we move the lab. I was going to wait for a couple of days, but I'm no longer sure we have the time," Alfonso said.

Pablo nodded but then said, "I haven't come to talk about the body: One of Luis's men said that someone is on his way to see you."

217

Alfonso frowned, and Pablo indicated they should leave the room with a small tilt of his head.

"I'm going to stand outside for a moment," Alfonso said to Carmen.

Carmen's eyes widened, and fear shot across them.

"I promise I'll be right outside. See?" Alfonso said as he went to open the door. "I'll even leave the door ajar."

Carmen nodded, and Pablo stepped out first, followed by Alfonso.

"Who's coming?" he murmured.

"Harry Wilson," Pablo whispered. "According to Luis's man, he's the one who abducted the girl. Again, according to him, this woman, River Swift, has stolen details of our operation from Harry, and he wants them back."

Alfonso fell silent for a moment and then said, "It's too late. We need to move the operation now."

Pablo frowned. "The chemists are cooking the last batch, and the girls are on their way. They'll be here tomorrow morning."

Alfonso took a step away from the door he'd left ajar and surveyed the landscape in the distance. "But the weather is turning."

The sun had just dipped below the horizon, but the light of dusk was enough for him to see an accumulation of clouds in the west. The rain would come. Alfonso just didn't know when. He'd consider the move once he'd had his conversation with Harry and plan accordingly.

Pablo's cell buzzed. He read the text. "Harry's here."

"Bring him to me. I'll sit outside."

Pablo turned around and made his way to the main building. Alfonso sat on an old bench he used only at night. There was no other chair or place to sit, and he wouldn't ask Harry to share the bench—sharing wasn't the way business was done in the cartel world, and today he felt like upholding that tradition. Harry would stand to hear what Alfonso had to say. He thought about getting his gun, but that would be overkill—literally.

Night had fallen and so had the temperature. The moon was only visible intermittently, which confirmed to Alfonso that thick clouds had gathered in the sky. There would be just enough light coming from inside his bedroom to see Harry as Alfonso informed him of his decision.

A silhouette appeared a few yards away. Alfonso would not have recognized Harry, but he recognized the man who was walking a few steps behind him. Pablo was following Harry in a way that suggested Harry hadn't come to the lab to speak to Alfonso but to Luis.

Harry's lean face was turned upward as he climbed the small slope that led to Alfonso's room. He stopped abruptly but was shoved forward by Pablo. He turned around in anger, but he had almost reached his destination and realized it was too late to turn back. He kept going without a word until he stood a few feet from the head of the Cruz Cartel in the United States.

"You and Luis kidnapped this young girl, Carmen. Why?"

Harry wasn't expecting such a direct question. His mouth opened a few times, yet he was unable to utter a word.

"What is it that you want in exchange for her?"

Pablo moved to the left of Harry, standing a few feet away—the perfect angle for a direct shot. Harry looked at the two men, and for the first time Alfonso detected fear on his face.

Harry coughed and then said, "A woman called River Swift has taken a few important items from me, and I want them back."

"I suppose we're not talking about matters that are personal to you, like the name of your mistress, or the fact that you have a child no one knows about, because that would be abusing the Cruz Cartel's assets."

"No, of course not," Harry blurted out.

"Then it must mean that you have lost valuable information that belonged to the Cruz Cartel, and that isn't right, is it?" Alfonso was enjoying making this worm of a man wriggle and squirm.

"Well," Harry said, running a finger inside the collar of his shirt, "at least the USB drives she took are password-protected."

"Any password can be cracked, and if the feds get those drives, a password isn't going to stop them."

Harry's permanent frown deepened. "My contacts at the feds in

Salt Lake City are telling me that there is no alert concerning Saint Ab."

"At least not yet," Alfonso said.

He leaned back against the bench and took his time to observe Harry. Alfonso couldn't be sure, but he thought the man was shaking.

"What is on those USB drives, anyway?"

Harry was about to answer when Alfonso lifted his hand. "Don't think about lying to me. I'll look at what's on these drives, and you better not have left out any details."

Harry took a moment then said, "There are three drives—one with the names of the cartel's informants and helpers as well as potential recruits, one with a list of the drug shipments as they pass through Saint Ab, and one with a list of the girls trafficked, either as mules or sex slaves."

Harry looked as though he might be sick.

Alfonso leaned forward, elbows on knees and head bent. He had already decided what would happen next, but getting Harry to suffer the excruciating pain of not knowing what his fate might be gave Alfonso a small sense of justice.

"How did it happen?"

"This woman River Swift got into my office, forced the drawer on my desk open, and stole the drives."

"Any alarm in your office?"

"State-of-the-art."

Alfonso nodded. "She must be pretty smart."

Harry didn't reply, and Alfonso could sense that Harry was at a loss.

"And you decided that kidnapping the young girl would prove you're as smart as she is? Or was it desperation?"

"Luis thought it would work."

"Luis isn't known for his sharp thinking," Alfonso replied with a cold smile. "So you were desperate. And if I hadn't discovered the girl, you would have recovered the USB drives, killed the two Swifts, and hoped that would be the end of it. But it didn't happen that way, and so now I'm going to tell you how the story ends."

Harry gave a small nod.

"You will take Carmen to the meeting point and recover the drives. Pablo will come with you to make sure Carmen isn't hurt. And then you will disappear—leave Saint Ab, leave Utah, and, if you're smart, leave the country. Because if I or my men come across your name or your face ever again, I will have you killed, and your death won't be quick."

Harry froze. Alfonso imagined with satisfaction that Harry's mind was racing.

"But she's seen this place—and you."

"I'm moving this operation tonight. We're almost done here, and if you think about contacting the feds for protection, you know how it will end, don't you?"

Pablo got closer to Harry, a silent yet overwhelming threat.

"I'm going to get Carmen now. Pablo will look after her as you make the exchange. You try anything funny, and he will gun you down like the dog you are."

Alfonso stood up and walked the short distance to his bedroom. The door was still ajar, and Carmen was still curled up on his bed, wrapped up in the blanket he'd given her. Alfonso walked to the bed, and Carmen sat up. She looked scared again, and Alfonso couldn't bear to see the fear in her eyes.

"You're going back to your mama," Alfonso said.

Carmen nodded slowly, not sure whether she should believe Alfonso.

"Come on," he said, extending a hand toward her. Carmen slid from the bed, still hugging the blanket. He took it away from her gently and wrapped it around her shoulders. They both walked out of Alfonso's bedroom toward the small yard where Harry and Pablo were waiting. Carmen didn't recognize Harry until they were near the bench on which Alfonso had sat to deliver his judgment. She recoiled and hid behind Alfonso.

"Don't worry. You're not going with him but with Pablo, and Pablo will take care of you, just as I've done."

Carmen looked at Pablo, whose face she couldn't quite see. He moved a little closer and nodded with a smile. "You're like my little sister," he said.

Carmen looked at Alfonso for guidance and then one more time at Harry.

"In a couple of hours' time, you'll be with your mama," Alfonso said, indicating that she should go with Pablo.

Carmen hesitated, but she suddenly ran the short distance between Alfonso and Pablo and clung to Pablo's side.

"Where is your meeting?" Alfonso asked.

"The Devils Playground arroyo, next to the Ledge," Harry said, his voice trembling.

"Off we go," Pablo said. "You go first, and no funny business." He opened his jacket to reveal his gun holster.

Harry started to walk down toward the labs, and Alfonso asked, "Are you taking the car?"

"I am, and Harry is traveling in the trunk."

"I'll see you later," Alfonso said.

He watched as Carmen and Pablo disappeared into the night. The air had become a little thicker, and he said, almost to himself, "A storm is coming."

Pablo lifted an arm in acknowledgment—a storm was indeed coming.

The second crack of thunder came with the first raindrops. The rain had moved in steadily from the west and was now over her. River was almost at the meeting point—the Devils Playground arroyo, near the Ledge. She could see the sheer drop of the cliff getting closer and understood where the place got its name from. She'd kept her helmet on but now lifted the visor just enough to shield her face from the rain.

She'd checked her watch a moment ago, and it was five to seven. She'd be at the rendezvous point just on time. She stopped and surveyed the landscape once more. She was arriving at the narrowest point in the gorge. The cliffs on each side resembled an unassailable rock face. Her plan had to work, or she'd become a sitting duck at a fairground stall.

In the distance, three silhouettes appeared. She could already tell that one of them was Carmen. She felt a pang of relief and forced herself to keep moving forward at a slow pace. The earbud in her ear crackled, and Miguel said in a low tone, "In position." The helmet was a good way to hide the earbud, and they agreed to keep conversation to a minimum. What she now knew, though, was that Miguel and the other three men had settled along the ridge of the cliff. She hoped they had chosen well and perhaps identified the places along the ridge the cartel men had themselves selected. Gary, John Lewis's son, was on his way back to Salt Lake City to get a larger team and help intercept the Cruz Cartel's new shipment of girls and drugs.

River moved into the open, making sure that the two men had seen her. She recognized Harry's tall and thin frame, and anger gripped her in a way it rarely did. The rain lashing at her in a sudden vigorous burst reminded her that her priority was Carmen and nothing else. She took a few more steps and then stopped. Something must have changed in the cartel's plan. Carmen wasn't supposed to be at the Devil's Playground arroyo, where River was due to surrender the USB drives she'd stolen from Harry's office. Carmen was supposed to be released later, at the Sand Mount.

"If you have a gun, it would be a good time to drop it to the ground," the cartel man said. "And do it slowly."

River moved her hand to her back, where the Glock was sitting. She pulled it out unhurriedly and then showed it over her head, holding it by the butt, finger away from the trigger. She then dropped it to the ground and waited.

"Anything else I need to be worried about?"

"No," River shouted back. "I need to pull something out of my jacket, though."

She took a small plastic bag that contained the flash drives out of her jacket pocket. She held the bag high so that the two men could see she had what they were looking for. The man she didn't recognize spoke to Harry. Harry seemed to hesitate, but he took a few steps forward. The light had dimmed even further, and parts of the gorge were plunged into total darkness.

"Harry's going to collect the items that belong to us and check that they are the right devices, then we'll release the girl," the other man shouted. He had a slight Spanish accent, but he didn't hesitate when choosing his words in English. His voice bounced around the walls of the arroyo, although their echo was dampened by a new bout of rain.

"So you're going to let us go?" River shouted back. Whatever he said, she wouldn't believe him, but it gave Miguel and the others time to spot the cartel man and make sure he came down if he drew a gun—or at least that was the plan.

"Yes," he replied.

Harry had started to walk. He would reach River in a minute or so. She concentrated her attention on Carmen. She was wrapped in a blanket, but her dark hair had started to cling to her face, wet with rain. A clap of thunder startled everyone. It bounced in a strange way around the canyon. Harry seemed to vacillate, and then River understood. Someone had used the thunder rumbling to cover the sound of the first shot.

She ran past Harry toward the cartel man. He'd grabbed Carmen in his arms and was running for cover. The shooting had started in earnest. Flashes of light along the rim of the cliff above River illuminated the night. She didn't stop to check on Harry but turned left and accelerated to reach Carmen. A couple of shots almost got her, and she started to zigzag, hoping it would help her evade the gunfire. The light down in the arroyo had become so dim that any shooter would need night-vision goggles to make an accurate hit.

The cartel man had reached the rock face and found a place to hide from the shooting above. Miguel hadn't contacted her on the phone.

"What's going on?" she said. "Miguel, are you okay?"

"I'm a little busy right now," Miguel said. "We've got two groups of shooters, one on each side of the cliff. John is doing well, with one down already. I can't speak for Dale and Loren. These cartel guys were here way before we arrived—"

River heard the discharge of a gun—*bapbapbap*—and then Miguel's "Gotta go."

She carried on running and slammed against a boulder. She rolled to the ground from the impact, swearing.

She crawled behind the boulder and tried to figure out where Carmen was. She thought the cartel man had dipped to the left of her but couldn't be sure. Harry was still hobbling away, trying to escape the canyon altogether. Part of her wanted to drag his sorry ass to jail, but it would have to wait. The fighting above their heads was still going strong, so River risked a low call.

"Is Carmen safe?" she said in the direction most likely to reach the place where they hid.

"She is," the cartel man replied just loudly enough so she could hear.

"I still have the drives," River said. "We can do the swap."

There was a silence, and then he said, "Are some of the men shooting above us yours?"

"Are some of the men shooting above us *yours*?" River replied.

She thought she heard a chuckle. "They are cartel men, but not ones I'd want to rely on," the man said.

"Then I won't feel so bad if my people kill some of those people," River said, and then she added, "Are they on Harry's side?"

"That's one way to put it."

"What's your name?" River asked, hoping to establish some level of trust.

He hesitated but then said, "Pablo."

A low rumble that didn't resemble thunder stopped the conversation. As the sound became louder, Pablo broke cover and shouted in the direction of River, "A flood is coming. We need to get to higher ground."

River ran in his direction, and he started to speed along the steep walls of the cliff. The roaring sound that came from upstream as the flood moved rapidly toward them told River they had only moments to flee. Pablo didn't run past the arroyo's gully but stopped and started to climb with Carmen on his back. A moment later, River reached the place where Pablo had started the climb. Her hands felt the rock, and she detected indentations cut in the stone. No doubt an escape route carved by traffickers. She followed Pablo as a stream of dirty water started to flow into the arroyo.

Pablo was doing well, and she was impressed with how well he was managing to keep moving up with Carmen clinging to him like a baby monkey. She followed in his footsteps, taking more time to find the footholds that had been carved in the rock. It had become slippery with rain, and she slid a couple of times, barely able to keep her balance and still hold on.

A cry of anguish made her raise her head abruptly and almost lose her footing. She worried that Pablo had slipped, but another desperate cry told her that the sound was coming from below. Harry had been caught by the rising water as he tried to make his way toward the escape route. Debris was now rushing past in the rising water, hitting everything that was in its path. He kept fighting the current but making little progress. River surveyed the landscape below her. There was a space between two large rocks. If he could reach it, the boulders would protect him from the debris.

River hesitated, but the part of her that wanted him judged in a court of law got the better of the part that wanted to see him dead.

"To the right," she shouted. "Go to your right."

Harry raised his face toward her and seemed to understand what she meant. The sound of rushing water intensified all of a sudden, and Pablo shouted, "Hurry up. The bulk of the flood is coming."

River accelerated, focused on the climb. She cast an eye to the left and saw a wall of water moving in a single swoop, mercilessly hitting the sides of the cliff. She kept going as fast as she could, but she'd lost some precious time. Pablo shouted again. "Go to your right—come on."

The sound was deafening, and the water hit her feet and legs. She could feel the pull of it. She pushed up, but the water seemed to be rising faster than she was. She felt her foot slip. She was losing her balance and raised her arm in desperation.

A hand grabbed her and pulled her up in one go. Pablo clung to a rope that must have been there to help climbers scale the last few steps over the edge of the cliff. River grabbed the rope, too, and managed to find purchase again. She climbed the last few steps and rolled over the rim, exhausted. She removed her helmet and fell on her back.

Someone dove onto her and squeezed her tight. River folded her arms around Carmen and scooched to the side, away from the precipice. They huddled for a moment, Pablo crouching next to them. The shooting seemed to have stopped, but there was no way of knowing which side had won.

"What happened to Harry?" he said.

"Gone," River replied as she sat up, Carmen in her lap.

He shrugged and waited a moment. The rain had subsided, and so had the flood below. They could hear the rush of water, but it somehow felt calmer.

"Where are your people positioned?" he said. "I'd like to avoid being their next target."

"I'll speak to them," River said as she pushed her earbud back in position and took her phone out of her jacket.

"Miguel," she simply said.

"Madre de Dios, I thought you were gone."

"I've got Carmen with me, and Pablo saved me from the flood just in time."

"We got two cartel guys, but I'm not convinced there aren't more. The shooting has also stopped on the other side, and John tells me that they got three guys on that side."

"Okay, I'll be careful," she said. "But please don't shoot the guy next to me. Carmen and I owe him one."

"I'll let the others know."

"We're good," River said.

Pablo and she rose slowly. The blanket had been lost in the climb, and Carmen was shivering. She needed to get out of her wet clothes.

River knelt in front of her, taking off her own jacket so she could put it over Carmen's shoulders. But the crack of a gunshot made her dive to the ground with Carmen in her arms.

Pablo opened his eyes wide and stumbled forward until a second shot pushed him toward the edge. His arms whirled around, trying to find something to hold on to, but it was too late. He fell backward, and his body was swallowed by darkness and the floodwater.

"No," River shouted.

A flurry of retaliatory shots and the sound of Miguel swearing told River that it wasn't her camp who'd shot him, and though she was sure Pablo's killer was now also dead, it was only a small consolation. She hadn't even thanked the man who'd saved both her and Carmen.

Chapter 19

"Are you hurt? Are you okay?" Miguel was shouting in her earbud. River had dropped her phone to the ground when she dove down to protect Carmen. She kept her niece tight in her arms, picked up the phone to ensure they were still connected, and replied to Miguel, "We're unhurt, but we need to get away from the ledge. It's too exposed."

"I'm coming to get you," Miguel said. "Stay low."

Carmen was shivering in her arms, and River started to rock her slowly.

"We're going home," River murmured in Carmen's ear. "We're going to see your mom and dad—and Franklin."

Carmen squeezed River even tighter. River felt the sting of tears in her eyes. Loving, cheerful, and bubbly Carmen was incapable of speech.

The sound of crunching boots approaching refocused River. She pressed the earbud to her ear. "Is that you?" she murmured.

"Yes. I can't see you yet, but I'm close to the rim of the cliff," Miguel replied.

River spotted Miguel's head and shoulders emerging from the path. His entire body appeared, and River had to stop herself from standing up and running to him. Miguel held back for a moment, crouching. He saw them, forgot about his own safety, and hurried in their direction.

River sat up, and Miguel came to kneel next to her and Carmen. She hadn't noticed them before, but night-vision goggles hung around his neck. He brought them to his eyes and surveyed their surroundings.

"I can't see anything. You guys run and make your way to my car. I'll cover you."

River sat up slowly. Carmen clung to her, and River took a moment to decide how she could make sure Carmen was secure. Her arm was still complaining from the rock climb she'd inflicted on it, but Carmen needed protecting.

"I can't carry you, honey. It's not safe if I do. But I'm going to hold your hand all the way to the car. Is that okay?"

Carmen nodded, grabbed River's hand, and locked her small hand with River's. They ran the few yards to the end of the path and started to go down a slope that would have been easy to negotiate in dry weather. But the slippery ground made it more difficult than River had expected. She slipped a few times, almost taking Carmen down with her. The path widened, and the lights of a vehicle turning toward them made River stop.

"It's Lewis," Miguel said from behind. "He went back to collect his SUV and drove as close as he could to the path."

River accelerated and made her way to the place where the SUV had stopped. Lewis got out and went to the trunk. He opened it and got a blanket out, then handed it over to River just as she reached him. She crouched next to Carmen and wrapped her in the blanket, holding her tight for a moment.

"We're with friends now," River said.

Carmen snuggled into the blanket.

"What do you want to do with your bike?" Lewis asked.

"I'll have to come back to collect it later on," River said. "My priority is to return Carmen to her parents."

Miguel had come to stand next to them. "I can drive you there and back."

Lewis shook his head. "Let's think about that. I'd be surprised if your brother's house isn't under surveillance. Andersen must be eager to get the USB drives back."

"You've got a point. He'll know they failed if he sees me and . . ." Her voice trailed off, and both men nodded. She didn't need to mention Carmen's name in front of the girl.

"Someone needs to tell my brother," River said, "and then find a secure place for the family."

Again, the men nodded, understanding River's half-spoken plan. River then took out her burner phone and dialed a number.

"Dale. Are you on your way back to your car?" River asked.

"Almost there. Why?"

"I need you to help with a diversion."

Lewis had parked his car a couple of streets away from Luke's home. Neighbors were still returning from work or an early dinner, and the streets around the area were busy. He then drove past Luke's home with River and Carmen hiding in the footwell.

"They haven't tried very hard to hide," Lewis said as he identified an unmarked police car with two men inside.

"I guess that's the idea," River answered from the back seat, where she and Carmen were sitting.

Lewis returned to the spot where he'd previously parked and stopped. River called Dale, as agreed.

"We've got an unmarked car with two guys in it just opposite my brother's house," she said.

"We're on it," Dale replied. He killed the call, and River waited to see whether the plan was going to work.

Dale was to drive alongside the unmarked car, stop, and strike up a conversation with the police officers inside, whom he almost certainly knew. Askew was waiting a few cars away in case it all turned unfriendly. Dale was confident he could pull it off without alerting the two officers.

River checked her watch, and Lewis turned around from the driver's seat.

"Give him a moment. It has to look credible enough."

"You mean so-called dumbass Dale blowing a so-called undercover op?" River asked.

Lewis chuckled. "Is that what he is?"

"I never said that," River grumbled. "But that's what Andersen's men think."

"They don't like a cop not toeing the line. If you can't turn him, make him look as though he's an idiot."

The unmarked car rounded the corner of the street in which River, Lewis, and Carmen were waiting and disappeared out of sight. Lewis gave River the thumbs-up, and River smiled. Dale had delivered as he'd promised.

Lewis started his car again and drove to the Swift residence. He stopped in front of the house. Askew remained parked where he was as backup. Dale had parked around the next corner. Miguel had been tasked with returning the USB drives to the mobile home and putting together the evidence they'd collected.

"I'll wait in the car," Lewis said. "Whatever you decide with this little one's parents, Askew and I will help."

Carmen had dozed off in River arms, and River placed a few kisses on her forehead to wake her up.

"Wake up, sleepyhead. We're home."

Carmen sat up, bleary-eyed, and then stuck her nose to the window. She turned her face to River as though unsure it was real. River opened the door, and Carmen flew out of the car, ran to her parents' door, and rang the doorbell a few times, reaching it on her tiptoes.

River was now standing next to her. She heard hurried footsteps and voices. Rosa opened the door. Her eyes grew big, and she collapsed to the floor in front of her daughter. Carmen jumped into her mother's arms, and they squeezed each other tight. Luke joined them a few seconds later, dropping to the floor, too, to wrap his arms around his family.

River couldn't tell who was crying harder—the three of them had become so closely entwined. River stepped away. She, too, felt a sob rise to her throat, and she let tears flood her eyes. The pressure of a hand on her shoulder made her jump. Lewis was standing next to her.

"You should all go inside. We can't tell when Andersen's men will be back."

River nodded, wiped her tears on the sleeve of her jacket, and moved closer to her family. Lewis returned to his car, keeping watch. She knelt next to them and said in a shaky voice, "We must go inside. We need to talk."

Luke and Rosa nodded. Luke took Carmen in his arms and disappeared inside the house first. Rosa stood up slowly. Her face wet with tears; she stepped back and let River in. River closed the door behind her, and Rosa took her hands, squeezing tight.

"Thank you for bringing her back," she said. She swallowed a few times before continuing. "I'm so glad you made it, too."

River squeezed her hands back. "I'm sorry I brought all this on the family."

Rosa shook her head. "You're not responsible for the cartel and the drugs. I won't have you feel it's your fault."

"Thank you," River said before squeezing Rosa's hands one more time and then letting go.

River and Rosa went into the kitchen. They heard Luke's footsteps and turned around. He was still carrying Carmen in his arms, but he'd gotten her out of her wet clothes and into her pajamas. Franklin was cradled in her arms, purring louder than ever.

"Let's sit in the living room," Rosa suggested.

"I'll join you," Luke said.

He went to the freezer, opened it while still managing to hold Carmen and Franklin, took a Popsicle out, and closed the door. Then he sat on one of the sofas, unwrapped the treat, and gave it to Carmen. She took it and started eating it. River sat on another sofa, and Rosa sat next to her.

Luke hadn't said anything yet, and River didn't know how she should break the news to them that they no longer were safe in their home. Then Luke asked, "What happened?"

River cast an eye toward Carmen, and then Luke and Rosa understood that she couldn't give them all the details. She told them as much as she could, and they didn't interrupt, even when she subtly conveyed the news that Harry was almost certainly dead. She told them about the evidence and the plan to involve more federal agents. She brushed over the drugs and the new girls arriving, judging that they didn't need to know.

When River had finished her tale, Rosa saved her by asking the right question.

"If Andersen is still around, are we safe?"

River shook her head. "I don't think so, and neither does Agent Lewis, who's sitting outside in his car."

This time Luke didn't object when Andersen's name was dragged into the open again. River wondered whether he and Rosa had had a conversation about the subject as they were waiting for news. His question surprised River, though.

"What do you suggest we do?"

River took a breath and then said, directing her answer to Luke, "I suppose you know who Old Bill is."

"Retired police officer—lost his wife to cancer a few months ago."

"He's got a place in the mountains. A cave."

Luke's face dropped, and River hastened to add, "It's not what you think. It's been modernized and looks incredible. I've been there."

"Why?" Rosa asked. "Is someone else hiding with him?"

"Another of the girls who escaped, plus Jen, Miguel Lopez's wife."

"But don't other people know he's got a cave in the mountains?" Luke asked.

River shook her head. "He never asked for a permit to build. No one knows."

Luke nodded without objection. They remained silent for a while until Luke said, "I think Rosa and Carmen should go—and Franklin, of course." He stroked Carmen's dark locks, looking at his daughter with adoration, and then added, "I'll stay here."

Rosa was about to object, but Luke lifted his hand. "Someone needs to stay home so that Andersen and his men think we're still here waiting for news. It will confuse them and give you more time."

"We could put some of the lights around the house on timers," Rosa said. Her face was drawn with concern.

"That's not going to fool them for very long," Luke said. "I need to get out and do a couple of things like pick up the mail from the mailbox. It'll be more convincing."

River wouldn't interfere, but she knew Luke was right. Rosa got up slowly and said, "I'll go and pack a few things."

She left River and Luke on their own in an awkward silence. Carmen had finished her Popsicle. The wrapper was still bunched up in her hand. River stood up, hesitated, and took the paper from Carmen, saying, "Let me throw that away."

She hurried to the kitchen and hovered there for a moment. She couldn't believe how uncomfortable she'd become around her brother. They'd always been different from each other, but they used to have fun, too. River sighed and returned to the living room.

Carmen seemed to have fallen asleep. River was grateful that the ordeal was over and that she was now safe. River recalled how resilient children could be, even in extreme environments like war zones, always able to bounce back and find pleasure in life no matter what they'd been through. River sat where she'd sat before, waiting for Rosa to arrive with a bag, ready to go.

Luke cleared his throat, took a short moment, and said, "Thank you for bringing her back."

"No need to thank me," River said. She meant it. Despite Rosa's words of support, River couldn't help feeling that Carmen wouldn't have been in danger had she not insisted on fighting the cartel.

"About this afternoon . . ." Luke started tentatively.

Just then Rosa appeared in the doorway with a backpack and a carryall.

"I'm ready," she said.

River stood up again and took her phone out of her jacket pocket. She called Dale.

"Are you ready to drive Rosa and Carmen to the cave?"

Dale sounded pleased with the request. "Of course. I'm on my way."

"Dale will drive you there. He knows the way."

River left the room to check the outside. She walked to Lewis's SUV. He lowered his window. "What have they decided to do?"

"Carmen and her mom, Rosa, are going to the cave with Carmen's cat. My brother is staying behind to let Andersen's people believe that he and Rosa are still waiting for Carmen."

"Not a bad idea."

"Dale is going to drive them."

Dale parked his car next to Lewis's. He opened the trunk from inside and stepped out. Rosa appeared on the threshold of the house and nodded a collective hello. She slung the suitcase and backpack into the trunk. Dale closed it and opened the back door. Rosa went to give River a quick hug and then slid into the car. Luke appeared on the threshold, holding Carmen in his arms. He gently transferred her onto Rosa's lap. Franklin was sitting right outside the door, observing the scene. He looked as though he was waiting for instructions, ready to follow his human.

"One moment," Luke said. He rushed back in, returned with a harness that he quickly fitted around Franklin's body. "I'm sure Old Bill won't mind," he said as the cat jumped into the back of the car.

River nodded. She wasn't so sure, but Carmen needed her little animal with her for comfort. Old Bill would understand that, she hoped. Luke squeezed Rosa in his arms without waking up Carmen. He kissed his daughter on the forehead and then pulled back. Lewis coughed a couple of times. It wasn't a good idea to linger. Dale shut Rosa's door, got into the driver's seat, and was off.

Luke stood on the threshold for a moment and then said, "You call me as soon as you have news."

"As soon as," River replied. They waved at each other, and then he closed the door.

"Let's go and get your bike," Lewis said.

River got into the passenger seat next to him. "And then we make a battle plan."

Pablo would never be coming back. Alfonso sagged to the ground under the realization. The moment heavy shooting echoed along the ravine all the way back to the lab buildings, Alfonso knew that he and Pablo had been betrayed.

Alfonso called Ernesto, another of his trusted men, and three others and made his way to the Ledge. By the time they arrived, the floodwater had receded, and the arroyo looked calm. The force of the flood showed on the banks of the stream—trees and other debris lay there, discarded by the surge. They spotted bodies along the top of the Ledge, and every time they found one, Alfonso thought he might be confronted with Pablo's.

Luis's men seemed to have encountered a greater adversary than they'd bargained for, proving as foolish as their master had been.

"They're all dead," Ernesto said.

"No sign of"—Alfonso swallowed a few times to bring himself to say the name—"Pablo or the girl?"

Ernesto shook his head. "If the floodwater has taken them, they'll be way down the arroyo, perhaps miles away."

Alfonso walked to the edge of the cliff. The moon was now clear in the sky, obstructed only by a few clouds. He stood on the rim of the precipice, hovering between despair and rage. Another step and he would fall to his death. Alfonso felt Ernesto at his elbow and stepped back.

"What do we do now?" Ernesto asked.

"We go back to the lab," Alfonso said. "You take two men and load the drugs we've cooked in the past few days onto the trucks and then go to the mine."

"What about the last batch?"

"I'll deal with it."

Alfonso walked down the path and returned to his SUV. He made his way to the Devil's Playground lab, fighting back tears. Why had he not seen it coming? The thirst for revenge after Luis's death.

Among his own people, there'd always been two factions, Luis's and his. Luis had always had the approval of his father, Señor Cruz. Alfonso was still too new in the organization to have earned their respect.

Alfonso drove as fast as he could and arrived before Ernesto. He ran to his room, packed his few belongings, then went to Pablo's room and did the same. He pushed away the desire to delay and packed the SUV with the two bags he'd gathered. He then picked up his cell phone and dialed a number he'd never liked calling in the first place.

"Alfonso," Sheriff Andersen said, puzzled. "What can I do for you?"

"Harry didn't succeed in recovering the devices on which information about our operation was stored. I'm sure you are aware of the theft."

Alfonso let that hang. The silence at the other end of the line told him what he already suspected—that Harry Wilson, Sheriff Andersen, and Luis had decided to keep the problem to themselves.

"Perhaps I can help. If I speak to Harry—"

"You won't be speaking to Harry anytime soon—unless, of course, you want one of my men to put a bullet in your head," Alfonso enjoyed saying. "Harry is dead. Some of my men have been gunned down in the process, too. You are the police, but I can't imagine you telling your people to kill mine."

Alfonso waited for a confirmation.

"Of course not. I never would. I mean, we're on the same side." Andersen's voice wobbled.

"Then it means that either the feds or another cartel was on to them," Alfonso concluded.

"I haven't heard—"

"Whatever you've heard and whoever is informing you is irrelevant," Alfonso snapped. "I'm now short of men. I expect you and the people you trust to turn up at the mine this evening to receive the shipment arriving in the early hours of tomorrow. I won't have it going astray because you and Harry have been useless at your job."

Alfonso could feel that Andersen wanted to protest but must have thought better of it. "I'll gather my men, and we'll see you at the mine."

"And make sure you use the agreed-upon signal when you approach the mine. My people are getting rather nervous." Alfonso killed the call and made his way to the lab.

Ernesto had started to load the drugs onto a pickup truck, helped by two other cartel men. The young man in charge of the lab walked to them, face mask around his neck.

"We haven't finish cooking yet," he said, puzzled.

"Speak to Alfonso," Ernesto replied. He heaved a couple of bags full of pills over his shoulder and walked off.

Alfonso appeared on the threshold of the lab and said, "Stop what you're doing. Pack up everything as fast as you can. Then set fire to place."

The young man frowned. "You mean—"

"Yes. I want the place torched. We're not leaving any evidence behind. It's likely the feds know where we are."

Mentioning the feds focused the young chemist's mind. He started giving instructions to the other chemists and helpers who worked around the lab. Everyone hurried, clear on what their next task should be. Alfonso left them to it and went to seek Ernesto.

"We're almost done," Ernesto said as Alfonso approached.

"Get your gear before you leave. I'm burning the lab and the rest of the place down. I don't want any evidence left behind."

Ernesto didn't question Alfonso's decision. He'd seen the men who'd been gunned down on the Ledge. He knew someone was coming for them.

"Andersen is bringing his own men to the mine, since we're low on numbers. He'll use the agreed-upon signal when they get closer."

Ernesto nodded and hurried around to finish the loading. Alfonso returned to the buildings farther away from the lab. He went into the largest and found a few of his men resting from the evening rounds.

"We're moving out," he said to the most senior one. "Tell the others. I want everyone to go to the mine, but one of you should stay behind with me."

The men stood up and started to get organized. Within half an hour, the place would be empty. Alfonso returned to his room, now bare apart from a bed, table, and chair. He sat down on the floor, back against the wall, and pulled his knees up. He rested his head against the wall. His path was now unclear.

His father must have felt it when he favored Luis over him: Alfonso wasn't born to be a cartel man. Pablo had been the anchor that kept him there, but now Alfonso couldn't tell what he wanted—or perhaps it didn't matter what he wanted. What mattered was what Señor Cruz wanted. Alfonso held back tears.

Someone knocked at the door and said, "We're almost done, Alfonso."

"I'm coming," he shouted back.

Alfonso gave himself another few moments and then stood up slowly. He went to the door, took a few more seconds, then opened it.

"Gather the solvents stored at the lab and empty the cans around every building."

The man at the door looked a little surprised but nodded and walked back toward the lab. He crossed paths with Ernesto, stopped and spoke to him, then carried on.

"Everyone is ready to go," Ernesto said.

"Only a couple of cars at a time. I don't want a convoy—too visible. I'll catch up with you later."

Ernesto looked a little puzzled. "I could stay back and set fire to the buildings."

Alfonso shook his head. "My decision, my doing."

Ernesto hesitated, but Alfonso pointed to the lab, where the drivers were waiting for instructions. Ernesto took a few steps back and then turned around. Alfonso watched as he disappeared past the buildings on the far side of the old ranch. The smell of accelerant drifted past him, heavy in the air. Alfonso went to his car. He picked up a bunch of papers he intended to shred and took a lighter out of one of his bags.

He stood outside the dilapidated barn, twisted one of the papers into a long, compact cylinder, and flicked the lighter, watching as a small flame appeared. Alfonso angled the paper to help it catch fire. He waited a few seconds to make sure the flame was strong enough, walked to the building that contained what used to be his room, and opened the door.

He threw the paper inside, stepped back quickly, and slammed the door shut. The *whoosh* that followed told Alfonso that the fire had caught and would be spreading fast. And for some reason, he enjoyed the thought of destroying it all.

Chapter 20

River parked the Ténéré next to the trailer and waited for Lewis to park his SUV next to it. Miguel and Askew were already inside. River went to the door and knocked a few times. The dirty curtain that hung in the window closest to the door moved aside, and then she heard footsteps. Miguel opened the door, and both River and Lewis stepped in.

Askew was sitting at the table, a laptop open in front of him.

"Did they return?" River asked him after removing her helmet.

"Unfortunately, they did," he said. "I think it was a good move that your brother stayed behind. I didn't wait long. I didn't want Andersen's men to realize they've been fooled yet again."

"He doesn't even own a gun," River said.

"He shouldn't need one," Lewis said. "What matters is that Andersen's men think he doesn't know anything and still expects his daughter back."

River leaned against the table; not sure she shared Askew's view. "The cartel chief must know his people are dead by now, and he'll be talking to Andersen."

"But what will the head honcho's priority be?" Miguel asked.

Lewis joined them at the table and said, "Cut and run. He's got to save the drugs and the next consignment of girls."

"Retreat to the mine?" River said.

Askew nodded. "And if he has lost men, perhaps call on Andersen for reinforcement."

They all grunted in agreement and fell silent to consider how the situation was developing.

"Have you spoken to Gary about the feds' reinforcements?" River asked Askew. "If it's going to be the cartel and the sheriff's men against us four—or even five with Dale—it's not gonna happen."

"They'll be with us early tomorrow morning. Gary said they would arrive just before daybreak," Askew replied.

River looked at Lewis, not wanting to interfere with what was becoming a fed operation, but he smiled at her, welcoming her thoughts.

"I think we should go on a recce to the mine," River said. "I know the way and can get you there. I can't bear the thought of letting these SOBs get away and losing Dolores for good."

Lewis thought for a moment and said, "But we need to protect the evidence. Someone either stays here or finds a better place to wait it out until we're done with the Cruz Cartel down at the mine."

Miguel and River exchanged a look, and then Miguel said, "Old Bill's cave."

"Sounds like a good idea."

"We need to call him, though," River said. "Dale would have called when he was on his way with Rosa and Carmen."

"I'm not calling him," Miguel said, hands in the air, concerned that he was pushing his luck with the old man.

River picked up her burner phone from her jacket pocket, checked her watch—11:24 p.m.—and then dialed Old Bill's number.

"Who's coming now?" he grumbled as he picked up the call.

"I'm glad I'm not waking you up," River said, rolling her eyes as the others were listening.

"Old guys like me don't sleep much. So are you gonna tell me?"

"Miguel Lopez and a ton of evidence we collected to send Andersen and his crew to jail."

"Attagirl," Old Bill said with a smile in his voice. "I'll get Dale to wait for him at my old ranch. The cave is not easy to find in the dark."

Old Bill hung up, and River gave a thumbs-up to the crew. "Dale will be waiting for you at his ranch."

Miguel looked shocked. "That was easy."

"You tell an old cop about evidence and Andersen going to jail, he ain't gonna say no, right?"

Lewis nodded. "Once a cop . . ."

Miguel stood up and started packing the laptop onto which he had transferred the photos he'd taken at the lab and the photos River had taken of the mine. He checked that the USB drives were where he'd put them in his backpack. Miguel looked at River, Lewis, and Askew in turn and then said, "I wish I could be there with you when the feds book these motherfuckers."

Lewis was the first to extend a hand and say, "Be safe."

Askew was next. Miguel shook his hand and clapped Askew's shoulder.

River walked to the door with Miguel and gave him a brief hug.

"I'll see you tomorrow," she said.

"If you need me," Miguel said, "you know what to do."

River smiled and opened the door. She waited until Miguel was in his car to shut the door and return to the dining room.

"How about we go on that reconnaissance mission?" she said.

The heat of the flames that reached high into the sky was still on Alfonso's skin. He'd taken a few extra minutes to contemplate his handiwork. The run-down ranch had caught fire like kindling, and the memory of the blaze filled him with an odd sense of freedom. He tried to concentrate on the drive to the mine even as his attention still turned back to the fire. Pablo's loss was still too raw and incomprehensible. He couldn't yet begin to think what it truly meant to him.

Alfonso slowed the SUV to a crawl as he approached the mine. The terrain had become more rugged, and the car was bouncing off the rocks that littered the ground. No vehicle could get close to the mine without being heard—one of the reasons he'd decided on the location in the first place. He stopped the car as he was about to enter the narrowest part of the ravine and flashed his headlights—two short bursts, a three-second wait, then three short bursts.

The response came almost immediately, a flash of light matching his signal. Two men were positioned in the recess of the cliff. He started the SUV again, waved as he drove past, but didn't stop until he reached the mouth of the mine. Andersen had arrived already, and he was leaning against his own SUV, his meaty arms crossed over his chest.

Alfonso parked near the broken-down structure that stood next to the mine's entrance. He stepped out of his vehicle and waited for Ernesto to show up first. Andersen needed to be reminded what the pecking order was in the Cruz Cartel.

Ernesto emerged from the inside of the pit and went to greet his boss.

"We're ready," he said. "The fentanyl pills have been offloaded, ready to be transferred into the Vegas truck. I checked with the coyote before reception got too bad. He's on track and should arrive in the early hours. Same with the Vegas men."

Alfonso nodded. "Looks good. Where are the men positioned?"

"Three of our men are on top of the cliff. Two are guarding the drugs."

"And Andersen's men?"

"Two at the entrance of the gorge and one at the back, where the Vegas truck should arrive," Ernesto said. He moved closer to Alfonso and continued. "I've seen them speak to Luis before, so I'm not ready to trust them yet."

"Agreed," Alfonso said. "Keep an eye out."

Ernesto nodded, and Alfonso slapped his shoulder. The gesture brought memories of Pablo, and Alfonso stepped away from Ernesto, fearing his face would betray his emotions. He gathered himself and then made his way to Andersen. When he reached him, he asked, "Anything new about the identity of the men who gunned down my people?"

Andersen shook his head. "I've put some of my men on the case, but we won't have an answer until later on in the morning."

Alfonso stepped closer to Andersen in a single stride. Andersen straightened up, and they took each other's measure. The moon was now clear in the sky, illuminating the fear in Andersen's eyes.

Rage gripped Alfonso as he spat, "What? Are you too frightened to get a hold of your fed contacts in the middle of the night? Or don't you have as much control over them as you say you do?"

Andersen seemed taken aback by the force of the accusation. His eyes flicked toward the top of the cliff. He was a sitting duck, and his defiance melted away.

He put his hands up in mock surrender. "I just don't like to sound desperate when I speak to my pals. That's all."

"I lost a lot of men a few hours ago, and I want to know why."

"I'll need reception to make a call. That means leaving the gorge." Andersen hesitated.

There was a hint of desperation in his eyes that Alfonso recognized.

Good try, but not good enough.

"If you climb to the top of the cliff, you'll have enough reception," Alfonso said. He jerked his head in the direction of the stairs carved in the rock, and Andersen's face froze. He seemed transfixed by the staircase. Something must have happened there, and the thought made Alfonso want to probe harder.

Andersen was about to protest, but he must have thought better of it. He ran a hand over his forehead and lumbered toward the steps. Alfonso watched as the heavy man took a while to get to the top of the cliff. Perhaps he would slip and come crashing down. Alfonso enjoyed the thought, but Andersen finally raised himself over the edge and disappeared.

Alfonso's mind drifted again toward Pablo. He looked around and felt oddly detached—the mine, the drugs, the Cruz men. He thought about little Carmen and wondered whether she, too, had been taken by the flood. Another girl he wished hadn't been so brutalized was waiting inside for the next batch of trafficked immigrants to arrive—Dolores, ready to be delivered along with the others to the Vegas crew.

Movement at the top of the cliff drew Alfonso's attention. Andersen was on his way back down. He almost slipped, and Andersen's muffled cry made Alfonso smile.

Sweaty and out of breath, Andersen approached Alfonso. "Nothing out of the ordinary on the feds' front, but my contact is making some calls."

"When is he calling back?"

"A few hours," Andersen stammered.

Alfonso probed further. "What are you not telling me?"

Andersen took a breath.

"Two of my men are surveying the Swift residence, and they encountered someone called Dale Jackson, one of the few police officers I don't control."

"Go on," Alfonso said, eyes drilling into Andersen's.

"He wasn't driving his usual car," Andersen blurted out. "So my men decided to find out where he was going. He was heading toward the mountain, not very far from here, and he had passengers with him."

"We're close," River said.

Lewis slowed the SUV. River was seated in the back with Askew in the front seat. She was focused on finding the trail that would lead them to the mine and hadn't noticed what lay farther ahead.

"Do you see what I see?" Lewis said.

A police car had stopped on the side of the road, lights off, waiting.

"Shit. Andersen has got some of his men guarding the trail," River replied.

"There's a blanket next to you," Askew said. "Drop down to the floor and cover yourself with it. I'll stop and ask what's going on."

"Got it," River said. "Better if they don't see me."

She hunkered down behind Lewis's seat and covered herself with the blanket as the car came to a stop. Lewis rolled down his window, and she heard him ask, "Is the road ahead safe?"

The officer rolled down his own window down and said, "There is some suspicious activity down in the canyon. We're just making sure no one gets hurt. Where are you going?"

How professional . . . saving Andersen's ass.

"We're on our way to Salt Lake City," Lewis said.

"Might be a good idea to turn around," the officer replied. It didn't sound like an invitation.

"Will do," Lewis replied. River felt the car turn around and waited until Lewis gave her the all-clear.

"You can sit up," he said.

"Andersen is covering his ass. He knows you guys are on to him," River said. "We're going to have to go to the mine on foot."

"How long will it take?" Lewis asked, looking at River in the rearview mirror.

"A couple of hours, maybe a little more. We can take the first trail we find and park the car as far down as we can. Then we walk."

Lewis nodded and waited for River to tell him where to turn.

"Here," she said, pointing to a place at the side of the road that anyone unfamiliar with the area would miss.

Lewis drove past, slowed down, and turned around. He killed the headlights and drove down a steep path that led to a narrow platform overlooking the ravine. He turned off the engine, and they waited, listening and watching. The sound of a car driving past made River hold her breath for a moment.

"Andersen's guys are checking on us?" she whispered.

"Or it might be another car," Askew murmured.

"At one o'clock in the morning?"

"Never mind," Lewis said. "Let's get moving."

They all got out of the car, careful to minimize the sounds they made. Lewis checked his phone. He had just enough reception to read the text messages he'd received. Gary was confirming a dawn ETA.

"I'm texting him about the other police car. They'll need to tackle them before they can set up the operation around the mine."

River transferred the Glock from her jacket pocket to her waistband against her back. She checked that the spare clip was in her pants pocket and stuffed her binoculars into her jacket pocket. The men slung MP5s over their shoulders and checked the sidearms in their holsters—Lewis had a SIG and Askew a Glock.

River led the way as they started down a narrow path that wove between rocks all the way to the bottom of the canyon. They moved in silence apart from the occasional low swearing as they slid on gravel and lose stones. When they reached the bottom, they stopped. River took her binoculars out of her pocket and scoped the terrain.

"We can get there in one of two ways. Along the ravine, closely following one of the cliffs, or to the south, along a trail that'll lead us to the top of the cliff."

Lewis stretched his hand out, and River gave him her binoculars. He spent a moment surveying the landscape.

"I presume it'll take more time to get to the top of the cliff?" Lewis said, binoculars still to his eyes.

"That's right. But we won't run the risk of being spotted from above."

"You're right," Lewis said, glancing at his watch. "It's worth the extra time. And we're more likely to get reception on the cliff top than below."

Lewis returned the binoculars to River, and they set off again across the rocky terrain. River walked due south, away from the mine for a little while, until they reached the bikers' trail she'd ridden on her way to Old Bill's ranch. She stopped before they started the climb.

"When we're close to the top, I'll go first. I think the terrain is pretty flat, and I want to make sure we're alone."

Both men nodded, and they started the climb. The trail was steep, and River wished she was on her bike. She turned back a couple of times to check whether the two feds were following. Lewis and Askew were concentrating on the task but not lagging behind, so she accelerated her pace. She then stopped and turned back, calling Lewis in a low voice.

"We're almost there. Let me check and report."

Lewis nodded, and she made her way to a place where the ground flattened and opened onto the top of the cliff. River surveyed the landscape once more with her binoculars. She thought she saw movement in the far distance. She checked the terrain nearer to them and spotted a string of rocks and boulders they could use to get closer to their destination. She slid down and onto the path and crouched to the ground. Lewis and Askew sat on a rock, waiting.

"I can't be sure, but I think there's movement near the mine. We can follow a string of boulders and get close enough, but we won't be right on them," she murmured.

"That makes sense. Whoever leads these guys has positioned men on top of the cliff. Just get us as close as you can. As long as we can see what's happening down below as well," Lewis said. "We don't want to miss the trafficked girls when they arrive."

River stood up slowly and checked her Glock. She moved to the top of the path, used the binoculars once more, and then, confident that no one was watching, ran low to the first boulder. She flattened herself against it and waited a few seconds. All was quiet around them. She turned around and gave a thumbs-up to Lewis. He ran low toward her, and then Askew followed.

River gave the men another thumbs-up. Both men nodded. She started moving from rock to boulder, running low, with Lewis and Askew running behind her. They were halfway there when River stopped them from progressing by holding her fist up. She indicated she would progress alone. Then she ran to the next rock and stopped, listening.

She heard a low sound she couldn't quite identify. She slid to the ground and lifted herself a little so she could use the binoculars to survey the landscape. And this time she saw them—three men dressed in jeans with black T-shirts and Kevlar vests, muscles bulging out of their sleeves. Each carrying weapons she thought were

AR-15s. She couldn't make out their faces, but she was certain they were cartel men.

The sound intensified, and she used the binoculars once more to try to locate its origin. She scanned the top of the cliffs on both sides of the ravine and then turned to the canyon. The sound became a rattle, and then she knew what she was looking for. The truck that was carrying the trafficked girls was on its way.

Shit. They're almost at the mine.

River checked her watch. It was almost 5:00 a.m. The feds wouldn't be at the gorge and the mine for another hour. She trained the binoculars on the floor of the canyon, and she spotted a small shape that was growing larger fast. She estimated that the truck would take another fifteen minutes or so before it arrived at its destination.

She slid forward a little more to get a better view of who was at the mine. She spotted a tall man talking to someone she recognized—Sheriff Andersen, whose body language told River he wasn't happy. Another man came to talk to the tall stranger, who she decided must be the head of the Cruz Cartel. She couldn't get a better look without compromising her position, so she retraced her steps back to the place where Lewis and Askew were waiting.

"Problem?" Lewis asked in a low voice.

"The truck is on its way. ETA fifteen minutes max."

"I haven't received a text from Gary yet," Lewis said.

They fell silent for a moment, and then Askew murmured, "The one thing that could delay the transfer of the girls and the drugs is the late arrival of the truck from Vegas."

River and Lewis nodded, and Lewis said, low, "What have you got in mind?"

"The Vegas truck is not going to be loaded with cartel men. I'd say two, three at the most."

Lewis nodded again.

Askew added, "I took a good look of a map of the terrain yesterday and think I could avoid the three Cruz men near the mine by walking south and then heading northwest. I can intercept or at least delay the Vegas truck from entering the canyon."

"What if we need you here?" River asked.

"Even with our MP5s, we're not going to succeed in freeing the next lot of girls. There are too many of them, and we need a task force tackling them in the gorge as well as on the cliffs," Lewis whispered.

Lewis was right, River realized. Askew's presence with them wasn't going to make a difference.

Askew started to slowly retrace his steps, leaving River and Lewis on their own. Lewis took his phone out of his jacket, shielded the screen with the palm of his hand, and checked again. He shook his head—still no message from Gary.

Chapter 21

River and Lewis moved as close as they could to the Cruz men without being detected, following the edge of the cliff. Down below, the truck had arrived, and the girls were stepping out of it. Two men shoved them toward the mine, and River knew what would happen next. They would be chained to the walls and made to empty their bowels so the fentanyl precursors could be collected.

Lewis shook his head in disgust. He didn't want to miss the opportunity to stop this abuse. River checked her watch again: 5:37 a.m. Lewis took his phone out, cautiously shielding the screen, and this time he showed it to River: ETA thirty minutes. River grinned. They were finally going to move. Lewis texted Gary what he knew of their position and the number of men they'd seen on the ground.

But then Lewis frowned. "Shit—the feds've got enough men for a ground operation in the gorge but not enough to cover both sides of the cliff."

"Two of us against three of them," River said. "I like the odds."

Another text from Gary, and Lewis raised an eyebrow. "A helicopter is on its way."

River frowned. "The Cruz men are going to hear it way before it's on them."

Lewis texted something back and waited for a reply. "Too late. The fun starts in five minutes."

River and Lewis took up positions on either side of the boulder that was hiding them and waited. The faint *fap-fap-fap* of rotors drifted over the early morning air. The day was breaking, and the landscape contours were becoming defined.

"FBI Agent. You are surrounded. Drop your weapons and step out with your hands in the air."

A deafening silence followed, and then the cartel men opened fire. The men who'd spent the night on the cliff top dropped to the ground and crawled closer to the edge. The sound of a helicopter approaching grew louder.

"What are Gary's instructions?" River said as she racked her Glock.

Lewis, who had opted for the MP5, said, "Hold our position until the helicopter is above them. Shoot if the men come our way."

"Don't worry," River said. "I won't let any of these SOBs run past me."

"I thought you might say that," Lewis said with a sigh. "Then you'd better take this." He quickly took the SIG out of its holster and handed it to River. "You may need a second gun."

The gunfight below in the gorge was raging—a to-and-fro of weapons discharges that seemed to be going nowhere. On the cliff top, there was no movement. River glanced a few times toward the spot where the cartel men had stood and then she remembered the steps carved in the rock. From the feds' position, they couldn't see the stairs, and the men had almost certainly dropped down to the gorge below, covered by their pals.

"There are steps down to the gorge, carved in the rock. The three guys must have gone down that way," River said to Lewis.

Lewis slung his MP5 over his shoulder and texted Gary. The reply came back almost instantly, and Lewis said, "I'm going after them."

"You mean *we* are," River said. "You need me to show you where these steps are."

Lewis rolled his eyes. "You're not gonna listen to me if I ask you to stay behind anyway."

River grinned. "There's that, too."

Lewis got ready and nodded to River. She ran low toward a piece of rock too small to shield them, so she dropped to the sandy ground.

Lewis followed and dropped to the ground, too. The helicopter was now flying in circles over the scene, and River and Lewis ran straight to the steps. She risked taking a look, but she couldn't be sure of who might be waiting for them at the bottom. Lewis pulled her back.

"Too risky. Even with the guns in the helicopter covering us," he said.

River hesitated, but she knew he was right. The gunfight had moved, now centered around the mine, and River hoped the trafficked girls had been taken inside, where they would be sheltered.

Suddenly, the guns stopped on the cartel side and someone shouted, "You move any closer, and we execute these girls."

The guns of the federal agents grew silent, too, and on the ground, Gary replied through a megaphone. "I don't think ending this in bloodshed will do you any good."

"Won't be good for your reputation, either," the answer came. The voice sounded educated, with a very slight Latin accent.

"What do you propose?" Gary shouted.

"For starters, get the helicopter to go back to base."

"And then?"

"I want to know what happened at Devils Playground. Was it you?"

Lewis got on his phone and dialed Gary. "He wants to know who gunned down his men, but it wasn't straightforward. The shooting started on their side."

Gary shouted, "The shooting started on your side."

River turned to Lewis and said, "I need to explain. Tell Gary I'm coming down."

Lewis tried to stop her, but River was already on her way. He spoke to Gary again to warn him. "River is coming down some steps hidden in the rock. Get your guys to hold back."

When River got to the gorge, Gary was waiting for her, and the chopper had turned around.

"I'm still expecting an explanation," the voice shouted, impatient, from inside the mine.

Gary nodded, and River shouted back, "I don't know who you

are, but I am River Swift, and I was at the arroyo to collect my niece, Carmen, when the shooting started."

There was a short silence and then, "I know. I sent one of my men, Pablo, to hand her over."

River thought she detected a slight wobble in the voice.

"People started to shoot from above. Harry Wilson was hit, and then we ran for cover. But with the rain, a flash flood surprised us. Pablo carried Carmen up and over the Ledge. He helped me, too, and then . . ." River swallowed, recalling the moment Pablo was shot. "Then, when we thought we were safe, someone shot him in the back. But I'd already told the agents who were helping me to spare him."

There was another silence, and River feared the man wouldn't think she was telling the truth.

"You have to believe me."

"I do," the man said, his voice tight in anger.

Gary looked at River with surprise. "Then this isn't a vendetta," Gary said.

"The people who needed to die are dead," the man shouted. He then seemed to hesitate but said, "I am going to come out, no weapon, arms in the air. I have a proposition."

Gary signaled his men to hold back. The tall man River had spotted earlier appeared a moment later, hands above his head. He walked toward River and Gary in a slow, steady pace—someone who'd made a decision and was going to follow it through. He dropped to the ground gradually and lay there, waiting to be taken.

Gary called Lewis and said, "I have a situation. Is everything clear on the cliff?"

River couldn't hear the answer, but Gary nodded. "No sign of activity."

Gary called a couple of his men. "Get to the top and cover us. Agent Lewis is on his own up there."

Gary went to the man on the ground and said, "I'm going to cuff you. As long as you stay still, it'll all be smooth. Do you understand?"

The man tilted his head slightly and said, "I understand."

Gary knelt next to the man, locking the cuffs onto his wrists. He then helped him stand up. The man turned to face him and said, "I am Alfonso Rodrigo Cruz. My father is Gonzalo Carlos Cruz-Coronel, head of the Cruz Cartel."

River and Gary exchanged a look. Their exchange didn't go unnoticed, and Alfonso gave them a quick smile. "I am speaking the truth. Gonzalo Cruz is my father, and I want to tell you all I know about his business."

Gary removed the cap he was wearing and scratched his head. This wasn't the development he was expecting. River was as stunned as he was but said, "How about the girls?"

"They are safe," Alfonso said. "They've been moved to the back of the mine."

"And Dolores?"

Alfonso nodded, and River briefly closed her eyes in relief.

"What about your men? I don't want to be sending my men into an ambush to retrieve these girls," Gary said.

Alfonso shook his head, "No ambush—they're gone."

"Shit. What?"

"The mine is also a cave with a couple of exits."

Gary's face turned to thunder. He picked up his phone and called his dispatcher. "I need the helicopter back at the Silver Rim mine."

He was listening with a frown and replied curtly, "Don't care. I said now. Make it happen."

He cut the call and turned toward Alfonso. "They'll get caught."

Alfonso shrugged and looked to his right. "At least I gave them a chance, which is more than Sheriff Andersen did for his own men."

River's gaze followed Alfonso's. A couple of bodies lay on the ground a few yards away.

"How about Andersen himself?" River asked, realizing that he, too, must have fled.

"Gone with my men. What did you expect?"

River was about to march toward the mine entrance when Gary stopped her. "We still need to be careful," he said to her, then added, turning to Alfonso, "It'd better not be a trap, or I'll put a bullet through your head."

Alfonso nodded. "I can't guarantee that my men won't be waiting for you, but it won't be on my instructions."

Gary called one of his men, who took Alfonso away. River saw him turn back toward her, and she nodded her thanks. She hoped he would know she was grateful that he'd chosen Pablo instead of Harry to look after Carmen.

Gary and five FBI men briefly discussed how to enter the mine. They spread out, three on each side, assault weapons at the ready. Gary gave the sign, and they moved in at the standard call. "Federal Agents! Drop your weapons, hands over your head."

River braced for some form of retaliation, but nothing came. She ran to the side of the mine and peeked in. Gary's men were aiming their flashlights at the back of a large open space, and as Alfonso had said, a bunch of girls were seated on the floor, their hands and feet tied, and their mouths gagged. River took a few steps inside.

"Can I follow?" she called.

Gary didn't turn around but motioned with his arm that she could join them. River reached the six agents, who were already freeing the girls, and then River pushed forward to get to Dolores. She looked scared but unharmed.

She squinted in the harsh light of the flashlights the agents were using but then recognized River. Her eyes grew wide, and relief flashed through them. River went to her side and undid the gag.

"You came for me?" Dolores croaked.

River took her in her arms. "I made a promise."

One of Gary's men called out, "There are boot prints going deep inside the mine."

Gary joined his man and knelt. He stood up again after a moment, then walked out of the mine to give instructions to the remaining feds just as River finished removing the ties around Dolores's ankles and wrists. She helped Dolores stand up. "You need to go with the federal agents now. They'll keep you safe."

"What about you?" Dolores asked.

"I have a score to settle with Sheriff Andersen."

Dolores hugged River one last time and followed one of the agents who'd been dealing with the other trafficked girls. River went deeper into the mine. Gary had returned there and gathered the same group of men. One of them was holding a light high so they all could see.

"We follow the boot prints. We go slow. The cartel men know the passages better than we do, so we could be ambushed at any time," Gary concluded.

"Mind if I tag along?" River said.

Gary looked at her in disbelief. "You're not serious?"

"Couldn't be *more* serious."

"I don't like to be pushed around," Gary said.

"You and your men don't know the area the way I do."

"We're not above ground. We're in a cave."

"You'll be going out of this cave at some point, won't you? Or at least that's what you hope."

Gary still looked unconvinced, so River bent toward him and whispered, "And I promise I won't tell anyone about the incident at Silver Rim—you know, being cuffed to a tree with socks in your mouth."

Gary's cheeks reddened, and River gave him a crooked smile. "I won't cause any trouble . . . promise."

"You cause trouble, and I'll handcuff *you* to a rock," Gary grumbled.

"Deal," River said.

Gary and his men moved forward slowly, guns drawn and ready. They used their flashlights sparingly, only to identify any obstacles and traps that lay ahead. They made slow progress, and after forty minutes, they stopped when they came to a fork in the passageway. Gary and one of his men knelt to inspect the prints left behind in the gravelly soil of the cave.

"The group has split," Gary said. "Only one man went to the left."

River looked and said, "I can't be certain, but I think this passage will lead to the flat part of the cliff, whereas the other passage, where all the other men have gone, will lead to another canyon."

"In other words, whoever went left would be in the open," Gary said. "Why would he risk that?"

"Because he's got people waiting for him who may not look suspicious on the face of it," River said.

"You mean Andersen?"

"That's right. The other Cruz men need the cover of the canyon. It's daylight now, so they'll try to hide as much as possible."

Gary nodded, convinced. "We'll go to the right. I'll pick up Andersen later."

River let the men go and fell back to the rear of the group. She slowed down, then stopped and activated the light on her cell phone. She slowly backtracked to the fork in the passageway. If Gary was going after the Cruz men, she was going after Andersen.

Ten minutes later, she spotted a faint glow of light in the distance. She accelerated her pace, still mindful of the uneven terrain, and when she finally broke into the open, it was broad daylight. The sun was shining, yet still soft. She blinked and shielded her eyes with her hand. She waited until her eyes adjusted to the light, then scoped out the cave exit and its immediate vicinity. She couldn't spot anyone and decided to venture farther into the open.

River used her binoculars to give the terrain a thorough check. Andersen had perhaps half an hour on her, and he wasn't an agile man, but still there was no sign of him. The land was rising to her left, and she tried to figure out where it led. She took out her phone, clicked on the compass, and let the dial roll until it gave her the coordinates. The reading looked somewhat familiar, and she realized what it meant. She was only a short walk from Old Bill's cave.

River grabbed her burner phone and dialed Miguel's burner immediately.

"Are the girls safe?" Miguel asked as he replied.

"Yes—all of them, including Dolores," River said, "but you all may not be. Some of the cartel men have escaped, and that includes

Andersen. I'm out on the plateau, and I think he's heading your way."

"On his own?" Miguel said. "I don't think he stands a chance. Dale and I have got more than enough to deal with him. Even more so now that we're forewarned."

"I don't think he's on his own," River said as she made her way toward the incline. "I think he called some of his guys to pick him up. Lewis, Askew, and I met two of them when we were in the car on our way to the mine. They were keeping an eye on the road. There may be more."

"How would they know where we are?" Miguel asked.

"I don't know. Dale took Rosa and Carmen to the cave. You took the evidence with you there. You've been careful, but that doesn't mean you haven't been spotted."

"That's true," Miguel reluctantly admitted.

"I'm on my way," River said. "Speak to Old Bill and keep an eye out."

She hung up and accelerated her pace toward the top of the slope. She stopped as she was about to bridge it and dropped to the ground. She crawled over the rocks until she could see the other side. This time River didn't need her binoculars. Andersen was there with four of his men. She suspected that two of them were the ones Lewis had spoken to from the car and the others were the ones Dale had disturbed surveilling Luke's home.

River dropped below the crest of the slope and called Miguel.

"We're getting ready," he said.

"They're coming for you—four officers and Andersen."

"Shit." Miguel's voice wavered. "We won't be able to hold them back for long."

"I'm almost there, and I'll call Lewis. Hold tight."

River hung up called Lewis from her usual phone. He responded immediately.

"Are you safe?"

"I am, but Old Bill and the others aren't. Andersen is coming after them with four of his men."

"I'm on my way. I'll contact Askew, too. Send me the coordinates."

"Coming right away," River said.

She hung up and forwarded Old Bill's cave coordinates to Lewis. He was a good forty minutes away on foot, and she had no idea where Askew was. River crawled back to the top of the slope and took her Glock out. Andersen and his men had moved on. They'd left their cars behind and had disappeared behind another elevation. She stepped over the ridge and ran low to the nearest car, heart pounding.

Old Bill's cave was only a few hundred yards away. She tried to recall the layout of the terrain. The rock face that stretched above the cave was sheer and high. It wouldn't be possible to scale it without proper equipment. The narrow passage that led to the cave itself was long and easy to guard, but the rocks on the other side of the passage were easier for Andersen's men to overcome. Still, it meant that Dale and Miguel could concentrate on defending only one spot.

River waited a few minutes, but none of the men returned to their cars. She ran to the next rock elevation to hear Andersen shout.

"Police. You're surrounded. We know you are holding information that has been illegally obtained and that you are harboring an illegal immigrant. Surrender both, and you'll be unharmed."

River trained her Glock on Andersen's back, but she couldn't gun all the other four men down and had to resist the urge.

The cranky voice of Old Bill gave Andersen his reply. "Go fuck yourself, Andersen. You and your goons. You're all gonna go to prison for the rest of your days."

Andersen and his men roared with laughter. "You always were an old SOB, Bill. I'm gonna enjoy shooting every single one of you," Andersen retorted.

Andersen's men started to climb the rocks that gave them access to the front of Old Bill's cave. They would soon reach the top, where they would start using the heavy machine gun they'd brought with them. Andersen was positioned at the entrance of the passage, taking no chances, waiting for people to come out.

Once the four men started shooting, Miguel and Dale would find it almost impossible to retaliate. River hadn't expected them to bring the sort of weapon that spewed heavy-caliber ammunition. She recalled what Miguel had said: The military dealt with the cartels in Mexico, and one of the reasons was the high-grade weaponry they used.

She called Miguel again. He picked up immediately.

"The have a heavy machine gun with them. You need to take cover—all of you."

"Shit. That complicates things. I'll speak to Old Bill."

Miguel hung up, and River positioned herself so that she could aim at the men climbing. She could easily take down two of them, but then it would be three against one—although it also would give Dale and Miguel the opportunity to retaliate.

She called Miguel again and said, "I can gun two of them down. It'll even things out for you."

"You're on your own. This is suicide—"

River killed the call and thought about whom she needed to take down first. The man with the HMG would be the first, and then the one who was about to reach the top of the incline. She transferred her spare clip to her waistband, took a slow breath, and made herself ready.

The first shot got the HMG man in the shoulder and the second in the leg. The sound of gunfire bouncing off the rock face surprised everyone. She took advantage and went for the second man. She aimed at the legs, and his body sprang back as the two bullets hit him. River dove down as a deluge of retaliatory gunfire hit the rocks above her head.

She moved away from her position, running low along the ridge that shielded her, but the gunfire kept coming, spraying bullets all along the rock ledge. River stopped at the far end of the ridge; if she edged out any farther, she no longer would be covered. The shooting stopped, and then Andersen shouted, "Whoever the fuck you are, we're going to get you. So either you come out now and we'll make it quick, or else it'll be long and painful."

The crunch of boots on the rugged earth told River that two of the men were headed in her direction. She imagined each man walking along the ridge and trying to squeeze her out in a two-pronged attack. She might be able to take one more down, but after that it would be game over.

A memory flashed in her mind—her mother telling her about death for the first time. *When it comes, when you know it truly is coming—and you will—don't fight it. It's a passage, nothing more.*

But River wasn't ready for the passage yet. She thought of a gamble. Get over the ridge, gun one of the men down, and get over to the other side. The element of surprise might once more work in her favor. They wouldn't anticipate her coming after them—or would they? There was only one way to find out.

River visualized the move and made herself ready. The discharge of an MP5 and a man going down stopped her.

"FBI Agent. Drop your guns, hands in the air."

River recognized Askew's voice. She smiled. She was starting to rather like the feds' calling card.

"I won't say it again," Askew shouted, impatient.

"It's only two of you left, and it's the feds against you now," River shouted to give Askew the lowdown on numbers and position. "How does that make you feel, Andersen?"

Andersen didn't reply, and for a moment she thought he was the one who'd been gunned down. One of Andersen's men appeared on the ridge with his hands in the air, and River stood up and took a few steps back, gun trained on him.

"How many of them?" Askew shouted from behind the rock that was shielding him.

"Andersen plus four. I wounded two of Andersen's men," River shouted.

"The guy I took down isn't Andersen," Askew said, moving out in the open.

"Where is he?" River said, pointing the gun at the man on the ledge.

He hesitated, and she shot a round to his feet. "I won't ask again."

"Gone," the man replied with an incline of the head to his left.

Askew had almost reached her and said, "We'll pick him up with the helicopter."

River shook her head and turned to face Askew. "He knows this land like the back of his hand. I'm not letting him escape."

Askew frowned. "You're joking."

"I'm not. I'm going after him."

Chapter 22

River ignored Askew's call to stay put. She ran to the point where the sheer incline of the plateau met the void and saw there was a passage that wove its way between the rocks. She replaced the Glock against her back and started the descent. Rocks rolled under her feet, and the slope steepened. She kept going and then stopped for a moment. Did Andersen really go this way? She had taken his man's word for it, but perhaps Andersen had traveled a different route.

She held her breath and listened intently. The sound of rocks rolling farther down the path told her that someone was climbing down toward the canyon. She thought of calling after him but decided she needed to surprise him rather than scare him.

River resumed her descent until she hit a part of the path that met a rock face. She was amazed that Andersen could manage it, but the fear of being caught had apparently given him strength and agility she didn't think he had. He was nowhere to be seen, though, so she decided to take her chances. She would be exposed as she climbed down the rock face, but she had no alternative.

She managed to find purchase and started down the cliff. She was expecting gunshots from Andersen, but nothing came. Her foot finally touched the ground, and she turned around to resume her pursuit. A bullet missed her head by an inch, and she dove to the ground. She squeezed herself against a rock and shouted, "That's the problem with you, Andersen. You couldn't hit an elephant if it stood a foot away from you."

Andersen didn't reply. She risked casting an eye over the top of the rock and saw a silhouette running farther down the path. River took off, her heart beating fast. She was about to get him. She accelerated, stones shifting underneath her feet, almost causing her to fall. She steadied herself, accelerated again. The path was bending to the left. She hugged the turn and slammed into a wall of rock. The shock sent her flying to the ground, hard. Her head swam. The racking of a gun forced River to concentrate. Andersen was standing a foot away from her, smirking.

"For a local girl, you're shit at knowing the terrain."

River's eyes reacquired focus. She tried to sit up, but Andersen pointed his gun at her and said, "One move, and I'll finish you with a couple of bullets to the stomach. You're a medic. You know what that means."

River nodded. She knew that a gun wound to the stomach would need to be treated fast. If it wasn't, death would be excruciating and certain.

"What do you want?" she said, wondering why he hadn't pulled the trigger yet.

"I'm thinking. Perhaps I can make a deal. You might become a handy hostage."

"Why would the feds make a deal?" River asked, buying time.

"I know a lot of people. Even the list you found in Harry's office is nothing."

River shrugged. "You *would* say that."

Andersen's face hardened. "Don't give me a reason to kill you right away. It's tempting enough as it is."

River's attention was diverted to movement near the top of one of the rocks.

"What do you want me to do?" she said.

The question made Andersen smile, a vicious look in his eyes. At last, she was admitting defeat. Her Glock had fallen out of her waistband under the shock of the rock impact, and Andersen pointed at it with his gun.

"Slide that to me with your foot."

River extended her foot and kicked the gun toward him. Movement drew her attention once more, but this time she froze.

"Andersen," she said, barely breathing, "don't move."

Andersen arched his brow. "What now?"

"There is a rattlesnake on top of the rock."

Andersen grinned. "Nice try. But you can hear a rattler miles away with—"

The rattle that followed transformed Andersen's expression from contempt to dread.

"Don't move," River repeated, but it was too late. Andersen couldn't help a shudder of revulsion turning around, and the snake's strike was vicious. It bit Andersen on the face. Andersen collapsed to the ground with a heavy thud and a deafening scream. The snake rose again and bit Andersen once more. It then slithered away between the rocks.

Andersen was rolling on the ground, howling in pain. River stood up slowly, concerned that the snake may still be around. She took a couple of steps toward Andersen. His face had started to swell. His mouth was wide open, and his eyes showed terror. Poison was seeping through him fast. A bite to the face was the worst kind—a victim had only hours to survive. But River realized something else. Andersen was in anaphylactic shock—the venom had caused his throat to close, suffocating him.

River knelt next to him, and he grabbed her arm, desperate. She shook her head: Without the right medication, there was nothing she could do. "Don't fight it," she said. "It's only a passage."

Andersen's eyes started to roll in their sockets. His grip loosened. He came to again, gasping for air, each attempt more laborious than the last. His chest heaved a couple of times in a wheeze, and then he let go. River waited a moment, placed two fingers on his neck. She couldn't detect a pulse. She stood up slowly, Andersen's lifeless body at her feet.

It wasn't the end she'd planned on. Death had come, and yet she couldn't imagine what sort of passage it would be for Andersen. She knelt once more, closed his eyes, and made her way back to the cave.

When she arrived at Old Bill's hideout, Lewis was already there, and a helicopter was circling over the people gathered next to the entrance.

Dale, Askew, and Lewis were dealing with the prisoner and the wounded. Cristina, Jen, and Miguel were outside with Old Bill. She couldn't see Rosa but guessed she was still inside with Carmen. More scenes of terror weren't what the youngster needed.

Old Bill was the first one to notice River. He alerted the others and came to join her.

"Did you get him?" he said.

River shook her head. "No. A rattler did."

"One wearing a gun?" Askew shouted from afar.

"Didn't need one. Killed him in less than two minutes."

Everyone nodded, including Andersen's own officer.

The sound of helicopter rotors grew stronger, and a cloud of dust lifted in the distance.

"We're taking the wounded by helicopter," Lewis shouted over the noise.

Dale waited for River to reach the rest of them and extended a hand. "I'm off. I'm giving a lift to Lewis and Askew. We're gonna deal with the North Saint Ab Police Station, starting with this one." Dale pointed at the officer in cuffs.

River shook Dale's hand. "Thanks, Dale. Good luck with the butt kicking."

Dale smiled. He turned around and pushed the cuffed officer toward his car. Askew waved at River, and she waved back. Lewis was supervising the airlifting of the wounded. The medical team was already on the ground, and the evacuation proceeded quickly. Then the helicopter took off in a cloud of dust.

Lewis was already on his way to Dale's car. He turned back to say, "If you want a job with the feds, you know where to find me."

River raised a hand in acknowledgment. Old Bill came alongside her.

"Ain't your style," he said, waving back at Lewis. "You need the open road."

River sighed. "I think you're right."

Miguel, Jen, and Cristina approached.

"Let's go home," Miguel said to Jen, wrapping his arm around her shoulders.

Cristina stepped closer to Old Bill. "Am I staying here?" she asked, hopeful.

Old Bill nodded and finally smiled. "I'm gonna see what can be done to get you legal, young lady."

River smiled at her. She was glad Old Bill wanted to help.

"Let me go get Rosa and Carmen," River said as she stepped away from the small gathering.

She jogged to the door of the cave, pushed it open, and entered the spacious living area. She called Rosa's name.

"In here," Rosa said.

River walked along a short corridor. Rosa appeared in the doorway of one of the bedrooms, and they hugged.

"It's over," River said.

Rosa nodded, her eyes welling, unable to speak.

"How is Carmen?" River asked.

"Doing well, considering," Rosa said, closing the bedroom door. "Her cat has helped a lot. He seems to know she needs him."

"Let's go home," River said.

Rosa opened the door again. Carmen was on the bed reading a book, with Franklin in her lap. They both stood as River approached. River hugged Carmen tight, and the little girl hugged her back.

"Are we going home?" Carmen asked.

"We are, my angel," Rosa replied.

River closed her eyes briefly, relieved. River left them to get ready and then went outside, where Jen and Miguel had made their way to Miguel's old car. Cristina hugged River. Old Bill smiled once more and said, "Good luck on the road. Be safe. Be wise." River smiled back.

Rosa, Carmen, and Franklin appeared at the top of the passage that led to Old Bill's cave. Franklin was in his harness and happy, it seemed, to be following his human. It made everyone laugh. Rosa and Carmen hugged Old Bill and Cristina goodbye, and when the three got to the car, the back doors were already open. Franklin jumped in first. Rosa sat down, and Carmen sat on her knees. River was the last one to get in. She took a final look around, wondering whether she'd ever return.

Rosa called Luke as soon as she had reception on her cell phone, and River saw on her face that she could hardly contain her emotions. They all stayed silent during the journey, each reflecting on what had happened. Miguel briefly stopped at the trailer park on the way to Luke's. River picked up her bike and was glad to be riding alone as she followed Miguel's car.

Miguel turned into the Swifts' road and then stopped in front of their home. Once again, Luke was waiting for them, door open. As soon as Rosa opened the car door, he dropped to his knees, opening his arms wide. Carmen bolted out and ran into them. They hugged tight. Franklin followed and rubbed his face against them, sharing the love. Rosa got out of the car and joined Luke and Carmen, and the hug of two became the hug of three.

River parked the bike in the driveway. The Lopezes stood outside, waiting. No one spoke, and then they waved goodbye. The Lopezes' car pulled away, and Luke walked inside, carrying Carmen in his arms. Rosa followed, Franklin in tow.

River removed her helmet but waited before going in. She then closed the door gently behind her and hesitated. They needed space. Perhaps it was the right moment to go to the attic and check the contents of her parents' box.

She took the first flight of stairs, crossed the landing, opened a door that led to a second set of steps, then climbed them two at a time. When she reached the attic, she switched on the light and saw that the chaotic space she remembered had been replaced by a well-organized room. She had no problem spotting the box, which lay on a low table next to a trunk. River sat on the trunk and rubbed her palms on her thighs.

She inhaled quickly, then opened the box. Several envelopes were stacked in it, most labeled with words and phrases signifying mundane matters—official documents, insurance policies, a will. But then at the bottom of the pile River found an unopened envelope marked RIVER.

She frowned and was confused for a moment, but then she understood. Luke hadn't delivered the letter to her when she returned to Saint Ab for her parents' funeral, and now he didn't know how to tell her after all these years that a message from her dead parents was waiting for her in this box.

She bit her lip, torn between the desire to rush downstairs and confront Luke and the sadness that swelled inside her. She waited for the moment to pass, took the letter out, and made her way downstairs, hoping she could avoid her brother. Luke, Rosa, and Carmen were huddling in the living room, and River walked across the kitchen without being noticed. She entered the spare room and sat on the bed, letter in hand.

The envelope looked thin—the sort of paper she and her parents used to use for international correspondence at a time when letters were weighed to determine the cost of the stamp. She didn't want to damage it, so she went to the bathroom, found a pair of scissors, and returned with them to the bed. She cautiously sliced the top of the envelope open and removed the thin blue paper she recalled her mother using.

River unfolded the letter with trembling hands. She recognized her mother's handwriting and took a moment before she started reading.

> *To River, our most precious girl,*
> *This letter will get to you under what you might think are sad*

circumstances. We want you to look beyond this moment—death is only a passage. Look at our lives. What we have built. What we have given. But more important, look at who we brought into the world, and that is you.

We are so proud of you, dearest River, not because we nurtured you but because you have flourished to become who you truly are— brave, kind, and free-spirited. It's a beautiful combination, and we're sorry we didn't say it enough when we had the opportunity. But know that we now understand why you chose to become an air force medic and that we trust whatever choices you make in the future.

If we no longer are here to stand by you, remember that we'll always be in your heart.

Love forever,
    Mom and Dad

The letter fell from her hands. She curled up in a ball and couldn't stop the heavy sobs that rocked her.

It took a long while before she sat up. She wiped her face dry on her sleeve. She'd been waiting ten years for this message. There was nothing in it that told her about her parents' death, but there was much more—love, trust, respect.

What the letter confirmed, though, was that they both knew they were under threat. She knew who the likely culprit was, and now she needed to know why that man killed them.

River stood up slowly. She gathered the few belongings she owned and packed her duffel bag. Her backpack was still in the storage compartment of her bike. She zipped her jacket up and left the room.

In the kitchen, she could smell coffee and hear voices coming from the living room—happy voices. Voices of people who belonged together. River tiptoed her way to the front door, opened it, and closed it behind her noiselessly.

She strapped the duffel bag to the back of her bike, put her helmet on, and straddled the seat. She took a last look at the home she had once called hers. She started the engine and joined the late-midday traffic. She was riding north, where Karen, her old air force friend, lived. She would make a plan, then cross the Atlantic and go back to a place she vowed she'd never return to. And then she would deliver her own brand of justice.

River stopped at a gas station and filled up her tank. She picked up a bunch of flowers, paid for her purchases, and left the station. She rode to the Silver Rim canyon, turned onto the path that had led her there four days ago, and stopped right near the edge.

She parked the bike, removed her helmet, and walked to the place where she had spotted vultures riding the thermals. She laid the bunch of flowers near one of the large boulders that hung close to the precipice and spent a moment thinking about Teresa, Dolores, and Cristina. She hoped the two friends who'd survived the ordeal would find a path to the life they deserved.

She pushed away the memory of her parents' letter. It was too raw—and anyway, she had a score to settle back in Africa before she confronted Luke about it.

She returned to the bike, rode down the path, and then turned left, due north. The weather was clear, and the ride would be pleasant. She just had to concentrate on it until her sorrow subsided.

The traffic remained light on I-15. River let a few cars overtake her. She would keep going for another hour or so and then find a place to stop for a bite to eat.

She spotted a car in her side-view mirror that seemed to be approaching fast. By her estimate, it was way exceeding the speed limit, and River wondered why the driver was in such a hurry and whether she should be concerned. She returned her attention to the road until the car was uncomfortably close. Her instinct told her to speed up and put some distance between herself and the car. She pushed the bike and started accelerating, but then the car's headlights flashed.

The driver opened the window, waved, and then positioned the car alongside River's bike. Then the window on the passenger side rolled down, and a young boy waved his arm, asking her to slow down and stop. River then realized the car was Rosa's—and that Jack was sitting beside her.

She slowed down and chose a place to stop at the side of the highway that looked convenient and safe enough. She parked the bike, got off, and removed her helmet. Rosa stepped out of the car, and so did Jack. He came running to River with a smile and gave her a big hug.

"I'm sorry I was away for most of your stay with us, Aunt River," he said.

River's smile must have emboldened Jack, and he continued, "I really wanted to speak to you about your service in the military."

River's eyes widened, and she looked at Rosa quizzically. Rosa said, "He's got lots of questions, and I can't think of anybody else better placed than you to answer them."

Rosa placed her hands over one of her son's shoulders and said, "We'd like you to come back—me, Jack, Luke, and Carmen." She nodded as if to give more weight to her invitation to return and then added, "Whenever you feel the time is right."

River was at a loss for words. She smiled and nodded back at Rosa. "There's something I need to do . . ."

Jack's face dropped, but River put a hand on Jack's other shoulder and said, "But then I promise I'll come back."

"And River always keeps her promises," Rosa added.

River took a few steps back and then a few more until she reached her bike. She put her helmet on, straddled the bike, and kick-started the engine. She waved at them, and they waved in return. Perhaps there was a part of the world in which she belonged after all.

Acknowledgments

It takes many people to write and publish a book ... for their generosity and support, I want to say thank you.

Barbara Clark, my editor, for her immense knowledge of good language and of what makes a good story great. Lizzie Gardiner for her expertise in design and for producing a book cover no reader can ignore. Susan Hood for her proficiency in typesetting the text and knowing what it means to work under pressure. Jean Durbin for her precise proofreading.

To the friends who have patiently read, reread, and advised on all matters of this book: my friend and cousin Beverly Hurlburt, who kindly helped me discover spectacular places in Utah I'd not visited before. Kathy Vanderhook, my most wonderful supporter, on whom I can test my storylines, and, of course, my very cool ARC team.

Coming Soon from Freddie P Peters

Also Featuring River Swift

Trip Wire (spring 2026)

Dear Reader . . .

I hope you enjoyed *Savage Peace* as much as I enjoyed writing it! If you'd like to follow River in her new adventures, the next book, *Trip Wire*, is available for preorder. Check it out on the link below.

https://geni.us/TRIPWIRE

Wanting justice for her parents' death, River returns to a country she vowed she'd never visit again. She crosses paths with a ruthless arms dealer who holds the answers—and she takes a stand, knowing it could be her last.

Perhaps, too, you would like to know about my other series.

Check out my Nancy Wu Smart Woman Crime thrillers: https://mybook.to/NWCT.

Or delve into the Henry Crowne Paying the Price series, in which you'll also find Nancy, here: https://mybook.to/HCPTP.

On my website, you can gain access to the backstories that underpin the Henry Crowne series and get to know my creative process and how the books are conceived. You can also read opening chapters of each book and the prequel to the Henry Crowne series, *Insurgent*. Just go to https://freddieppeters.com/ and join Freddie's Book Club.

And now it's time to ask you for a small favor. Please take a few minutes to leave a review on Amazon, Goodreads, or BookBub.

Reviews are incredibly important to authors like me. They help readers decide whether they might enjoy my books and increase my books' visibility. So if you'd like to spread the word, get writing or leave a star review.

Thank you so very much.

Looking forward to connecting with you!

Freddie

Printed in Dunstable, United Kingdom